FOR THE LOVE OF HADES

SASHA SUMMERS

For the Love of Hades
Sasha Summers

Cover Art
Najla Qamber Designs

Interior Layout
Author's HQ

Editor
Candice U. Lindstrom/Sasha Summers

Sasha Summers re-release publication date August 2015

To Allison Burke Collins
& Angelyn Schmid,
Thanks for swooning over Hades.

Prologue

Hades glanced at the lily propped atop the mantle. The blossom was bright white against the black silk to which it was pinned, light against the darkness. He reached up, tracing one petal with an unsteady finger. He saw the tremor, cursed it, and clenched his hand, drawing back from the flower as if it had burned him.

Turning abruptly from the fire, he made his way to his chair and sat heavily. There was a sweetness to his burden, but it was no less a burden.

He leaned forward, rested his elbows on his knees and covered his face with his hands.

What had he done? How could he make amends now that his heinous act had been hidden so long? Using his powers to aid a mortal would seem trivial in comparison with the offense he'd committed against Demeter. Against Olympus.

And yet, he felt whole.

The raw emptiness that he'd held at bay, for nigh on an eternity, no longer threatened to consume him. Having her here, with her constant laughter and endless conversation, had changed his world irrevocably.

If not for her, he would have remained bitter and angry. He would not have interfered at Cypress. He would never have thought to champion the mortal, Ariston...

"My lord." Her soft voice interrupted his thoughts.

He lifted his head from his hands, surprised.

Persephone stood, beauty to behold, watching him with wide green eyes. In the blazing firelight her hair glowed copper, warm and rich. Her face, normally alight with smiles and laughter, was drawn. Was she not fully recovered? Or did the tension between them tire her as well?

His voice revealed nothing. "Persephone."

Her steps were cautious, but she made her way to him. "Aphrodite?"

So she had seen Aphrodite. "Has gone." And she should have gone with her fellow Olympian. He should have insisted she do so. He swallowed against the lump in his throat, ignoring the tightening in his chest.

"I thought as much." She stood so close he could see the front of her tunic. The fabric trembled, thundering in time with the rapid beat of her heart.

Was she disappointed? Was she ready to leave him… his realm?

She should go. She should have gone weeks ago. He knew it was right. Yet knowing it did nothing to soothe his agitation. He clutched the arms of his throne, clinging to control.

"I've not asked you for anything in my time here." She paused. "Have I?"

He shook his head once. No, she'd seemed happy, though he had little knowledge of true happiness, he supposed. His gaze found shadows beneath her eyes and a tightness about her mouth. He was a blind fool.

Have you been miserable? He could not ask the words aloud, fearing her answer.

Her voice was no steadier than her pulse. "Nor would I trouble you now, if my need were not so great."

"What is it?" he asked. His voice sounded harsh to his own ears.

She sank to her knees, glancing at him with an almost timid gaze. Her hands lifted, wavered, and covered his hands. He stiffened, stunned by her actions. She touched him… He swallowed. The feel of her hands upon him squeezed the air from his lungs.

"Show me mercy. Show me the same mercy you've bestowed upon the mortal… the soldier Ariston." Her hands clasped his tightly.

He would not reach for her, he could not. No matter how he might want to.

"Have I been cruel, that you feel the need to beg for anything from me?" His words were a harsh whisper. She shook her head and he continued, "Then why do you kneel before me?"

"It is a selfish request, one that may turn you from solicitous to," she paused, her cheeks growing red, "… sickened."

Was it possible for him to feel so towards her?

He stared at her hands, wrapped about his. He would not meet her gaze. He would not reveal his damnable weakness to her. He could not risk losing himself in the fathomless depths of her green eyes. "Ask me," he murmured as his traitorous eyes sought hers.

She drew in a wavering breath, ragged and labored. Her whispered words were thick. "My lover… Release him. Release the man who loves me, please." Her eyes sparkled, mesmerizing him while his heart, so newly discovered, seemed to shudder to a stop once more.

Chapter One

Persephone assessed the blackened tree trunk. Patches of white, bleached and fragile, peeked through the charred bark. She bit her lip. Was she too late?

She hesitated, her hand wavering as she pressed her palm against the pine tree. Her heart steadied, her chest lightened. She spoke with feeling. "I feared you'd left me, old friend."

The pine spoke, its musical words for her ears alone.

She listened, before answering, "I have no answers for you. Why do men lose sight of the majesty that surrounds them every day? How can they forget that the world is not theirs alone to conquer?" she teased. "They are foolish, perhaps?"

The pine was not appeased. It was wounded, beyond the injury man's arrows and fire had caused. It felt betrayed.

Persephone felt the weariness, the hopelessness, within the tree and sighed. She must cheer it for her healing to work. "I would see you heal and grow." She pressed both hands against it. "I would hear your branches creak in the wind, for it is the sweetest song. Watching your limbs grow heavy with leaves and fruit fills me with pride."

The pine tree was silent.

"Do not deprive me of my joy, I beseech you," she pleaded gently. "Let me help you. And while I work, you can tell me a story. You know how fond I am of stories."

The tree argued, refusing to be appeased.

"You're wrong. I don't know *all* of your stories." She stroked the trunk, wincing as bits of the scorched bark broke free beneath her hands. "Yours are the very best stories..."

The tree spoke again, rejecting her ploy to pacify it.

"I am *not* flattering you shamelessly..." She laughed, touching the naked trunk with careful fingers. She closed her eyes, willing her strength into its core. Bark formed, thickened and hardening beneath her fingers. "If you do have a story, I would hear it. Then I will sing to you." She continued to move her hand in long strokes, sealing and healing the angry gashes left by the warring mortals. She'd heard the pine's story before, but listened anyway. The language of the trees was fluid, carrying her along its lyrical current.

"Your stories fill my ears and heart with delight. Thank you." She stepped back, the healing, and the story, complete. "What song would you hear?"

The tree always asked for a song, the same song. It was the pine that had taught it to her years ago, patiently. And she treasured its gift to her.

She sang, in a tongue no longer spoken, using words she scarcely understood. She sat on the tree's thick roots and leaning against its trunk. This giant pine tree was older than her fathers, older than the Titans. And it was whole once more, because of her.

When the song was done, the tree thanked her.

"You're welcome," she answered. "It is my pleasure to give something to you, old friend. *I* will never forget you. You are a treasure."

She rose, stepping around its base with care. She must head home. If her mother learned how far she'd wandered...

A man stood, regarding her warily.

She froze.

His form was muscled heavily, his chiseled torso slick with sweat. He wore only a chiton, draped low around his hips. It, like the rest of him, showed signs of toil under the hot afternoon sun. His hands... they were red, bloodied.

His gaze would not hold hers, yet she sensed no threat in him. *Better to be sure.* She stepped back, pressing her hands to the tree trunk once more, seeking answers. The tree's quick answer eased her.

"Are you hurt?" she asked.

He glanced about him, his lips parting then closing.

She paused. The tree had told her this man was safe. She would not doubt her friend, no matter how imposing the man was. But there was a gravity to him... a weight that drew her in. In truth, she'd never seen a man like him, nor felt such a presence. She swallowed.

His skin was pale, lacking the golden kiss of the sun. His hair, blue-black in the afternoon rays, was thick and curling, caught back with a leather tie. His face was hard, rugged and angular... He was beautiful. If a man could be called such.

He shifted, the muscles in his calf and leg rippling in the sun. She swallowed again. There was no doubt this man had the strength to be most dangerous.

His hands clenched, drawing her gaze back to the blood that marred his pale skin. "Are you injured?" she asked, softer this time.

One black eyebrow arched as his guarded gaze met hers. "You speak to me?"

She nodded slowly. "Of course."

He seemed nervous. Or confused? Perhaps he'd suffered a blow to the head. Hermes had told her a fierce blow might disorient a man. She frowned. It would explain the blood on his hands.

His jaw tightened, the muscle bulging.

She stepped forward. "Are you injured?"

It was her voice that reached him first. Such a calming serenade would ease those souls newly sent to his realm, he had no doubt. But he did not seek out the songstress until he'd carried the last body, a seasoned soldier, to the shelter of the tree line.

When he found her he could do nothing but stare. Her form and face captured his attention so completely that he forgot grime and blood stained his chiton and dirtied his hands.

She was an immortal, he had no doubt. She glowed vibrantly, almost blinding in the sunlight. Her every movement was echoed by her aura, the pearly cast a faint ripple in the air.

But he did not know her.

She smiled at him, a sweet smile.

He frowned, confused. A comely woman, immortal or no,

should not wander unaccompanied. Not when Greece faced such an invasion. He'd heard her speaking to someone, surely she was not alone. Whoever it was made no move to reveal himself.

He stared about him, seeking out her companion. "Are you alone, lady?"

She did not answer, so he turned to her once more. Her green eyes were so brilliant he found it hard to hold her gaze... such green eyes, so lovely.

She glanced sidelong at the tree, but said nothing.

His eyes searched the tree, staring up into the branches. He froze then, understanding. His gaze bore into hers, his anger swift and sudden. He'd stumbled upon a secret meeting, between lovers. He'd heard her song and knew the words well. She'd sung of love. And promised never to forget him... Such a promise, given so eagerly, convinced him that she must be here with her lover. Her coward of a lover hid, leaving her alone.

She blinked, the line of her throat tightening as she swallowed.

He was staring. Why was he staring? He stiffened, his muscles going taut and hard.

"Your injury?" Her head tilted, her gentle features growing concerned. "Did you hit your head?" She moved closer to him.

She was too close, was coming even closer. He frowned, willing her to stop. Instead, she reached up, as if to touch him. He stepped back, stunned, holding his hand before him.

"Your hands." She pointed, blinking when his gaze met hers. "You've blood on them," her voice was soft, wavering.

His voice startled even him as he spat out, "It's not my blood."

A slight furrow creased her brow, her eyes going round. "Oh... Well," she ventured. "Good... that's good." She smiled, seemingly well pleased, and rattling him all the more.

The damnable urge to smile found him, though he pressed his lips flat. He'd no time for such distractions. First the souls wandering in the meadow, now this... this vision. He could delay no longer. Zeus had summoned him, had summoned all the Olympians, a rare event. And yet, he was here, staring at this peculiar girl, far from the Council Chamber.

"How did you... What happened?" she floundered. "Whose blood is it?"

Enough. He would ascertain that her cowardly lover was, in fact, hiding here and leave her under his protection. His eyes traveled over the tree, inspecting its mighty branches before searching the meadow again. "Are you alone?"

Her gaze followed his, her curiosity evident to see. She lifted her hand, shielding her eyes as she inspected the meadow. "Are you seeking someone?"

He sighed, exasperated. But her face stopped his sharp response.

Her green gaze lingered on the meadow. The bloodstained, flattened grass stood eerily still, too matted to sway in the warm afternoon breeze.

"You are a soldier." She glanced at his hands then stared up at him. "Were many lost?"

He saw the furrow of her brow, heard the sorrow in her voice, and answered gently, "Not many."

"Did you... Was it horrible?"

His eyes searched hers. "Horrible? Is dying for the sake of glory and honor horrible?"

"No, oh no." She shook her head. "But surely the fighting itself is neither glorious nor honorable?"

Her insight surprised him. Beauty was not her only asset, then.

She paused, uncertain. "I... My apologies. I've no knowledge of war or battle, glory or honor."

Yet she understood the truth, the travesty, of it. "No?" he asked curiously.

Who was she?

She blinked, swallowing as his eyes swept over her face.

His voice was hard. "I ask again, are you alone?"

She shook her head, staring at her feet.

He waited.

"I am not," she said slowly.

His lip twitched. There must be considerable objections to this lover, then, beyond his spinelessness. Why else would she protect him so? "Who were you speaking with?"

A baying howl filled the air, startling her. He bit back yet another urge to smile and turned, whistling once. His hounds raced toward them, their silken bodies undulating through the waving grasses. In an instant, they were at his side.

Hades saw her, stooping low to smile at his formidable hounds. She held her hand out, a welcoming smile at the hounds. The youngest stepped forward, sniffing her hand. "Hello," she whispered, rubbing the hound with dainty hands and graceful fingers.

He swallowed, tearing his gaze from her hands. "Will you answer my question?"

She glanced up at him, still smiling over the dog. "I'm not alone."

"As you've said." He was torn. Should he laugh or shake her? Was she testing him? He took a deep breath before asking, "*Who* were you speaking to?"

He watched, fascinated by the color that bloomed in her cheeks. She stared at the hound, then the tree. "A... a friend."

He sighed, not bothering to hide his mounting frustration. One word from her, a straight-forward answer, and he could be about his duty. If she would not tell him, he would find them. He moved, the hounds following. But he found no one as he circled the massive tree trunk, though his eyes searched every shadow and shrub.

"Where is this companion?"

"Not so much a companion as..." She paused, blushing again.

A lover. His eyes swept over her. *Lucky fellow.* He all but snarled, "As?"

She sighed, looking utterly defeated. "The... the tree."

He could not have been more surprised. "The tree?"

"Yes." She met his eyes, nodding. "This one, this glorious pine, is very old, you know."

This was the most peculiar conversation he'd ever had. His carefully blank expression gave way as true bewilderment settled upon him. Even as his gaze bore into her clear, green eyes he wondered what she'd say next. "Is it?" he asked softly.

"It is." She nodded, warming to her subject. "Older than most of the Greece we know, shading the Titans..."

"The Titans?" he interrupted, unable to stop himself.

"Even Titans need shade on a day such as today." Her smile grew. "Before the Gods overthrew them, they wandered these plains. The mountains, there." She pointed, her eyes roaming the horizon as she continued, "They were taller then, jagged and rough, as was the world. Man had yet to settle or thrive, the beasts were new and skittish. So the Titans would come here, to its green grass and young trees, and dream of what was to come. It was a more peaceful time. Or so I've been told."

He watched her closely, enthralled by the sincerity in her voice. She believed what she said. To hear her, to see the wistful look upon her delicate features, he might believe her too. "Peaceful?"

She nodded. "It was a very long time ago, before the Titans grew greedy, before war with the Gods, before man sought power... A long, long time ago."

He glanced at the tree. That she spoke of a tree, not a lover, pleased him. "Are you a nymph?"

"No." She shook her head. "My attendants are. Nymphs, that is."

He regarded the tree in silence. He'd thought not. She was too gentle, too guileless a creature to be a nymph.

"It's a lovely tree." She placed her hand on the trunk, stroking its bark with a satisfied smile. His lungs tightened. "The loveliest pine in all of Larissa, perhaps all of Greece. It will shade travelers, bring joy and comfort, for years to come," she added.

He marveled at the smile upon her face. He'd never seen such adoration. And yet she clearly held deep affection... for this tree? "Who are you, lady?"

A shout went up, startling her again.

He turned as the hounds leap to attention at his side. The hair between their muscled shoulders rose on end. Their ears flattened, and teeth, dangerously pointed daggers, flashed as the three growled as one. They were no longer alone on the meadow.

The clash of metal reverberated, then another cry.

He stepped in front of the girl as a hoplite soldier ran from the trees and into the field. His gait was awkward, as if one leg was too heavy to move with ease. Hades sucked in his breath when he saw why. His leg was cut, near hanging from the knee joint.

The hounds whimpered as two men ran after the injured soldier. Swathed in layers of colored silks and veils, these men were no Greeks. Persians, Persian messengers or spies, were gaining ground.

He searched the trees for some sign of reinforcements.

"Is there no one to help him?" she whispered.

But he could see no one. This soldier was likely a survivor

from the battle he'd tended earlier. And wounded as he was, Hades doubted the soldier would survive the day. Still, the terror lining the young hoplite's face grieved him.

Hades felt his fear. It churned in his stomach, demanding he act.

"Can you..." she paused. "I beg of you, sir. Help him."

He turned, his eyes traveling her face. She did not know what she asked of him. But he did, and he would suffer the consequences, later.

His hands throbbed, a spark of frigid cold scorching his palm and numbing his fingers. He fisted his hands, grasping for control. His hounds followed, their jaws snapping as they went.

He had a choice to make. Fight them, or use the gift the Fates bestowed upon him. He shook his head, bracing for the fight without thought.

He walked to the first Persian, blocking his path. The Persian, no small man, did not hesitate with his sword. Hades evaded the blow, turning to the side as the man rushed by. He threw his elbow back, landing a well placed blow to the Persian's side.

The man grunted, turning with his sword at the ready.

But Hades saw the other Persian, too close to the wounded hoplite, and knew he had no choice. This fight was done. His hands loosened, releasing the power as he met the advancing Persian.

He grasped the villain's shoulder firmly and pulled. The sound, a heavy rending of flesh, wet and fluid, filled the air. His grip tightened, his arms and chest taut. The tearing gave way to a scream, one that gargled and choked but would not end.

The pain, the agony of this man, filled him. He could not escape it, or ease it. He could only endure it as it went on. With a final tug, he parted soul from flesh.

He gasped, drawing in a deep breath.

He was vaguely aware of the girl's horrified cry as she clapped a hand over her mouth.

The pain began to fade. The Persian's body, bloodied and mutilated, fell to the ground before him. The soul, a wraithlike shadow, writhed in his grasp. Flickers of life, of the souls remembered sensations, seared his fingertips. He released it, uncaring where the wind took it.

The second Persian stood frozen, holding his hands in front of him to ward off such evil. He spoke rapidly, backing away from the meadow in surrender.

Hades turned, hoping the Persian's fear would carry him quickly from this place. He glanced at the girl, prepared for the horror he would find there.

Instead she cried out, frantically warning him, "Look out!"

Hades ducked, but not far enough to avoid the smooth slip of the dagger across his shoulder. He drew in a deep breath and grabbed the Persian.

Chapter Two

Persephone crouched on the ground, covering her ears and pressing her face to her knees. She could not listen, she would not watch, not again. There was little doubt that what she'd witnessed would haunt her dreams long after this day was finished.

She dared lift her head only after the grass beneath her assured her all was well. Peeking between her fingers, she saw him. He stood, breathing heavily, in the waving grasses. For an instant, he trembled. There was no pride or satisfaction about him. He seemed, to her, defeated. Yet the bloody evidence of his victory lay on the ground by his feet.

She turned away, her stomach roiling. Terror and disgust, astonishment and awe, sadness and relief, all warred within her.

There was no mistake; he'd done as she asked. And now he searched, following the trail left by the wounded soldier.

Did the soldier live?

Persephone stood, the fate of the fallen soldier taking precedence to all else. She scaled slowly down the hill, on unsteady legs, to aid the man and his hounds in their search.

Her eyes lingered on the broad line of his shoulders, the play of muscles beneath his pale skin commanding... and, she knew now, most lethal. Who, or what, was he?

For all that he was capable of, he was not a thing of evil.

The man stopped, staring down. His shoulders, all of him, drooped, revealing much.

Her chest grew heavy as she ran forward. The soldier lay, the blood from his near severed leg soaking the ground at his side. It was not his only wound. His stomach was pierced as well. His chest rose and fell, but it was labored and unsteady.

"He has little time left," the man murmured. "His wounds are too great."

She nodded, fighting panic. If only she were Apollo, she would heal him.

The soldier, a mere boy, moved. His hands contracted, claw-like fingers seeking some sort of anchor in the earth beneath him. She knelt by the soldier, taking one grasping hand in hers and leaning over him.

"You've honored Greece," she whispered.

The boy turned murky eyes upon her, fading already. "Have I?" His hand tightened about her. "I fought. But...there were so many... I ran..."

She smiled brightly, hoping to ease him. "You will have glory."

"In Elysium?" the boy gasped.

She squeezed the boys' hands, wishing she could do more. *Hades, hear me*, she prayed silently. "I'm sure of it."

The boy nodded once. His body seized, tightening awkwardly, sharply, before gradually relaxing. A faint smile crossed his face as his grip loosened upon her. His chest stilled then fell slowly, his final breath a hiss of air that wavered and stopped. His eyes cleared, the lines bracketing his mouth relaxed, and a thin stream of blood ran from the corner of his mouth.

He was gone.

She sat back, tears falling freely down her face. She sniffed, placing the boy's hand gently upon his chest. She heard the tremor in her voice as she asked, "Will he?"

"Will he?" His voice was softer than she'd expected.

She looked up at the man, astonished to see pain and anguish within the depths of his blue-black eyes. When his eyes met hers, his face stilled, becoming remote and distant once more.

She sniffed. "Reach Elysium? Will Hades find him worthy, I wonder? He is a child yet, too young to have earned true glory, too young to have fallen alone."

"This boy died for the honor of his country. That is worthy of

Elysium, is it not?"

"Yes? Surely it is…" She blinked, wiping her tears with an unsteady hand. "I hope so. But I am not Hades."

The man's mouth twisted sharply, surprising her. "No, you are not."

She turned back to the soldier. How still he was. Her tears fell, landing on the grass. A carpet of tiny blue flowers sprang up, embracing the boy in the thick, fragrant blooms. Her tears moved the grass and the earth, or perhaps this boy's sacrifice moved her friends as well. She touched the ground, murmuring her thanks at such kindness. This was his memorial.

She picked one, placing it upon the boy's chest.

"He must have a coin to pay the ferryman." She'd given her word that he'd reach Elysium. But she did not have the one thing he needed to make such a journey. She stared up at the man, pleading, "Do you have a coin?"

The man's face remained impassive, but his eyes were riveted upon the tiny blue flowers that continued to blossom. But she could not worry over it now. Who she was seemed of little importance next to this boy's eternal fate.

She scanned the boy's body, finding a small pouch tied to his belt. She reached for it, pausing to look at the man. "Can I?"

The man's brow rose. "You seek a coin for his crossing?"

She nodded. "I do."

The hard set of his face remained, but his eyes held no censure when they met hers. "He would thank you for it, I'm sure."

She pulled the pouch free and poured the contents into her hand. Two coins, a smooth rock and a very thin, pointed stick were inside. She took a coin and placed the rest back in the pouch, tying it back to the belt.

She stared at the boy, her hand shaking as she touched his cheek.

The man moved forward, kneeling at her side. He closed the boy's eyes, took the coin and placed it under the dead soldiers tongue.

He handed her his cloak then, looking pointedly at her hands. She took it, startled by the amount of blood that covered her fingers and palms. She swallowed, her hands trembling fiercely. She wiped the cloak across her palms, wincing as it smeared and streaked her arm. She continued rubbing her hands and arms until her skin felt raw.

She glanced at him. "I am indebted to you."

His eyes seemed to pierce hers, holding her gaze. He was both curious and... angry. With her? But he said nothing.

"My thanks," she continued, somewhat breathless, "for coming to his aid."

His gaze shifted, settling on her mouth for the merest of moments. His jaw clenched. He stood, breaking his hold on her.

She stood too, awash with such sensations, such feelings.

She stared at his retreating form and then ran after him. She followed him back to the edge of the meadow, careful to avoid the bodies of the other men. She would not look upon them.

Images of the battle, if it could be called a battle, of what he'd done, flashed in her mind's eye. But what he'd done, what she'd seen. What did it mean? His actions were not those of a mortal man, none she'd ever heard of.

"You... How..." She paused, thinking of the fallen soldier. Mortal or not, he'd done it to help her, to help this boy. "I thank you."

He stopped, turning to face her once more. There was an edge to his voice, "You thank me? For this?"

The weight of his gaze pulled hers to him. Oh how her heart leapt in her chest.

"Persephone?" Was someone calling her name? Surely it was a trick of the wind. She ignored it, wondering at the darkness of his eyes and the almost braced stance he took.

"Persephone?"

No trick of the wind, then. It was Myrinne, one of her attendants, calling.

She glanced at him. Would he know who she was? Would he know her name?

His brow furrowed, and then his blue eyes widened. Yes, he did.

"Persephone? Are you finished yet?" Crysanthe joined in.

His eyes swept over her slowly, from the fiery red tresses atop her head to the bare toes peeking from beneath the hem of her robes. When his gaze found her again, his lips were pressed flat and his eyes... His gaze was haunted, suffering. Yet something lingered in his dark eyes, calling to her.

"Come on." Myrinne was closer. "Your mother will be angry if we're late again."

"Persephone!" Crysanthe yelled loudly, closer now.

She answered, "I am here," but she could not pull her gaze from his.

"We found all on your list," Myrinne said.

"Your mother will never know what you were up to," Crysanthe laughed. "Or where you ventured..."

They were smiling as they reached her, but fell silent when they saw him. She was faintly aware of the nymphs as they stared, wide-eyed, at this man. They should stare. Had they ever seen such a man before? Even in her limited experience, she thought not.

"You would do better not to leave your mistress so ill-attended. Demeter would see you punished for such carelessness with her daughter." His words were sharp, demanding their attention and commanding their acquiescence.

The nymphs stared at him, their eyes growing round before they quickly bowed.

"I sent them on their way," Persephone spoke, surprised by their reaction to this man.

Stranger still was her own response. What was this inexplicable need to touch him, to ease his temper? She did not deny herself, but moved forward to place her hand on his arm. Her tone was soft, soothing as she assured him, "They've done nothing wrong."

He was surprisingly warm beneath her palm. She stared at his arm, watching the shifting sinew in his forearm, the black hairs sprinkled across his pale skin... She felt the strangest pulse, a heady, consuming pull, where her flesh met his.

She glanced at him. Did he feel it, too?

Her heart thudded loudly in her ears. Had he heard it?

His gaze fell to her hand upon him. He swallowed, his blue-black eyes peering into hers with fierce intensity. He was displeased. "These are dangerous times, lady. You would be wise to keep your attendants at your side."

She nodded, her fingers curling about his arm as her gaze locked with his. "I will."

Breathing seemed a challenge.

His eyes wandered, tracing her brow, her cheek, her mouth, without any hint of his thoughts.

She could not think. Indeed, very little seemed to exist beyond the strengthening pulse they shared. Such warmth radiated up the length of her arm, spreading into her chest. Surely he felt this? He must.

His hand fisted, the muscles of his forearm flexing under her touch. He moved quickly, shaking her hand from his arm.

An ache, new and heavy, filled her chest. Where had it come from? What was happening? She felt off balance, unsteady on her own two feet.

He inclined his head, eyes flashing briefly, and turned from her. "Go now. I have work to be done." He paused, whistling once. The youngest hound stood, stared alertly at the man, then joined Persephone and her attendants. "He will see you safely home."

She could think of nothing to keep him, though she sought any guise to call him back. She felt the strangest pull, the need to call out to him, but held herself quiet. Yet he walked purposefully, swiftly, to the tree line. Each step took him further away, making her heart thunder and twist.

"Come on," Myrinne grabbed her arm and began pulling her from the meadow.

"How did you come to find *him*?" Crysanthe asked, her words whispered.

"He was doing his duty," Myrinne kept moving, glancing back over her shoulder with wide, nervous eyes. "He was collecting those that had crossed over. Did you not see the meadow, Crysanthe?"

"He must know who you are," Crysanthe said, hurrying along. "He would never have spoken to you if he thought you a mortal woman."

Myrinne finished, "Any woman."

"You know him?" Persephone gasped, turning to the nymphs. "Who is he?"

They looked at her in surprise.

"Why he is Hades, Persephone," Myrinne sounded incredulous.

"The Lord of the Dead." Crysanthe shuddered.

Persephone's eyes searched for him in the distant meadow,

but he was gone. "Hades." She let his name slip, too warmly, from her lips. She could not help savoring the feel of it upon her tongue.

Hades stood astonished. Rarely was the Council Chamber in such chaos. The room, a circular chamber of the whitest marble, echoed and shook from the Olympians' overlapping conversation. Twelve marble thrones, a rainbow of colors and shapes, faced one another, but all were empty.

Hera, Demeter and Artemis stood together, their murmurs lost beneath the roar of the rest. Hera, Goddess of marriage, would hear many prayers in the days ahead. Husbands, wives, and children alike, all would worry over this war's toll. He would hear them too.

Demeter's harvest had been plentiful, easing the concerns over provisions for those fighting and those left behind. But the next crop might suffer, if none remained to tend it... or the Persians burned the fields to ash.

He understood why Hera and Demeter looked grief stricken and concerned. Even wild Artemis looked resigned, holding her bow tightly to her chest.

Hermes, Zeus, Ares and Poseidon carried on loudly, their voices rising and falling to be heard. Athena stood amongst them, more at ease amongst the Gods than her fellow Goddesses.

His eyes swept the room. It seemed only Apollo and Aphrodite were absent.

So he was not the last to arrive. He strode into room, prepared for a set-down from Zeus. But the others were lost in their debate, too embroiled in matters of war to note his late entrance. For that, he was grateful.

"They'll have no more success this time than the last," Hermes spoke.

"Better to drive them back," Ares added. "Better to crush them once and for all."

Hades sat in his little-used throne and waited, considering their words.

Hebe, the Goddess of Youth, offered him refreshments. Her normally bright smile was forced, and her eyes stared upon the floor. This was the effect he was used to having upon women. This was as it should be.

He stared at the ambrosia. He did not like the taste of it. It was a cloying meal, weighing down his limbs and thickening his tongue. The drink, nectar and wine, he downed quickly enough and set the cup aside. He would welcome another cup, if Hebe dared offer him more.

His hands ached, chilled still from their work on the meadow. He flexed his hands, noting that bits of dirt and blood still clung to his fingers. He had washed quickly, knowing his lateness would provide meat for his fellow Olympians to feed upon. And after the morning's events, he feared his patience too far gone to tolerate their heckling.

Truly, this morning had seemed to tilt his world completely. Now he must forget, and right it once more.

Athena's voice rose, filling the Chamber and grabbing his attention. "Athens' hoplites are strong, trained well to defend the city."

"You would refuse my aid? You think your mortals can thwart the numbers that Persia will place upon Greek soil?" Ares stared, shaking his head. "This is war, Athena. My realm..."

"Olympus will have no need to interfere or offer aid, you will see," she snapped.

He thought of the boy he'd left, his body surrounded by tiny blue flowers. His aid had done little to help the soldier.

"We must decide such matters carefully." Zeus turned a pointed gaze upon Athena, then Ares. "That is the purpose behind this meeting, to ensure Greece, and Athens, victorious."

"Our soldiers would do better without such a storm." Apollo swept into the Chamber, his golden face tight with anger. "I fear we've lost more to the waves than to their mortal adversaries."

He'd encountered no storm. The sun, Helios' sun, had set Persephone aglow. Persephone. He stiffened, searching for Hebe and another cup of nectar. But Athena's face, her flaring nostrils and red cheeks, caught his eye instead.

"Storm?" Athena glared at Poseidon.

Poseidon shrugged. "None of my doing, niece. I am here, as you plainly see."

Hades' eyes traveled between the two, marking Athena's narrowed eyes and Poseidon's contrived innocence. It was an old rivalry, one that seemed to have no end.

Would Poseidon ever tire of scheming? Surely provoking Athena grew tiresome. And how could Athena, Goddess of Wisdom and Reason, not see how shameful such pointless squabbling was?

Why did he continue to expect changes from them? Hades let out a sigh of exasperation. Olympus was beyond his control. He would stay for as long as Zeus required, no more. Until then, he would be wise to focus only on the matter at hand. The war, the mortals... Greece.

He fixed his gaze upon Apollo.

"And yet a storm wreaks havoc on *Greece's* ships." Apollo ran a hand through his gilded locks, smoothing the rain from his head.

"Is it so grave?" Zeus sounded astonished, causing Hades a moment's sympathy. He did not envy his brother dominion over all.

"It is." Apollo nodded. "For its temper is unleashed upon the Greeks while *sparing* the Persians."

"What?" Zeus roared.

Hera gasped, clutching Zeus' hand in her own. "Who would do this?"

Who indeed? Hades wondered at such foolishness. Surely even Poseidon... From the corner of his eye, Hades saw it. A quick smile of victory flickered across Poseidon's face.

But Poseidon covered his mouth as he rubbed his chin in mock consideration.

What ruse was this?

"Phorcys..." Poseidon began, leaning forward with a sparkle in his eye.

Does no one see the bastard's pretense?

Hades' gaze swept the Council Chamber in hopes his brother would be caught. If anyone suspected as he did, he saw none of it. He sighed again, clenching his fists in his lap. If the others were so obtuse, he would not deign to enlighten them. Likely they would accuse him of seeking vengeance or retribution.

"That spineless Titan would not *dare*!" Athena cried.

"Justice," Zeus intoned, his voice hard, his anger palpable, "will find him. It seems we've no time for debate. I fear this day will bring many to your realm, Hades. See that you are ready."

Hades stood, all too eager to depart. While he had not learned the reason behind his summons, Apollo's news demanded action.

Zeus spoke with gravity. "Poseidon, go and end these storms."

Hades watched Poseidon, his eager nod, the heightened color of his cheeks and smile on his lips. Whatever scheme he'd set in motion, Poseidon was most pleased.

Hades moved quickly, wishing to put some distance between them.

This day was far from over. He *knew* what this war would reap, knew Charon's purse would grow heavy with coin and his ferry would bring many across the rivers to his home.

"I'll accompany you, brother." Poseidon appeared at his side, smiling. "As we've both been sent to do Zeus' bidding, we might make the journey together."

Surely he'd been tested enough this day? But to endure his brother's company, alone...

Poseidon whistled. His giddiness, gravely misplaced in the face of such news, strained Hades' fraught nerves. He held his tongue, broadening his step to speed his descent.

"Can we not find some common ground to remark upon?" Poseidon shook his head, looking comically disappointed. "I would think you'd be eager for some companionship, even from me."

"You are mistaken," Hades answered.

Poseidon laughed loudly, falling in step at his side.

The words were out before he could stop them. "I've seldom seen duty please you so."

Poseidon turned the palest blue eyes upon him, smiling broadly as they continued down the mountain. "Saving those poor souls from a Titan's wrath is surely enough to please me."

Hades caught his bitter smile. To reveal anything to Poseidon – a twitch, a sigh – was to reveal too much. "For you? No."

"You are far too shrewd, brother. I fear you'd ruin my fun if you visited Olympus more often." Poseidon laughed again, clapping Hades on the shoulder. "I think you'd learn the root of my sport before the rest had begun to suspect anything was amiss."

Disgust rose within him, and anger that should have long ago extinguished, blossomed anew. He stiffened, ignoring the urge to shake his brother's hand from his shoulder.

His voice revealed none of his conflict as he murmured, "I far prefer the peace of my home." *Learning the root of your so-called sport turns my stomach, brother.*

Poseidon shuddered, clapping his shoulder again. "If you have peace it's because the company you keep are dead, Hades. Unlike the lady I will call upon shortly."

Hades froze, the disgust in his voice unmistakable. "A woman?"

Poseidon laughed, shrugging. "Not just any woman..."

Hades stepped forward, his words hard and sharp, "Will she help you calm the storm? Save Athens' finest?"

Poseidon's brow quirked as his lips curled into an amused smile.

Hades stepped back then, cursing his temper.

Poseidon's pale blue eyes narrowed, assessing Hades with interest. "I will settle the storm for the mortals." Poseidon rubbed his hands together, staring at Hades. "And she *will* settle the storm raging in my cock."

Hades stood still as stone. Poseidon need not know that he longed to pummel him senseless. That he would have happily thrown his arrogant bastard of a brother down the mountain. It would do him no good. Such actions could offer him no peace. There were times immortality was the cruelest sentence. He would never be able to extract the revenge he longed for.

Hades took the last steps from Olympus in silence, moving quickly, ahead of Poseidon. Once they stood at the mountain's base, he stopped. He did not look at Poseidon as he spoke; he could not risk it. "I charge you to remember your lot, brother. Those soldiers, Greece, should not look to luck in times such as these."

"No luck is needed, for Greece, her soldiers or...my lady." Poseidon met Hades' eyes with a taunting smile. "Luck would do the lady no good, for she has no choice." With those words, Poseidon melted into vapor and blew towards the city.

Hades felt bile flood his mouth. Fury, hot and churning, quickly followed.

She has no choice... He sucked in a ragged breath, rolling his neck to release the tension that knotted and pinched his broad shoulders.

His eyes followed Poseidon, a swiftly moving shadow, drifting towards Athens. Would he do his duty? Hatred, his constant companion, mixed with grief for those that would suffer under Poseidon's care.

Charon would ferry soldiers to the Underworld's shores this eve. Soldiers Poseidon should have spared.

That his brother was selfish was no surprise, most of the Olympians were. But where the others might find a way to justify their actions, Poseidon felt none was needed. He was an Olympian. His every action and word was for his purposes and none would stand in his way. He reveled in his self-indulgence.

In the time since they'd drawn their lot for life, Poseidon had changed little.

And Hades' loathing for his brother had changed not at all.

Chapter Three

"You have nothing to say?" Demeter stood before him, her face alight with amusement.

Erysichthon of Thessaly stared open-mouthed at the deity before him. He shook his head. "For once, I'm speechless, Goddess."

She laughed. "Your words prove otherwise, oh mighty King."

Her laughter stirred him, pulling a smile from him.

She'd not changed since the first time he'd looked upon her. Nor had the love he felt for her... But such sentiments were one sided. The love she bore Erysichthon came from his complete loyalty to her as his Goddess, nothing more. But this? She knew of his affection for her, his devotion for her. Surely she was mocking him.

"You are in earnest?" he asked, surprised by how tight his throat had become. She must care for him then, to suggest such a thing. "It is a surprise, Goddess."

Her brown eyes narrowed as she regarded him. "A pleasant surprise, no doubt?"

He nodded quickly, "Yes, yes. Pleasant can scarce describe such a... gift." He paused, still stunned by her words. "I swear by my honor, I will esteem to earn her."

"If Hermes will not," Demeter cautioned. "I would see her marry from the Olympians first, of course."

He nodded, taking no offense. He was, after all, a mortal king's son. He may rule all of Thessaly, but he was only mortal. He could hardly find fault his Goddess for wanting an Olympian match.

"But if Hermes will not have her, I would see that you do."

He should be pleased. No, more than that. What she proposed was a rare honor...

"She is young." Demeter moved forward, staring down at him. "And innocent. I would have you remember that. Such a gentle soul will need a show of affection and time to accept this match."

Erysichthon watched a faraway look claim Demeter. His eyes wandered over the Goddess, curious to know if his young wife would be as fair as her mother. None had seen Persephone, Demeter was fiercely protective of her. Some said it was because the girl was hideously disfigured, that Demeter thought to save her daughter from the ridicule or malice from those that should respect her.

He prayed that was a rumor. He would do as Demeter asked, wed and bed the young Goddess. But it would be easier if she was comely. If she resembled her mother, it would be... He felt heat rush to his loins.

Her brown eyes bore into his, causing his heart to thunder within his broad chest. "I know what you are, what appetites you have. Your skills are your sword, your loyalty, and I value them. But I must know, can you be gentle?"

"I will be whatever you ask of me," he promised. If he was to marry Persephone, he would lose Demeter. He knew it and ached.

Demeter smiled at him, tilting her head slightly. "And that is why I chose you."

"She is in favor of this match?" he asked.

Demeter shrugged. "My daughter has no notion of you or my wishes when it comes to this marriage. But she will, soon. There will be, however, some changes within your kingdom."

He waited. Demeter had shown him mercy since his reign began, more than twenty years before. In return, he'd been careful of her, taking pains to keep faithful to her and those she cherished. When he'd learned of her affection for barley, for it reminded her of Persephone's hair, he planted fields of it. When her beloved cypress grove was threatened by fire, he fought the blaze without a single tree lost.

"Speak them, Goddess, and they will be made."

"You will have no more mistresses." She watched him closely as she spoke. "And your daughter must leave. Marry her to your neighbor. His holdings are almost as grand as yours, are they not?"

Such a notion had crossed his mind many times. But Ione was young, a comfort to him. He'd thought to pass more years with her at his side. He'd hoped as much.

Demeter sighed, as if she could hear his thoughts. "Besides your Goddess, there can be only one woman in your heart, Erysichthon. I demand it."

Her words cut deeper than a sword. While he'd only ever loved Demeter, his daughter Ione was the only one who'd ever loved him. Pain, and anger, twisted his gut.

"I know you are fond of her," Demeter continued, "as I am fond of my own daughter. If I am to give you Persephone, a Goddess, you will send your Ione to the north."

He could not meet Demeter's eye, not when his anger burned so. But he nodded, his voice only slightly husky as he acquiesced. "It shall be done, Goddess."

Demeter touched the top of his head. "Come now. You will have more daughters, demi-gods at that. Your Ione will not be dead or punished, just gone to live a new life of her own. How proud she will be, for you will both marry well. How pleased she will be to see such honor bestowed upon you. Much better than losing favor with the Gods, surely? Better than two such loyal worshippers suffering the Olympians' wrath? Is it not? Think on it that way."

He said nothing, for his anger burned brighter. She threatened him? His Ione? When he had been nothing but loyal to her?

But he must be careful. For Persephone would live with him, away from her mother's influence. Once the vows were done, he would find a way to bring Ione home again, somehow.

Until then, he must remain Demeter's most devoted servant. He took a deep breath, speaking calmly, "You do me, and my daughter, the highest honor a mortal can hope for. I thank you."

She smiled down at him, patting his bearded cheek. Her palm lingered, one finger stroking his thick brow. "You are welcome, Erysichthon. See that you do nothing to make me regret such generosity. Won't you?"

He shivered from her touch, ashamed when he turned into her palm. He inhaled, pulling in her scent. Earth and honey, flowers and grass, woman, all swirled in his nostrils. His attempt to stifle a groan was unsuccessful, but she did not scold him for his lust. Instead she tilted his head back, her brown eyes bright.

"Can you be gentle, mighty Erysichthon?" She ran her fingertips over his mouth, watching her movements with heavy-lidded eyes.

He swallowed, desperate to pull her to him. Did one seduce a Goddess? Did one dare try? For her touch upon his mouth was more potent than any coupling.

"I can be," he murmured, daring to add, "I would show you."

She smiled, her hands cupping his cheeks to tilt his head forward. She placed a kiss upon his brow, whispering, "Show my daughter."

He closed his eyes, the throb of his hunger pounding in his ears. When he opened them, she was gone and he was alone, kneeling on his floor.

The cave dropped, a mere shelf of rock that hung over his realm. Hades stood, peering at the world that stretched before him. Tartarus glowed red from here, a wasteland of pain and suffering. Only those most evil and cursed were sent there. Such was fitting company for his mood.

He grasped the edges of the ladder, climbing swiftly down. The ladder swung, suspending him precariously in the thick blackness separating Tartarus from the rest of his realm.

The Erinyes, those he charged with Tartarus' keeping, would have followed his orders by now. They never tired of tormenting their charges, of bringing suffering to the damned. It was their way. But his mood made him restless and he sought any distraction. Tartarus offered much in the way of distractions.

The smell of sulfur, blood and smoke welcomed him. Heat wafted from the tunnels leading to the earth's core, spewing steam at irregular intervals. He dropped from the ladder, landing on the warm, black dust with a thud. His eyes narrowed, adjusting to the red flickers of light and lengthening shadows.

"Didymos," Hades greeted Tartarus' master guard, chosen by the Erinyes themselves.

Didymos bent low, his booming voice echoing, "My lord."

"Hades," a woman's voice stirred the hair on his neck. "What do you think of your reinforcements?"

Hades turned, glancing at the Erinye before him. He took care to reveal none of the aversion her appearance evoked. They may assist him in his realm, but theirs was a fragile friendship. Erinyes were spiteful creatures, easily offended and quick with their retribution. Only a fool would make an enemy of an Erinye.

"More guards have been placed, as you ordered." The Erinye's voice was deep.

Vaporous forms, hardly recognizable as men, lined Tartarus' wall. Their eyes, black holes that flamed and sparked, did not rise to regard him. To look upon him would set the Erinyes' wrath upon them.

He nodded. "Good."

The Erinye added, "We shall reinforce the wall next, my lord."

The Erinye bowed, returning to the shades. She paced before them, her whip snapping with threat. She moved, a true hunter, like one stalking its prey. Hades' eyes traveled over the souls that were once men. Whatever their crimes among the living, there was no escaping punishment in death. She would see the wall twice as thick, and enjoy it.

In truth, those that fell under a Persian sword would not enter Tartarus. Few that fought for their country, died for their country, were sentenced to eternal torment.

War brought sorrow to all. How many wives and children, mothers and fathers, would Charon and Cerberus drive back from his realm when war brought their loved ones here? How many mortals and souls would cry out in anguish, reaching even his ears, when they were denied?

What would it be like to have someone so devoted? That they would travel into the Land of the Dead, to plea for your release or one last glimpse of your face?

It was a sorrow he would never know. He should be glad of it. His life had seen enough sorrow. He would not seek more out.

He set off, prowling the tunnels with a sharp eye. All he passed bowed. The shades trembled, falling to their knees while the Erinyes stooped low.

He wound through every passageway, following the corridors those within Tartarus had made with a small hammer and pick.

They were endless, opening on to tunnels, cells or vaults. On and on they went, winding back and forth, towards the main cavern.

It seemed that man had an affinity for evil and Tartarus would need to grow. He left the tunnels, watching the shades work.

They were gruesome to behold. More spirit than flesh, their eyeless faces and bent, twitching movements were the stuff of nightmares.

If he were mortal, would he be sent to Tartarus? He'd done terrible things in his time.

"Will Hades find him worthy, I wonder," Persephone's voice reached him.

She'd looked to him for reassurance that the young soldier would find peace, not knowing he would be the one to give it to the boy. Or take it from him.

The days since he'd returned had done little to dampen his memories of her, or the troubling effect she'd had upon him. He could feel the throb of her, the pull of her touch upon his arm. Indeed, the air seemed to come alive, searching for her... aching for her, if he thought on her too long.

He moved forward, grabbing up one of the large boulders meant for the wall and set to work. It was not the first time he'd toiled alongside those in Tartarus, but it had been years since the need was as great as it was now.

He would chase away her presence, or go mad from it. She lingered in his mind's eye and haunted his dreams. Why, he did not know. But he would banish her.

He worked on, until his back ached under the weight of the massive black rocks and he grew weary from the heat.

"My Lord," Didymos spoke from behind him, "Judge Aeacus calls."

Hades nodded, set the last stone and straightened, flexing and rolling his neck and shoulders.

Didymos backed away, his eyes downcast as he returned to his work. This man had been a monster in life. Even now, the man's corded muscles and layers of scars displayed his earthly sins. He'd earned his eternity in Tartarus, the deeds of his life beyond forgiveness. But Hades had found his skills useful. Monster or no, Didymos served Tartarus well.

And Hades valued Didymos. All who served him, loyally, deserved as much.

Hades entered the chiseled tunnels rising gradually to the only opening into Asphodel. The gated hole, a sudden gash caged by leaden bars, was constantly watched over by a dozen guards. No one would leave Tartarus and no one would fall from Asphodel. The gate opened for him, though he had no key. It was the Fates' doing. He was all powerful in his realm, and only slightly less so in the Land of the Living.

The murky sunlight that greeted him was blinding when compared to the red darkness of Tartarus. The air was clean and cool, a balm upon his dry throat.

The guards bowed their heads as he passed, expecting no acknowledgement from him. None was given, for Aeacus was waiting.

"My lord," Aeacus greeted him with a slight bow.

Hades clasped the man's arm. "Aeacus. What troubles you?" He set off towards the crossroads, Aeacus at his side. The Judges of the Dead held court at the crossroads, enabling those new to the Underworld to take the path to their given place.

"One who demands your audience." Aeacus did little to disguise his disbelief.

"Demands?" Hades regarded Aeacus with surprise.

Aeacus shrugged. "With no disrespect, to be sure, but he is most insistent. As he is a hero from Athens, we sent him ahead to your home, to wait for you."

"Why?"

"He would offer up a bargain of sorts."

"A bargain?" Hades stopped, stared briefly at Aeacus then set off again. "Who is this man? A hero? That finds fault with Elysium?"

"His name is Ariston," Aeacus said, keeping stride with Hades once more. "An Ekdromoi of Athena, soldier of Athens and son to Rhodes' high counselor."

"Is he as arrogant as you make him out to be?"

Aeacus shook his head, laughing. "No, my lord, he is not. That is why we sent him to you. He is noble, truly, but not arrogant."

Hades regarded Aeacus, weighing his words. This promised to be an interesting exchange.

"Tavli this eve, my lord? You may try to beat me." Aeacus smiled at him. "Though I will bring my own astragals, for your dice are weighted, I think."

Hades snorted, dismissing him. "If your pride is less injured then bring them, Aeacus."

"More arrivals come, my lord." Aeacus walked at his side. "Boat after boat of soldiers. Some lost to the storm, others to the Persians, off Athens' coast."

"Too many will be lost in this endeavor." Hades shook his head. This was a young war yet, with many battles to come. His ghosts had learned the truth; the Persians were determined to win Greece for themselves. Their numbers were great. He feared they might win in their conquest, if Olympus did not intervene soon.

Aeacus nodded. "I know there were wars in my time, but none so wasteful as this."

"War is always wasteful, Aeacus."

Aeacus conceded as they reached the crossroads. "Perhaps you are right. It is easier to see such folly now."

"Bring your dice." Hades clasped arms with Aeacus in farewell and headed home, alone.

His home rose, stark and black. Carved into the side of a huge mountain, its parapets and arched windows were set into the rock face. He had no courtyard, as was common in Greece and Olympus. But his chambers were grand, connected with sloping passageways and intricately carved doors. All had been constructed with long balconies, extending the length of every room so that he was able to look out over the Underworld if he pleased. It was the first thing he'd built in his new realm, to honor his new station and his new life.

He paused by the river's edge and bathed his face and hands before crossing the bridge and entering his home.

He studied the man that awaited him. A young man, Hades saw, powerfully built. He'd fallen in battle. He bore an angry puncture, from stomach to back, and a jagged cut across his chest. Painful wounds, one that ebbed life slowly and caused suffering.

This man was for Elysium.

Hades walked past the man to sit in his black stone throne. "You have a bargain to offer me?"

The man straightened, drawing in a deep breath.

What would drive a mortal man to seek Hades out? When all others cowered at his name, he would demand an audience.

Hades found a peculiar sense of anticipation settling over him. "You asked for an audience; you have it. Where do you belong?"

The man swallowed, staring into the white-blue flames with a furrowed brow. He spoke a single broken word. "Athens." Ariston of Rhodes lifted pale gray eyes, revealing his pain... so much pain.

Hades spoke carefully, keeping his tone aloof and distant. "You died with honor and glory. Is that not what every soldier wants?"

"My wife..."

His wife? Hades was surprised. "Lives. You do not."

"She is in danger."

Hades heard the pleading in Ariston's voice, and the torment. But he would remain firm in his resolve. "Earthly danger," Hades said. "She is no longer your concern."

"The danger she faces is not earthly, far from it..." Ariston's voice was hoarse, edged with a desperation Hades could feel. Ariston took a wavering breath before he began again. "She is everything to me. I am proud of my death, and the honor it brings my family, but it means nothing if she is in peril. I must know." Ariston kneeled. "I beg you. I beg you to return me to Athens."

Hades stared into the fire, unable to deny the impact of this man's actions. He was here, humbling himself without shame, for the honor, the love, of his woman. Hades was in awe. Would that he was able to feel such devotion, without fear of recrimination?

"Who is this wife?" Hades asked, angered by the hoarseness of his voice.

"Medusa of Athens," he paused. "Now of Rhodes."

Hades was silent, his thoughts racing. Could he help this man? He could help Ariston. This was his realm. But should he? Should he give this man a reprieve?

"When I die," Ariston began.

"You are dead," Hades assured him.

"When I return... die again, I would serve as guardian to Tartarus. I am a skilled warrior, a skill I might offer you." He spoke with confidence.

Hades could do little but stare at the man. Was he mad? Did he know what he was offering? For a woman?

"You vex me," Hades murmured, his brow furrowing at this strange proposal. Surely there was more to this offer. "You offer this to me for a woman?"

Ariston nodded. "She is worthy."

Hades was silent, for his chest seized with anguish. It encompassed him, raw and sudden. It was a pain he'd long denied, buried deep for his own protection.

Ariston continued desperately, "As Olympus has my arm and sword, she has my heart... a mortal, and perhaps weak, heart. My words may not ... adequately express the love I have for this woman. But I cannot leave her when she is at risk."

Ariston would return to his wife, to protect her.

As Hades had once done.

Would Ariston's wife welcome him home? Would she be pleased to have him at her side and in her bed?

Or would she cry in terror and beg him leave her forever?

His hands clenched at the memory, faded but no less excruciating.

Hades nodded. "It is a weakness that is not reserved for mortals alone, Ariston of Rhodes. I understand." Perhaps this mortal would have what he could not.

Ariston was silent, his body rigid as he waited. Hope, hope and excitement, flared in his startled grey eyes. It was more than Hades could bear.

"I will return you to your ship so that you may lead your men to victory. Too many have fallen in this war and I would see it end. When that is *done*, you may go to your wife." The words came quickly, but he did not censure them. He could justify this, for every soldier was needed. He paused then added, "And when you return to this realm, I will expect your fealty when I demand it."

"You have it," Ariston vowed earnestly, and Hades believed him.

Six days of disappointment passed. She'd spent the better part of each of those days needling and prompting Myrinne or Crysanthe. She was far too eager for any insight or knowledge she might learn about him, she knew, but she could not stop herself.

Hades.

His burning blue eyes haunted her.

But her efforts were in vain. The nymphs were afraid of him, Persephone surmised. The few things they had shared with her were uttered in hushed tones. All the while, their eyes had flitted this way and that as if he might appear and drag them screaming into the bowels of the Underworld.

What she'd managed to extract had done little to aid her in searching him out.

He had four monstrous horses, a gift from his brother Poseidon.

He was evil, the bringer of death.

He was cruel and unfeeling...

Such news was useless to her, for she knew most of them to be falsehoods. She'd seen the pain in his eyes. If he was unfeeling, or evil, such pain could not exist. Yet it did, she'd felt it, she knew it. And when she'd asked for his help, he'd not hesitated to give it.

She'd seen his power and understood it. He did not wield it lightly.

No, he was not cruel or unfeeling, he was good and generous and beautiful...

"Persephone?" her mother called to her, distracting her from her thoughts.

"I'm in the courtyard," she answered.

Her mother arrived, wearing the white robes of Olympus. "You missed dear Hermes, Persephone. He had no time for a visit as he was sent by Zeus to summon *all* to Olympus," she said. "I fear there's been little progress in this siege..."

But Persephone heard no more of it. If Zeus had summoned all the Olympians, Hades would be traveling too. And if he was traveling to the mountain, she might find a way to meet him.

"... so stay close to the house as your attendants will not be back for some hours yet," Demeter finished.

Myrinne and Crysanthe had set out this morning under the pretext of collecting wool. She knew better, there was wool enough for half a dozen new garments. Her companions were hunting an altogether different kind of companionship. And when they went to their lovers' beds, she had the day to herself.

Excitement bubbled up within her. She would *see* him. This very night.

"Take your spinning inside," her mother continued. "And lock the doors."

Persephone said as little as possible, knowing her voice would betray her anticipation. She collected the spindle and whorl, as well as the basket of raw wool she'd been spinning. She'd planned to weave this afternoon but it would wait until tomorrow.

Her heart was in her throat and her hands began to tremble, so she paused to steady herself. She must be careful.

While preparing her mother's hair, she took pains to keep her touch light and steady. If her mother suspected she was ill or out of sorts, suspected her of anything, Demeter would defy Zeus and stay with her.

"Why call upon all of us?" Demeter shook her head. "Ares and Athena, certainly, and Poseidon as well, for much of this war is on the seas. Hades will come, poor fellow, as his realm will grow greatly if things do not cease. But why me?"

Persephone found her voice. "Poor fellow? Hades?"

Demeter met her daughter's eyes in the looking glass Zeus had given her. "Imagine how he must feel. To be called up, tempted by the sights and sounds of this realm, only to be cast into the gloom that is his domain once more?"

"Is it so bleak?"

"Bleak? Persephone, the man lives in eternal darkness. His only companionship found with the dead. It explains his grim disposition. He is a churlish fellow."

Persephone made a non-committal noise, hoping her mother would go on. Her mother's description did not sit well with her. Did none see him as she did?

Demeter shook her head, her finely arched eyebrows rising as she spoke. "Poseidon declares him senseless, that his time away from humanity has driven him mad... I say, if Hades is so, then Poseidon must bear his part of the blame for it. It was Poseidon who rent the first wound upon his gloomy brother. Who can blame him if he is mad? His life has afforded him little comfort. And, he is the ruler of death."

Persephone shivered at her mother's words. Death... Had she

not jolted awake these last few nights, remembering the shade being torn from its mortal shell?

But what of this other?

How had Hades suffered at his brother's hand?

Demeter stood, kissing her daughter's cheeks. "Remember my words, Persephone. Stay in the house and lock the doors. I would not risk losing you."

Persephone hugged her mother and waved her off, closing the door with shaking hands and leaning upon its carved wooden surface to calm herself.

She waited as long as she could bear it, all the while her heart racing in her chest. Winding her heavy chlamys about her shoulders for warmth, she borrowed the scarf she'd embroidered for her mother and covered her tresses with the delicate eplibema. She might venture off alone, but she was reasonable enough to cover herself.

Pulling the heavy doors shut, she teased the climbing vines high, to cover them. Only then did she turn, half running towards the roadway.

Her hands trailed along the tall grass as she went, listening closely.

He would come this way. The grass had seen him many times, this was his path.

She walked on, her fingers stroking the grass as she went. She smiled, encouraging the shoots an inch taller with her simple touch.

It was sunset when she made her way to the crossroads.

She touched the base of a towering fig tree, seeking answers. He would pass beneath the trees branches, it assured her. She rubbed her hand over the smooth bark, watching the leaves green and plump at her touch.

"Thank you," she murmured.

The tree entreated her up, into its branches for safety. Hades was not the only man who traveled this road. She climbed high, settling amongst the sturdy branches until he arrived.

Mayhap she'd missed him. Mayhap he was already there? But the tree told her he had not traveled this way in many weeks...

Her heart thundered wildly. *Then I shall wait a bit. If he does not come, I will retire before the sun.*

Chapter Four

The chargers flew, their heavy hooves tossing up earth in their wake. Hades held the reins loosely, giving the horses their head. They had been too long confined and found their newfound freedom exhilarating.

He smiled, savoring the simple joy of racing with them. Faster they went, galloping across the plains without pause. They hugged the base of the mountain, and tore across a wheat field. As they drew close to the main road, he gripped the reins more firmly.

He sighed, straightening his shoulders and tightening the length on the reins. The horses resisted, as did he. But they eventually responded to his hand upon them, slowing to a slight trot.

Orphnaeus shied suddenly, the massive black horse turning into his three running partners in his move to get away. Hades drew the team up, searching for the cause of his stallion's distress.

Then he saw her. She was sitting in the tree, her foot dangling from the limb.

And he felt Orphnaeus' urge to flee, too.

She'd tortured him most sweetly. Every day since their meeting he'd forced her from his thoughts. She was a Goddess, virtuous and protected by both Demeter and Zeus alike. No good could come from this fascination. He wanted none of it.

That the memory of her voice found him to whisper his name, that he could still feel the silken touch of her hand upon his arm, meant nothing.

She meant nothing. She would never mean anything to him. He would not allow it.

And yet his eyes lingered on her, hungrily taking in every inch of her.

Damn her. Damn her copper locks and dazzling eyes. Damn her round curves, her welcoming smile... and damn the slight ankle that dandled before him, swinging back and forth playfully.

Damn her for such beauty.

"You came." Her voice startled the animals anew, making them rear and whinny. "I am sorry," she said as she slipped from her perch to the ground.

"No." He jerked the reins sharply, knowing his team would mow her down without thought.

But the four grew still, blowing hard with ears pricked forward. They made no move against her.

"No?" she asked, standing beside the horses, fearless. Her brow rose. "You didn't come? But... but you are here, sir."

Hades stared at her, exasperated and enchanted all at once. He found nothing fitting to say, so he said nothing.

She smiled, a blinding sight to one who was seldom in the sun's light. "What a team you have. So fine and proud," she whispered to the horses, extending her hand to Aethon.

Before he could utter a warning, the horse snorted into her hand.

Persephone laughed as Aethon lowered his nose to her touch.

Hades was stunned. Mighty Aethon, known to bite and tear flesh, would yield to her touch? Perhaps the beasts could sense her as deity? Perhaps she was capable of magic? Did she cast all living things in her thrall?

His memory had not captured her lovely face, the curve of her lips and sparkle of her eyes well enough. And now, she seemed to beckon to him.

Yes. Yes, she was magical. He could feel her power creeping over him; it was most unsettling.

She spoke to Aethon, stroking the stallion's forelock with gentle fingers. "You are a handsome beast."

Enough of this. "He is not meant for such company." His voice sounded cold and distant, which pleased him. "He is not a pet. He is a charger."

She nodded, not in the least offended, as she continued to run her hands along animal's neck. "He is indeed one of the more fearsome creatures I have ever seen."

He was at a loss. "Why are you here?"

"I was waiting for you." Her green eyes met his.

Her answer startled him, rendering him speechless. His chest felt unaccountably heavy and strangely warm, but he ignored it. She had waited for him. She had waited... for him?

"My mother was summoned by Zeus, you see. She said all had been summoned. Which meant you might also be called upon." She smiled again, her green eyes never wavering from his. "I hoped this would be your route. The grass told me it was, and they were right. They normally are. They have no need to deceive, I suppose."

He remained silent, contemplating her purpose. What game was she playing?

"Does it trouble you, my lying in wait?" She blushed then, further disorienting him. "I only thought... I wanted to..." She shrugged, growing redder with each uncertain word.

Finally her gaze fell from his, releasing him to breathe and think once more. He raked his hand across his face and drew in a ragged breath.

This would not do.

She wanted what? He swallowed. Why had she waited for him? Why did it matter to him? His hands fisted, clenching the reins.

His words were hard, "You are alone again?"

She should not be alone. It was not safe... He stiffened. She was none of his concern.

She nodded. "Mother is on Olympus already. And my attendants are off collecting wool." She paused. "Rather, that's what they told my mother. In truth, they've gone to meet their lovers, I think. Myrinne was missing hers greatly, or so she said last night. It would be taxing, if one was used to such... companionship, to go without. Don't you think?"

Hades could not contain the small smile that her words stirred. "You are fond of speaking."

She laughed. "It's necessary to become acquainted with someone. If you have an interest in making new acquaintances, you should converse with them. I should think. Do you agree?"

His smile was irrepressible. "That is why you're here? Lying in wait for me? So that we might become better acquainted with one another?"

She blushed, but nodded.

He found no artifice, or coy affectations. Either she was a master at such games or she spoke the truth. But it could not be true, for that made no sense. He shook his head, hardening himself. He pressed the smile from his face and turned his gaze toward the mountain.

He would end this now. "I see no need. You would be wise to return home before your mother finds you out, alone... again." He glanced at her, though he knew he should not.

Her face fell, a strangely vexing expression. He did not like to see her so. Nor did he like to be the cause of such displeasure.

No. No, he was in the right. She would be well rid of him and he must be rid of her.

"I have matters on Olympus..." he started.

"The war? So many have fallen."

"I've returned a soldier to the Land of the Living." Why had he told her?

Her green eyes regarded him, her sweet smile returning. "Why?"

He tore his gaze from her, but not before he'd noticed how her eyes tilted slightly or that her upper lip was kissed by a perfectly round mark, inviting him to look his fill at the plump lips beneath. His voice, when he spoke, was soft, distracted. "He was a leader of men. He led his men to victory."

"Then you were wise to return him. Mother worries over this war for the battles will be long and costly. Greece has seen enough wars, she says." She watched him, an unsteady smile upon her mouth as she added, "He will help Athens?"

"One man cannot fight an army, but he can lead one to victory." Hades cleared his throat. His tone was too soft for his liking. He spoke again, lacing each word with an abrasive edge. "And his skill is surpassed by few, so yes, he will help Athens."

It was true. He'd discovered all he could about this Ariston, to know more about the man he'd freed. He was a worthy soldier, commander to the Ekdromoi, the most skilled of Athena's warriors. And while that should have warranted Hades' consideration, it had not been what decided matters for him.

But he would not share that with her. Or Olympus.

"You will be praised for such an act."

It took an effort to keep his face calm, for a bitter sneer longed to surface. "You have never visited Olympus?"

Her brow furrowed. "No, though I would make the trek if mother permitted it. I long to learn more of the world and its happenings."

"While I long to escape it," he murmured.

She paused, pushing her long braid from her shoulder. He could not help but notice the golden curve of her shoulder, exposed now, as she did so. The sun had kissed her, gilding her a most enticing color. Her neck, long and slim, was the same color, as was the slope of her jaw...

"Perhaps you are right."

"Am I?" he asked unsteadily. About what? What had he said?

"Perhaps being there is not necessary. For it's not the being there that excites me, it's the stories. I am fond of a good story." She walked towards his chariot, her hand resting upon the blackened edge.

He swallowed, fighting the urge to push her hand away. She was too close to him. His nerves were frayed enough without her standing so near him. "I must go. The sooner I arrive, the sooner I may leave."

"It will be a short visit then?" Her finger trailed over the engraved demons on the chariot's basket, her eyes narrowing as she studied their faces.

"Too short to be called a visit, if I have my way. I would not make the trek if my brother had not demanded my presence." He watched her curiously, aware he said too much.

"Then I will wait." Her eyes found his.

"Why?"

"To hear what they say. I would hear about the battles from Ares. What Apollo has spied from his place with the sun. Is Athena pleased or quarreling with her uncle? Is Aphrodite present? Mother suspects something is afoot with the Goddess of Love as she's been absent of late. Is Zeus ready to intervene on the mortals' behalf? I would know these things, and anything else you learn, trivial as they may seem to you. Will you tell me?" She paused, blinking at him. "Please?"

He shook his head, entranced by the shift of expressions that crossed her beautiful features as she spoke. She was truly a sight to behold.

"No?" She considered his face, her smile dampening somewhat. "If you return, we can exchange stories. I am a master storyteller, it's true. Even Mother is enthralled by my talent."

She had enthralled him without the use of a story. He could imagine her, absorbed in her tales, animated and lively as she wove a spell with the husky timber of her voice.

His thoughts troubled him, greatly. He should have ridden past her. He should never have stopped.

"What makes you think your tales would be of interest to me?" He did nothing to hide his irritability from her. His words dripped with forceful sarcasm. That he was irritated with himself, and not her, seemed irrelevant.

She sighed, clasping her hands in front of her and stepping away from the chariot. "As I said, I've a gift. I believe one should share their gifts. Don't you? I vow, even you in your concentrated solemnity will be diverted." She paused, smoothing a wayward curl from her forehead absently. The smile she sent him was warm as the sun. "I've kept you too long already. I will wait for you here."

It took great effort to breathe normally. It took a greater effort not to beg her to leave him be, to let him return to his life without wanting...

Or was it too late already?

He did not look at her as he flipped the reins against his team's flanks. He did not turn when they climbed the base of the mountain.

It was only after he'd settled the chariot onto the flat of the road that he glanced back. She grinned at him, waving happily from her perch in the tree.

He was well pleased that he caught himself before he waved in return.

"You would be wise to marry her, dear Hermes." Demeter's words were the first he heard.

But then, only Hermes and Demeter sat in the Council Chamber as yet.

"Hades." Hermes rose, clasping forearms with him. "I fear you will be plagued more regularly by me in the days to come."

Hades nodded. "I will tolerate it."

Hermes laughed.

Demeter did not.

Hades glanced at her briefly, hating the mix of pity and disdain that marred the lady's lovely brow. His gaze remained as he considered Demeter. As lovely as she was, she could not compare to her daughter, in face nor form. Persephone was rounder, softer, she smiled...

"You wound me, sir. Or do you bear me a grudge for losing to me at tavli?"

"I bear you no grudges, Hermes," Hades admitted. "You've skill with the dice."

"Even Hades finds little to fault in you." Demeter took Hermes arm. "I entreat you, consider my offer. Would it be such a chore, to have my beautiful daughter as wife?"

Hades froze.

"And I tell you again Demeter, Persephone deserves better." Hermes shook his head, a warm smile upon his face.

"Is there better?" Demeter asked, fluttering her eyelashes shamelessly.

If he'd had the urge to flee from Persephone, it could not compare with his desire to do so now.

"There is, I assure you. While I am fond of your sweet daughter..." Hermes began.

He knows Persephone? Hades sat in his throne, assuming a pose of casual interest.

"... I would not care for her heart as dearly as she deserves," Hermes continued, "For I've a wandering eye, Demeter. My passion will not be tamed by one woman, no matter the woman."

Would a man want another if Persephone was his wife? He stiffened, angry with himself. He leaned his head against the back of the chair and closed his eyes. He could see her hair in the sunlight, how her eyes sparkled when she smiled.

"Hades, I implore you. Come to my aid," Hermes spoke. "Demeter thinks me a fitting husband for her daughter."

Hades opened his eyes to find them both staring at him. "Is there a man worthy of her?"

He saw the widening of Demeter's brown eyes, the quizzical turn of Hermes' mouth. Had he uttered such words, aloud?

"You should be honored, Hermes, if Demeter thinks you are worthy of her." He waited, watching Demeter smile with pleasure and Hermes sigh in defeat.

He relaxed.

"Demeter thinks you are worthy of who?" Poseidon asked, sauntering into the Council Chamber.

Hades stiffened, as did Demeter and Hermes.

Poseidon smiled. "I've interrupted a scheme? One you wish to keep from me?"

Hades knew his brother would not rest until he was answered. But Demeter was struck silent with shock and Hermes red with embarrassment. None would have Poseidon on Persephone's trail or know that Demeter sought to wed her daughter.

"It is no business of yours." Demeter's eyes narrowed as she spoke. "Must you always meddle?"

Poseidon's grin widened, enjoying Demeter's frustration. And Hades' chest tightened so that his breath grew short.

"A scheme that turns you ferocious, Demeter?" Poseidon asked.

"A nymph, wasn't it?" Hades asked with disinterest. "She spotted fair Hermes and..."

"A nymph?" Poseidon was skeptical. "You discuss the worthiness of a nymph?"

"Young and untried, so it would seem." Hermes was quick, thank the Fates.

Demeter spoke sharply, "An innocent. One in need of protection from you."

Hermes laughed, albeit nervously. "I am flattered, to be sure."

"And well you should be, for she is a lovely creature." Demeter nodded eagerly. "Sappho was struck by Hermes when he visited."

"Sappho?" Poseidon shook his head, staring amongst the three of them with narrowed eyes. He sighed, apparently losing interest, and took a cup of nectar before sitting on his throne. "Still dallying with nymphs, Hermes?"

Hermes laughed, shrugging.

Hades watched closely, but could find no cause for worry. It appeared that Poseidon was satisfied, for now. And then Zeus appeared, followed by the rest of the Olympians.

It began as it always did, pointless bickering and endless boasting. There was never an end to it. Why they felt the need to compete amongst themselves, Hades knew not. The Fates had designed them to serve in harmony, one complementing the next.

But the Fates had been forgotten here, blurred in a haze of indulgence, nectar and ambrosia.

When Zeus finally brought all to order, talk of the war began. It was true, Greece struggled against their foe. Even now, troops of Persians invaded Greece's countryside.

He saw a flash of Persephone, sitting peaceably in her tree.

This was taking too long.

"What can you share, Hades?" Zeus asked him, drawing every eye in the Chamber upon him. "Are the losses so great?"

Hades stood, confirming that Greece's losses were staggering. He continued, "Between those brought by Chiron and Hermes I fear none will be left for Greece." He shook his head. "If I had not seen the toll I would never have considered a reprieve."

A murmur went up. He'd never offered a reprieve, never.

"You pardoned a soul?" Zeus was as astonished as the rest.

Hades nodded.

Again, a murmur filled the Council Chamber.

"Did you not feel it necessary to ask permission for such an act?" Poseidon regarded him.

He met the ice cold eyes of his brother and shook his head. "The Underworld is my realm. It is my choice."

"Who is pardoned?" Zeus asked, waving a hand at Poseidon.

"Ariston of Rhodes, then Athens. A mighty warrior, I hear. He served Athena in Athens, as well." He continued, his voice calm. "He petitioned to return, to fight and serve. He asked only to be returned to his wife once the Persians are gone. I agreed."

"It was a wise choice. He is an Ekdromoi. His skill will be needed at Salamis." Ares nodded as he spoke. "If more could be returned,

50

our odds would be greater."

Hades shook his head at such a suggestion. He tested the Fates as it was.

Zeus mused, "A leader can make a great difference amongst men."

Hades nodded. Had he not said as much to Persephone? Persephone, who waited for him in the tree... Alone.

"Then we must pray that Ariston is such a leader," Poseidon spoke, taunting Athena with a smile. "Did he show such initiative while serving in the Temple?" Poseidon's voice rang out, his enjoyment evident to all.

Hades watched them. Did Poseidon know Ariston? Did Athena? He feared he'd embroiled himself in something more. For Athena stared at Poseidon, her face flushed with unspoken fury. All waited, he thought, for her retort. But she said nothing; an odd turn of events, for Athena was never one to hold her tongue.

He cared not. He would leave.

"He had little chance to prove his prowess while playing caretaker," Ares snorted. "But I've seen him fight. His death was *glory*. He will bring down the Persians."

"Apparently he has the incentive to do just that." Hera smiled. "A rare husband indeed."

"It is, I think, rare to find such loyalty. Be it mortal or immortal," Aphrodite agreed.

Hades silently agreed. Such loyalty, to a woman, was puzzling. He had yet to decide whether he pitied or envied Ariston.

"I, too, have seen this Ariston in battle," Apollo's words interrupted Aphrodite. "He resembles our Ares, only slightly less immortal."

"You've done well, Hades." Zeus praised his younger brother before all.

Hades face remained impassive, shielding his impatience. "Then I shall leave you," he spoke softly as he rose.

Poseidon rolled his eyes. "You rarely venture to Olympus, brother. Why do you feel the need to quit it already?"

Hades refused to be baited by his brother. It would please Poseidon too much.

"Have you captured some nymph and stolen her away to the

Underworld?" Ares teased.

"Not that I have seen," Apollo joined in.

Hades stifled the urge to sigh. Were duty and honor so trivial? No nymph, no woman, had such a hold on him. He would never allow such trivial things to drive him.

"If the rays of your sun were as well-reaching as the cast of your eye, then Athens' crops might fare better." Demeter patted Apollo's hand gently.

As gentle a rebuff as it was, her point was made. Duty trailed their pursuits for entertainment, their curious preoccupation with gossip. Hades applauded her silently.

"Can my brother be tempted with sins of the flesh?" Zeus asked, inspecting him with too much interest.

Could he? Green eyes flashed before him, making him rigid. He could not meet Zeus's eyes.

"You tease him," Athena snapped. "Is that not excuse enough to leave?"

Hades turned, startled by her exclamation. Indeed, all eyes turned to regard Athena.

She looked greatly troubled, more so than he'd ever seen. But her city was threatened and her people at risk. She had reason to feel troubled.

"May he prove himself worthy of your bargain," Ares said. "Ariston, that is. I thank you for returning him to the living, Hades."

"He was most persuasive." He had never seen a man more desperate. It had startled him, and humbled him. Who was he to deny this man? He knew all too well the pain Ariston suffered...

"Love can be most persuasive indeed." Aphrodite smiled.

"Or distracting," Demeter added.

Hera shook her head. "Love can be dangerous, too."

He held his tongue. *I know this, all too well.* But love was not his lot in life.

Persephone could not stop smiling. He was here.

He shook his head, but drew the horses up when they reached the meadow.

She jumped from the tree and ran to them. "You tarried."

He turned to her, surprised. And she saw his smile before it disappeared. Oh, what a smile. She took a steadying breath as she drew closer, watching as he stepped down from the chariot car and began unlacing the team's harness. "What of your hounds? Are they close?"

"The hounds are with Thanatos, hunting shades, or guarding Tartarus. They know their duty without my constant guidance." He glanced at her as he spoke, but she refused to be chastened.

"Let me help." She skipped about the chariot, sliding her hand along the flank of the horse. "And who are you?" she asked the animal.

"He is Nyctaeus, beside him stands Alastor." Hades' eyes met hers over the horses' backs. "And you've met Orphnaeus and Aethon."

She nodded, feeling her lungs tighten under the weight of his gaze. Her hands fumbled briefly before she managed to slip the straps from the harness. "You have the most beautiful horses I've ever seen."

"They will run," he warned.

She ran back, jumping into his chariot as he pulled the harness free.

They bolted. In a thunder of hooves and flying earth, the horses ran. She laughed, catching no more than a glimpse of their tails, streaming on the wind behind them. She narrowed her eyes but in the dusk of twilight, the animals were quickly lost to the shadows.

"They know these hills." His voice startled her.

"You give them leave to run here?"

He shrugged. "Not often enough."

She climbed down from the chariot and walked to him. "You should… You should bring them more often. Soon." That she would delight in his company she kept to herself.

He regarded her, but said nothing.

She stared back, smiling slightly. "How did they receive your news?"

And still he stared at her.

She swallowed.

"Your mother would see you married." His words were low.

Her heart stopped and her lungs tightened in anticipation. How could he know such a thing? Unless… her heart began to pound…

Had her mother asked Hades? She'd never thought her mother would consider such a match.

But why not? Where else would she be as safe? Her safety was all Demeter wanted. There was no place safer than the Underworld.

Her heart rejoiced. Never had she felt such joy.

She longed to place her hand upon his arm. Instead she clasped hands tightly together, saying, "Yes. She would."

"To Hermes." His voice remained even, though his gaze turned to the sky. "Tell me, do you know him well?"

She released her breath, fighting the sorrow that flooded her. *What a silly fool I am.*

"You know him?" he repeated.

She laughed, a nervous breathy laugh. "He has always been kind to me. He visits mother often, for Zeus or matters of import."

"Are you pleased with his suit?"

Persephone turned from him, walking through the tall grass to pluck a white lily. She had too little time with him to let her disappointment ruin it. She turned back to him and shrugged. "I suppose one is no different than the rest? At least Hermes is immortal. I could not bear to wed a mortal, to watch him fade before my eyes. Such pain would be unspeakable, I think..."

His face grew hard at her words.

She tried again. "I have not given Hermes much thought. I have no special affection for him."

"Then why would Demeter be so set on the match?"

"She is a mother, sir, the mother to a daughter, no less. She worries over my safety. She fears I will fall victim to capture, abuse, injury, love, lust, passion, man, *or* ... Poseidon." She laughed, but saw his hands clench.

She moved closer, watching his face in the failing light. While he would not meet her eyes, his agitation was plain enough. His jaw was rigid and a slight crease marred his forehead.

"Is Hermes a friend?" She could find no other reason for his sudden mood. "I've not meant to offend you."

He shook his head, holding himself straight. She could see the throb of his pulse in his throat. It seemed rapid to her.

She swallowed. "What of your soldier? Was his release met with praise as it should have been?" How she longed to take his hand in hers.

He glanced at her then. "It seemed to please them."

She clapped her hands. "If they will not applaud you, then I will."

His smile appeared again, and she matched it with her own. Her heart felt so full.

She handed him the lily, letting her eyes soak in his every detail. "I must leave you now. My mother will carry on if I am not there waiting when she gets home."

He took the flower, holding the offering with care. "*She* will not tarry?"

"No." She laughed, surprised at the hint of teasing in his voice. "*She* will not tarry."

He lifted his blue-black eyes to hers and she feared she'd drown in them. It was a pleasing thought.

She found breathing difficult, but forced the words out. "I owe you a story." Was that her voice, so husky and low?

He shook his head, his dark gaze steady upon her. "You owe me nothing."

She swallowed. "I do not mind... Truly." If only she could stay. She wanted to stay with him. She moved closer, too close perhaps, searching for some word from him, some sign.

His brow creased again, endearing him to her all the more.

She tilted her head, wishing she knew his thoughts.

Before she could stop herself, she smoothed her fingers across his forehead. His nostrils flared ever so slightly, in distaste or restraint? She hoped it was restraint...

She had none.

She moved quickly, rising on tiptoe and pressing her lips to his. His lips were surprisingly warm, surprisingly soft against hers. His breath fanned her cheek, tingling, and his scent filled her nostrils. She sucked in her breath sharply, drawing him in. Her lips clung for a second longer.

She spoke against his lips, savoring his closeness. "Oh Hades, I do not mind."

She swayed, overcome with such warmth and... happiness. She rested her forehead against his chest for but a moment, steadying herself. She could say no more, her lungs would not allow it. Nor could she look at him.

What would he think of her now?

Her lips tingled.

She stepped back, running from him, from the meadow, past the fig tree, until her lungs were gasping. Still she ran, torn between shock and delight, through the ravine that hid their home. Only when the doors were closed and locked did she consider what she'd done. Her fingers brushed her mouth, and she shook her head. She'd kissed him and, she thought, he'd kissed her back.

Chapter Five

The catch in her voice moved Hades, forcing his eyes to hers. Under her gaze, he felt something dangerous shift inside him. He felt vulnerable. He felt lonely. He should feel nothing. "You owe me nothing."

He saw her swallow, heard her whisper, "I do not mind... Truly."

Her eyes held him. His body responded even as confusion plagued him once more. What did she want from him? Why did she torment him so?

Her fingers were cool upon his forehead, soft as silk. Her wrist, the inside of her arm, was lightly fragrant.

She moved suddenly, swaying, pressing the curves of her chest against him. He shuddered, completely unprepared for the touch of her full lips upon his.

By the Fates, she was warm and lush.

He could not bear it. But he must. His hands fisted, denying the urge to pull her to him. He closed his eyes. He would not catch her hair in his hands, or clasp her curves to him. His hands throbbed, clenched tightly.

But his lips would not be denied. They fitted to hers briefly, hungrily tasting her.

How she threatened his control, enticing him mercilessly. He could not give in to this temptation. But her words were as sweet a torture as her kiss.

"Oh Hades, I do not mind."

Her head rested upon his chest, her hair brushing his nose. Her scent filled his nostrils, lilies, earth, and sun, inflaming him. He must hold himself still, keep his eyes pressed shut. One look into her eyes would defeat him. He would not be able to set her away from him.

But now, in this moment, he could think of nothing more than the sweetness of her against him. He was not strong enough. His hands lifted to cup her head, to press her lips to his once more. He drew in a ragged breath and opened his eyes.

But before he could touch her, she ran from him, a flash of white and copper in the moon's rays. His hands gripped only air and then his chest. He breathed out slowly.

He should not feel such things.

He watched her go, aching yet angry. None could compete with her grace, her charm and femininity. He could not keep the smile from his lips as he watched her disappear into the still night.

He must not see her, ever again.

If he'd never stumbled upon her, it would not trouble him to know he must see no more of her. How he wished he'd never seen her.

He sighed, staring at the flower she'd given him. He should crumple it, throw it down and leave it. He smoothed the petal and stem of the flower, tucking the white lily into the clasp of his chlamys with care.

"You've lived too long alone, Hades." A voice spoke, amused.

Hades spun, alert and ready. Was this a trap then? Had she played a part in it?

Hermes stood at a distance, his arms held up in submission.

Did he dare feel relief that it was Hermes who'd come upon him? If it had been Ares or Apollo or Poseidon that had found them so... Self-loathing found him, raging within him. No, he would spare her that.

Hades ran a hand over his face, releasing his pent-up frustration with a low growl.

"Surely that was not the fair Persephone, pressing kisses on your dour face?" Hermes joined him. "It is said that the night can fool the eyes. I've laughed at such a claim many times. But now I wonder, is there truth in it?"

Hades cast a sidelong look at Hermes. To be discovered in such a state of admiration was disconcerting. To be discovered in such a state by the Gods' messenger, a devoted gossip, was another matter altogether. He would try. "If I said there was truth in it, would this night be forgotten?"

Hermes shook his head. "I fear I could not forget such a tableau, my friend." His words were a mix of humor and sympathy. "I am overcome."

Hades' words were a hard whisper. "*You* are overcome?"

Hermes laughed. "Less than you, of course."

Hades shook his head. Would Hermes goad him? Tease him? Reveal this... this interlude to Olympus?

"You care for her?" Hermes asked, no longer teasing.

Hades laughed, a hollow, bitter sound. He had no heart, it had been crushed so long ago he scarce remembered it. "How can I?"

Hermes countered, "She would be easy to love."

"If one was given to such emotions, perhaps."

Hermes chuckled. "Ah, I see. You want her, then?"

Hades glared at Hermes, but said nothing.

Did he want her? The memory of her pressed against him made him burn. Even now his hands ached to cup and stoke her. It was answer enough. He could hardly deny Hermes' query, but neither would he answer it outright.

"She would have you," Hermes continued. "It was plain upon her face. She would welcome you, I doubt it not."

Hades shook his head, ignoring the yearning Hermes' words stirred. "Have you followed me out of curiosity, Hermes? Or were you sent to me on some errand?"

Hermes regarded him, sighing deeply as he spoke. "Zeus bid me give you this. You left too swiftly. Now I see why."

Hades took the scroll Hermes offered. He opened it, reading the missive with growing amazement.

"He thought it would please you, as reward or payment. You acted wisely, releasing one of Athens' finest to fight anew. All of Olympus agrees."

"*This* is how he chooses to repay me?" Hades asked, astonished. "To slake my pleasures with a maid of my choosing? In Aphrodite's pleasure chamber? I was satisfied with their thanks. I need no more.

And I want none of this."

Hermes' gaze did not waver, though he took on a thoughtful expression. "How long has it been?"

He turned his most forbidding scowl upon the young messenger. "It will *never* be that long."

Hermes spoke haltingly. "You may be the Underworld's lord, but you've a man's passions..."

Hades rolled the scroll back up and handed it back to Hermes. "You may return this with my thanks. I have no appetites for such companionship. He would be wise to bestow such a gift on one more appreciative."

"Some are worried, Hades. It's unnatural, this isolation you insist upon."

"This is *worrisome*? That I am ruled by discipline, not lust?"

"What of companionship?"

He felt loneliness, but it was tolerable. "I have enough."

Hermes regarded him with wide-eyed wonder. "You could petition Demeter and Zeus. You might have her yet, Hades... Persephone, I mean."

"She cannot want that." He shook his head, wishing he'd not spoken at all. He bit off the rest, furious for his slip. "No. I will not have her. Ever."

"Why? You are a loyal mate. I know of none on Olympus as faithful to his wife as you..."

Hades moved swiftly, grabbing the front of Hermes' cloak to silence him. "Do not speak of her." He pressed the scroll into Hermes' hand and shoved him away. "Take it and go. Paint me as you will to those on Olympus, but have a care, Hermes." He'd said too much already, so he continued. "Leave Persephone's name from their minds and ears. The thought of corrupting her would be too sweet a temptation for some."

"You speak of Poseidon?"

He paused, speaking with care. "She is innocent. She is, by all appearance in word and deed, gentle and good. It is as you told the lady's mother; Persephone's heart deserves tender care."

Hermes studied him. "I will pass your message on to Zeus, with your thanks and nothing more."

Hades clasped Hermes' forearm in parting. Would Hermes keep

silent? Could he? If tonight was revealed, it would be Persephone that suffered for it. He would spare her that. He would keep her as she was, with sparkling eyes and joyous laughter.

Persephone heard her mother's arrival, heard the front door closing and the murmur of voices. Demeter wasn't alone then, a small relief. If they had company, her mother would be distracted and less likely to notice her mood. Assuming her transformation was a visible thing.

And no doubt about it, something had changed within her. She twisted the wool, humming as she did so, hoping the joy in her heart was safely hidden.

"Let that be the last Council meeting for some time. I tire of such... episodes," Demeter was speaking.

"As do I, Demeter." Hermes' voice joined her mother's, causing her smile to widen. Hermes was a teller of tales and a friend to her.

"Too much ambrosia or too little?" she called out to them.

She heard Hermes laugh, heard him as he made his way to her in the courtyard. "Neither. The Persians were the meat and drink of this night." He paused, smiling down at her. "What have you occupied yourself with this long night, songbird?"

Persephone felt her cheeks warm, but she smiled easily enough. She knew she'd be smiling for days to come, this night promised that. "A new eplibema for Myrinne, I think."

"Your fingers will chafe, child." Demeter joined them, shaking her head. "You've been at it since I left."

Hermes took her hands and looked at her fingers. He winked at her, startling her. "I think they are chafed, indeed. Come, talk with us, Persephone. The Council was not all gloom and strategy." He pulled her along with him.

Demeter sprawled upon her kline and leaned back, relaxing against the couch's thick cushions with a sigh. "Truly, Hermes? I found the talk of nothing *but* gloom and strategy."

Hermes released Persephone, offering her a padded stool to sit. She did, waiting to hear Hermes' rendition of their meeting.

"Come now, Demeter," he spoke, laughing. "Surely Persephone would have interest in the events prior to Zeus' arrival?"

Persephone turned to her mother and watched with piqued curiosity as her mother's brown eyes narrowed dangerously.

"Ah, I see you remember now." Hermes flopped onto the floor, lounging comfortably. "You were the topic of discussion, Persephone."

"I?" She turned from her mother, her curiosity mounting.

"Your mother is determined to find you only the finest of husbands," he began.

"You're a shameless cad, Hermes." Demeter chastised him half-heartedly, smiling all the while.

"So mother was pressing you to marry me?" Persephone shook her head. "Again?"

Hermes nodded. "When Poseidon ventured in."

Demeter scowled once more. "And demanded to know who I would have Hermes woo."

"Oh." Persephone bit her lip. She'd never met Poseidon. She had no desire to *ever* meet him.

Hermes smiled easily. "But Hades was sharp."

His name slipped softly from her, making her wince. "Hades?"

Hermes' gaze was fixed upon her. "Yes, Hades. He was quick to spare you. As Poseidon had not heard your name mentioned in your mother's plot, Hades led him on a completely different trail."

"It was rather gallant of him." Demeter nodded. "Surprisingly so."

Persephone shot a look at her mother, displeased by this disparaging remark. She turned back to find Hermes watching her.

"It is not such a surprise," Hermes assured them.

She blinked. Why was Hermes watching her so closely? Or was he? Mayhap it was her guilt leading her mind astray.

Hermes continued, "He's not the monster all would believe him to be."

She grew uncomfortable under his gaze. "But why would Hades do such a thing?"

"Because of Poseidon," Demeter spoke softly.

"There is bad blood between them?" Persephone longed to know all she could about Hades.

Hermes' smile dimmed and he exchanged a long look with Demeter.

Persephone turned to her mother. "What happened?"

"A sad tale," Demeter murmured. "Too sad and too long to begin at such an hour, child."

Persephone's heart dropped. She would know more. "Is it so late?"

Hermes sat forward, smiling at her. "It was late when I left Hades in the meadows and found your mother coming home to you. I imagine Helios will rise soon."

"The meadow?" Persephone blinked. "You did not travel with my mother?"

"Oh no, Zeus had sent me after Hades, for he had quickly quitted the Council Chamber before he was rewarded for his cunning."

Persephone bit back her smile. He hurried from the Chamber? Because of her? Or was he simply eager to return home?

"He surprised me twice this night." Demeter laid her head back, closing her eyes. "It's a shame he would not accept his reward."

"What was it?" Persephone asked, still considering Hermes' words.

"His deed or his reward?" Hermes asked.

Persephone knew what he'd done, but she could hardly say so. "Both."

"He returned a hero to Athens' battle front," Hermes paused. "So Zeus rewarded him with a woman, a pleasure chamber and the night to enjoy himself."

Persephone swallowed. Too many disturbing images flashed through her mind. And anger, hot and quick, wrapped about her. She frowned.

"But when I found him in your meadow, he had no interest. In fact, he seemed greatly distracted." Hermes shrugged.

Persephone glanced at Hermes and understood. Her heart was in her throat as she waited for him to reveal all to her mother.

"Poor man." Demeter sighed without lifting her head or opening her eyes. "He is too alone."

"Mayhap that will soon change?" Hermes spoke, staring into Persephone's eyes. "We should hope he will find someone who might help him forget the ghosts of his past and find some warmth and laughter."

Persephone blinked.

What was he saying? Was he speaking for Hades? Had he come on his behalf?

"I hope so," she whispered cautiously.

Hermes searched her face, asking, "Do you?"

She nodded.

She could do nothing more than stare at Hermes, swallowing the questions that begged to be asked.

"You are right. He has grieved long enough. We must hope he finds peace," Demeter murmured, her voice fading as she dosed. A thin, reedy snore rose from her, and her posture relaxed in sleep.

Hermes leaned forward, whispering, "His heart is hard."

She shook her head.

"No?" Hermes' brows rose.

"Guarded, yes. But not hard."

He smiled at her. "Guarded, then."

She blushed fiercely. "Do you... Did he send you?" She felt such hope, such promise.

He shook his head. "Never. He would not think it."

Her face fell, but she nodded.

"He will fight you." Hermes held his hand up, further buffering their whisper from Demeter's slumbering form.

"Will he? Fight? Me?"

He nodded. "He will not give up his heart easily. No matter how eager it might be to leave him."

"Is it? If only that were true," she whispered. "I have no wish to... torment him with my ... affection. But I do... I am, most fond of him."

Hermes covered his mouth, shaking his head. "Persephone," he sighed. "He's forgotten what a heart is for."

She felt sadness at such words. "I would show him. I would help his heart find its way... to me."

He studied her for some time, then said, "Then I will help you..."

Demeter sat up, jolting sharply awake and making them jump apart.

"Persephone? I forgot to tell you. In one week's time, we journey to Thessaly. You will meet Erysichthon, King of Thessaly. He is most loyal to me. Since Hermes will not have you, I've decided that Erysichthon may." She yawned, stretching before she rose to her feet. She reached for her daughter's hand, pulling Persephone up with her. "It promises a fine match. For he can protect you when I am away."

Persephone was too stunned to speak or resist.

Erysichthon?

"You may sleep here, Hermes. But my daughter and I must find our beds alone."

Persephone stared blindly ahead, stunned. How could such bliss turn to misery?

Erysichthon watched the last of the revelers go, and with them his daughter Ione. He'd done as Demeter demanded, sent his daughter to wife with a man older than his own father.

His Ione had smiled throughout, a fine daughter.

"A good wedding," a man said, his pale blue eyes assessing him with ease. "I hear the father is soon to marry?"

Erysichthon looked at the man. A fit specimen, well-muscled and agile, Ione would have fancied him. But that he knew of his impending marriage? This was troubling. Few knew he was considering it, and none who he might wed.

"Do I know you?" He knew he didn't. He cut too striking a figure. And he wore fine robes, too fine for an unimportant man. "You were a guest? From Haemon's family?"

The man shook his head. "I come for other business."

"Oh?"

The man's eyes narrowed slightly. "I seek Erysichthon. The great King of Thessaly, warrior of Greece."

"You have found him." Erysichthon paused. "You are from Olympus, then? What does my Goddess want of me now?"

The man smiled, a most magnanimous smile. "Fealty."

He scowled, waving the man to follow. "When have I not given her fealty?" He entered the great hall, waving off attendants and servants. "I have done all she asked, without the promise of her daughter's hand."

He poured two cups of wine, offering one to the man. He paused then. The man regarded him with a furrowed brow, his jaw tight.

"My apologies," he murmured quickly. He would not lose

Demeter's patronage now. "I fear today has been trying. I am honored to do whatever Demeter would have of me, with or without Persephone as my bride."

The man smiled broadly then, his pale blue eyes regarding him closely. "Sometimes the Gods forget what it is to be mortal. It is rare for an Olympian to make any sacrifice, but they do not hesitate to ask for such examples of devotion."

Erysichthon felt the truth behind the man's words. And yet, he knew his Goddess was different. "Demeter is a rare Olympian, I think. She has never asked for anything indulgent of me, until now. And, truth be told, she asks for what I should have already done. Marry and ally my father's kingdom with that of our neighbors."

"You are loyal to Demeter." The man's eyes were too sharp.

"I am." He nodded, treading carefully. "And I will remain so."

The man's gaze wandered, regarding the wine with sudden interest. "Have you met your bride to be? The fair Persephone?"

He near choked on his wine. "Is that your message? Has Hermes refused her hand?"

"Hermes?" Again the pale blue eyes narrowed, a strange smile playing upon his lips. "He has."

Erysichthon smiled. "Well, then, this day grows more promising." He patted the man on the shoulder. "I have not seen her. But she must be a beauty; there is none more lovely than her mother."

"Would that the mother was as eager to marry as her daughter?" the man offered, laughing.

Erysichthon could not laugh. His smile faded, for that had been his dearest wish for so many long years. "I will learn to love her daughter as I love her mother."

The man regarded Erysichthon with a peculiar twist to his mouth. "You *are* a loyal subject indeed, mighty Erysichthon. I can see why Demeter would place her daughter in your care."

He nodded, "We shall see, friend. We shall see."

Chapter Six

"Sweet vines," Persephone whispered, clasping the fragile shoots delicately. She knelt, not caring that she'd be covered in soot. She shuddered with worry. The vines did not call out to her, they were too still, too quiet. "Hear me."

There was no answer from the vines, but the faint scrape of claws on rock reached her.

She was not alone in the vineyard. She sucked in breath, peering into the gloom. Between the low lying fog and dying plumes of smoke, she could see little. The hair on the nape of her neck stood.

"Come away, Persephone," Crysanthe implored softly. "There's too much damage. We will tell your mother there was nothing to be done..."

She heard Crysanthe and Myrinne, but her eyes sought out their silent companion. She found him, eyes warm and golden, watching her. She knew the broad slope of his shoulders and the line of his velvety black snout. Hades' hound...

Was Hades here? Her heart thumped rapidly, causing her to suck in her breath.

She'd not thought he'd venture out, not when his realm was filled each day by the never-ending flow of casualties. The Persians were a fierce foe.

As her eyes wandered the charred vines and stakes, she wondered if this was how Hades' realm would look. Black, dark, despair, and defeat. Is that what the dead had to look forward to?

She would ask him… if he was here. If he was here, if there was a chance of seeing him, she would prefer to do so alone.

Crysanthe and Myrinne complained, anxious to leave this place.

Myrinne was finishing, "If rain finds us, we'd best be home."

Persephone glanced at the sky, unable to separate the smoke from the clouds overhead. Rain was not her enemy. She welcomed the showers for they brought life. She spoke carefully. "I cannot return to my mother with such news. I can save them. They are Dolopian grapes, needed for nectar. I must try."

The hound moved, capturing her attention once more. He disappeared amongst the vines, a ghost in the gloom.

She shook her head. No matter how her heart leapt at the thought of seeing Hades, she must remember her duty. She must do what she'd come to do. She brushed the brittle leaves away from the vines roots. She scraped at the earth, clawing the dead debris away, to plunge her hands into the moist brown soil beneath. It hummed weakly, life flickering.

She smiled up at them, overcome with relief. "There is hope here. I cannot leave it untended."

Myrinne sighed. "What shall we do?"

"This place… It unsettles me." Crysanthe's voice quavered.

Her companions were discomfited. She understood. All around them lay evidence of man's worst abilities. The vineyard, once well tended and abundant, had been annihilated. Such destruction was wasteful and thoughtless.

"Go back." She raised her hand when they both began to argue. "I must do what I can here, to help those still living, those I can save. Listen closely. Gather whatever seedlings have long roots. I've at least six ready for planting, but leave the rest. And bring soil from my pot; it might be needed to repair such devastation."

Such an errand was necessary for the repairs these grapes would need. And it would give her the time to seek out Hades.

"Crysanthe should go," Myrinne said. "It's not safe for you to be alone."

"No, no, Myrinne, you go," Crysanthe shook her head as she spoke.

Persephone shook her head. "Both of you go. One of you cannot carry the seedlings and soil without damaging one or both. Besides, rain is coming. I would have the planting done before it leaves. Go now, hurry."

They'd scarce left when Persephone sensed the hound's return, the dark edges of his shadow moving through the grey-black tangle of the scorched vineyards. She sat back, waiting.

The hound came to her, with drooping ears and tucked tail.

She held out her hands to the animal. "Hello, friend." He crept closer, nervously circling her before rushing forward with a slight whimper. He rested his head on her lap, sighing deeply as he relaxed against her.

She laughed, running her hands over his head. "Are you seeking shades for your master? A hard and heavy task, I'm sure."

What kind of life was lived seeking death? How could joy be found in such employment?

The hound stared up at her, his tail thumping slightly in the blackened earth. Each thump dislodged a cloud of black and grit, making her cough. The hound sat up, cocking his head at the sound, whimpering.

"The dust," she explained. She paused then, her eyes narrowing. "I've no notion whether you can understand me or not. I can speak to the trees, the grasses, and all manner of growing things. But you've no roots." She caught one silken ear between her fingers, rubbing it softly.

The golden eyes drooped, his mouth lolling open in a canine grin. She laughed in return, the sound carrying on the wind.

The faintest plea reached her, silencing her. She waited, rigid. Her laughter... she'd woken the roots and the vine cried out, in sadness and pain. She felt it and called out, "I am here, I am here..." She withdrew her touch from the hound and moved down the vines until she'd found it. She set to clearing the debris from the base of the vine stalk. Only then did she dig into the dirt, pulling and turning the earth with her long fingers.

The sweet sound of the vine was louder then, more reassuring. The roots ran deep, securely anchored below the topsoil. She pressed her hands flat, letting the warmth of her power seep into the earth and the roots. The roots pulled it in, drinking deep of her energy and sighing with pleasure.

69

She listened, moving along the vine stalks. She was deliberate, clearing the area, digging deep and pressing her energy deep. The hound, she noted, went with her.

"There now," she said to the hound. "See how it plumps?" She pointed a dirt-encrusted finger at the stalk she'd just healed.

The dog whimpered, staring at the stalk.

"You're right." She nodded. "It's still a sad sight. But it's a start." She sounded hesitant. The hound came to her side, pressing his nose to her cheek. "I won't give up on them, don't worry."

She moved on, ignoring the discomfort of her nails tearing free in the earth. It made no difference that her chiton grew heavy from soot and dirty ash. She had to answer the call of the vines. But the pleas grew faint, then silent, as she reached the end of the row. She stood, covering her mouth to stifle the cry. The vines had disappeared.

No vines, no grass, no shrubs or trees. Only the smoldering remnants of half of the vineyard remained. The destruction ran the entire hillside. Even the great house atop the hill had suffered.

"Why is such a thing necessary?" she asked the hound. She reached out, comforted by the feel of his head under her palm.

She turned back to the vines, crouching by the silent stalks to weep. "I am sorry," she murmured, sifting through the dirt. She dug in vain, scooping the dirt away and pressing her hands to the plant.

"Take my strength... Let it reach you," she whispered even as the stalk cracked and splintered from her touch. She winced, pulling her hands away as a sob choked her.

The hound whimpered, pressing his nose against her cheek. She wrapped her arms about the animal, accepting the comfort he offered.

"Persephone?" Hades' voice startled her.

She turned, wiping the tears from her face with grubby fingers. How could she feel such sadness... and such joy at his mere presence?

His voice was laced with contempt. "You should not be here."

The dog whimpered, but stayed at her side. Her hands kneaded the animal's fur, all the while assessing Hades' mood. He was angry, truly angry. The tension in his stance, the rigid line of his jaw, made him even more fascinating, and glorious, to look upon.

She could not speak, not yet. Her gaze fastened on his face, remembering the caress of his breath upon her cheek, the press of his lips upon hers... Her hands clung to the hound, keeping her from swaying on her knees. Truly, her body seemed to rise, stirred by his presence. She had thought of him so many times. Had he thought of her?

His face was hard as granite, his jaw clenched fiercely. He would not look at her.

"Come," he bit out the word, startling her again. His gaze fixed on the hound at her side.

She sat back, releasing the animal. The hound shifted from paw to paw, whimpering, but did not leave her. His brown eyes looked between the two of them nervously.

"Go on," she murmured, smoothing a hand over her dirtied skirts. Her hands, she noted, trembled. She stilled, resting her clenched hands on her knees. She must steady herself.

Even his anger pleased her. He was here.

"Did Hermes send you?" his words were soft.

She could scarce contain the surprise on her face at his words. "No, no... No one sent me. Well, that's not true. The grass, the trees..." She hesitated, choked once more from their pain. "The fire was large. As was the suffering, such suffering that all things green and growing called out to me."

"And you came?" His eyes flitted over her face, so quick she feared she imagined it. "Did your plants tell you the cause of the suffering?"

She nodded, swallowing. "And that those responsible were gone..."

He sighed, shaking his head. "Persephone."

She stood, knowing she was covered in the filth and grime of her labor. "I have a duty, like you, Hades. I know it's trivial, perhaps, when compared with you or Hera... or my mother. But they, the plants, rarely ask anything of me. How could I deny them? I could not."

His gaze swept over her, lingering on her muddied skirts. When his eyes found hers, he winced. He drew himself up, stepping back, as if pained.

"Does your mother know you are here?" he asked.

She shook her head. "No. She was needed elsewhere. The Persians are nothing if not thorough in their travels."

He moved so quickly, she took a step back. His face was tight with fury. His tone was hard and bitter. "Go home, Persephone..."

She stared at him, his words all but lost on her. He stood so close she could smell the heady musk scent of him. She leaned forward, letting her eyes feast upon him. His eyes were blood shot, rimmed with black shadows. "You are tired," she said.

A sigh, hiss-like and exasperated, slipped between his compressed lips. "Persephone..."

"You should rest." She was scarce aware that her hand rose, reaching for him. But his hand caught her wrist and his grip upon her was bruising.

"Do not," he rasped, holding her still. "You play at things you know nothing of. You come here, to heal what needs no healing. Death is a renewal for life, is it not? Yet you would venture out, alone and unprotected, for adventure? Have you so little respect for your lady mother? For Olympus? You are a Goddess, albeit unnecessary, whose fate impacts us all."

She wanted to recoil, but his grip only tightened. His words, hot and biting, fell upon her shoulders like blows.

"If you are taken or injured, your carelessness would endanger all else. Demeter, and no doubt Zeus, would not let the matter rest. Those fighting this battle would suffer their indifference because of your selfishness." His nostrils flared and his blue-black eyes bore into hers. "Because of you."

Persephone blinked back tears. His words rang true. She would never forgive herself if she endangered another...

"Get you home, now." He released her wrist roughly, causing her to tip unsteadily.

She nodded, swallowing her tears. "I would never..." she paused, breathing deeply. "Forgive me..."

His expression twisted sharply, causing her heart to seize painfully. He was angry with her, yes. But he was disappointed too. And that knowledge settled coldly into the pit of her stomach.

He turned, glancing over his shoulder. "Come, I will see you home."

She nodded, overcome with pitiful sobs. She could not stop.

Had she chased any hope of his affection away? She sniffed, following behind him. Did he really think so lowly of her? Was she... was she unnecessary?

To him, perhaps. She glanced at the contoured lines of his shoulders, bare and pale in the sun. She had no anger. His burned too bright, with too much conviction, to doubt that she was the one at fault. So she followed, weeping, until they reached the main road. She could bear it no longer.

She lifted her robes and ran from him, for once eager to reach the walls of her isolated home.

"Tired?" Aeacus smiled as he rushed forward, sword held high.

Hades shook his head, kneeling to brace himself. His sword turned, deflecting Aeacus' blow at the last. He stood, spinning and raising his sword to strike. The sword froze, its tip pricking the back of Aeacus' neck.

"Yield?" Hades asked.

Aeacus looked back at the sword against his neck. "I have no need to continue. I am no match for you, as you've made clear this long and tiresome morning. But you seem no less agitated now than when we began."

Hades lowered his arm, shrugging.

Aeacus relaxed his stance, rolling his head as he drew in a deep breath. "What ails you?"

Hades looked at Aeacus with a lifted brow, his irritation clear.

Aeacus laughed. "While I would never dare to call you pleasant, you're not one to succumb to temper. Such fits are contagious, I fear..."

Hades stared Aeacus. "You blame me for what happened?"

Aeacus shook his head. "No, my lord."

"Explain your meaning." His words were hard.

Was Aeacus right? Had his mood presented an opening for these schemes?

Aeacus spoke carefully, "You are distracted. That is no secret. And those in Tartarus would test that, test their chances at freedom."

"Tartarus' borders are too strong. It was not an attempt at escape. They will find no freedom and they likely know it. They fought to squelch their boredom, the tiresomeness of their relentless existence."

Aeacus nodded. "So you were giving them a kindness? Engaging them in such a battle?"

Hades rubbed a hand over his face, his ire threatening to overwhelm him once more. He'd been thrilled with the fight, engaging the faceless, nameless inhabitants of Tartarus with lethal efficiency. A battle with the dead could not end in death, but he and Didymos could force them back to the pit fires, where they would burn and suffer until freed. He'd delayed the sentence long enough to vent some of the frustration that had plagued him since his return home.

Aeacus was right. His mood was foul. He had no patience. And there was nothing he could do… Nothing.

Hermes joined them, his ever present smile upon his face. "I fear I've brought enough new souls to pass this day in work, Aeacus. The judges wait." He clasped Aeacus' forearm first, then did the same with Hades. "Sparring?"

Aeacus nodded.

"If you can call crossing swords with Aeacus sparring." Hades attempted humor, but delivered an insult instead.

"Your timing is well received, Hermes." Aeacus bowed stiffly, saying, "I leave you then."

Hades sighed, watching his friend and ally move towards the Judges Court.

"Well done," Hermes chided him. "You have so many friends, Hades, why worry over insults or wounded pride?"

Hades scowled at him. "Aeacus is a Judge of the Dead. He serves me and the Underworld–"

"And is friend to you," Hermes interrupted.

"Why are you here?" The words were harsh, but he cared little. Why did all seem bent on tempting the bounds of his control?

Hermes laughed. "I, too, have duties to you and the Underworld." Hades shook his head.

"And I'm to invite you to a celebration." Hermes was still smiling.

"You push me to my wit's end."

"That is why you should come." Hermes clasped his shoulder.

"Your temper threatens the peace and balance you pride yourself upon. Surely you see it?"

Hades cast a wary gaze upon him. "Why would this celebration alter the state of things?"

Hermes shrugged. "Come and see."

"No."

"Why?"

"Because I have responsibilities that extend beyond your understanding, Hermes, and I cannot shirk those duties for such frivolousness."

"Is the impending marriage of a king and a Goddess frivolous?" Hermes asked. "Demeter requested you come."

Hades felt a sudden weight upon his chest. "Whose marriage?"

"You know," Hermes said softly.

Hades swallowed. "How will attending such festivities appease me?"

"If she means naught to you, as you claim, this will cause you no discomfort. Indeed it might do you good to see her wedded and bedded. You can move on, free of her."

His breathing became challenged.

"Demeter wanted to thank you for shielding Persephone from Poseidon. She has arranged offerings for you at the celebrations."

Hades wanted to hit something. Hermes was goading him, knowingly. He wanted to hit Hermes.

"Or you may stay here, reject the offerings, and brood over the loss of one that was never yours to lose. Not because she would not have you, but because you would not have her," Hermes finished, a taunting grin upon his face.

Hades roared, his anger evident, "You *have* come to torment me then?"

"You've assured me you cannot be tormented."

Hades stared at him, fighting his fury.

Hermes moved forward, picking up the sword Aeacus had left. "We could wager on it?"

"No."

"If I defeat you, you will accompany me."

"No."

"If you win, I will never speak of Persephone to you again.

Ever."

Hades' eyes narrowed. "Ever?"

Hermes lifted the sword, tossing the hilt back and forth in his hands. His face was expectant, enjoying himself immensely. "Ever. Though speaking of her should provide you no distress, considering your proclaimed indifference to her..."

Hades swung the sword, bringing it down upon Hermes with all of his strength. Hermes sidestepped the blow, laughing.

"He has children from his late wife," Demeter spoke to Persephone in hushed tones, leading her down the passage that led the celebration. "He will be in no hurry to have another."

Persephone heard her mother's words and felt nausea churn her stomach. Children? They were precious, to be sure. But she'd yet to experience any life of her own. The duties of a wife and mother would ensure nothing changed; life would go on as it always had for her.

No, that was not true. She'd go from being the sheltered daughter of a Goddess to wife of a man she did not love and mother to a child she did not want.

But perhaps that fate was better than to remain an unnecessary Goddess? She ignored the tug at her heart.

"Don't pout," Demeter scolded. "Look around you, daughter. All this will be yours."

That King Erysichthon was wealthy, there was no doubt. Yards of the finest linen hung over the marble walls, elegantly carved wax tapers were lit in each of extravagantly carved sconces, and fresh boughs of herbs and flowers were tied together and hung to scent the air.

"Why does he want to marry me?" Persephone asked.

Her mother turned wide eyes upon her, smiling a tolerant smile. "You are a Goddess, Persephone. You are beautiful. Why would he not want to marry the daughter of his patron goddess? Of course he wants to marry you."

As they rounded the corner, Persephone was hard pressed not to gasp at the vision before her. She'd never seen so many people gathered together, all draped in such finery.

Demeter turned to her daughter, arranging the mask upon her face with a critical eye.

"Is this really necessary, mother?" Persephone asked. The porcelain of the mask smelled musky and felt constricting against her face.

"He should not see you yet. Did we not discuss this before we left? We must determine if he is worthy of you, without your beauty acting as an enticement. It is a good mask."

It is a mask you wear to visit your lovers undetected. But Persephone said nothing, relieved that the mask was in place, for she knew her cheeks were red.

"You should use whatever feminine wiles you see fit," her mother continued.

"Feminine wiles? I have none. You've seen to that."

Demeter waved her hand in front of her, dismissing her. "You are my daughter. Such affectations and devices will come most naturally to you, of that I have no fear."

And if I do not want to use such tactics? If I do not desire this match? Again, she knew better than to speak such words.

Demeter smiled at her face. "You are not the only masked face here this night. We will not make this an easy conquest for our prince." She straightened the mask, adding, "You have nothing to fear this night, daughter. Erysichthon is a gentle giant, one most faithful to me, and therefore, to you too."

Demeter left her side, preceding her into the courtyard so that Persephone might remain unknown.

Persephone waited, resting her head against the wall as she drew in slow steadying breaths. How she wished this night was over. How she wished she was on the plains or meadows or in one of her trees.

She slipped around the corner and hurried towards a heavily draped column, avoiding the curious eyes of those milling about her. She clutched the fabric, peering around it to assess the room's company.

Faces, some masked, some painted, others free from any disguise, filled the room. So many, too many... After a life of living out of doors, of seeing few people, she felt caged.

She closed her eyes, remembering the whispered words of the

grass, the deep tones of the trees, and the sweet songs of the flowers.

She opened her eyes, somewhat soothed. She stared around the room, finding the man that was surely Erysichthon. And once again, panic descended upon her.

Men, the nymphs assured her, came in all shapes and sizes. Their appearance gave little insight into the spirit within. Persephone prayed this was true with Erysichthon. A gentle giant, her mother had said. The man was a giant. She would hold her mother accountable for the rest of her description as well.

The man was large, broad and thickly muscled. He was dark, with black hair and a heavy shadow on his angled jaw. He sat, so his height was indeterminate, but she assumed he would tower, as his knees were hunched to allow him his seat.

His face was well lined. A deep furrow marred his brow, presenting a daunting scowl. And yet the wealth of wrinkles layered at the corner of his eyes indicated he was equally fond of smiling. Even now, speaking to another, he was most animated.

She sighed. It was a small comfort, to discern his state of mind from the expression on his face. Unlike… No, she would not think of Hades.

She stared at Erysichthon. He was to be her husband. He was her mother's choice. She turned, her back pressed against the column as she tried to steady her pulse.

All about her people chattered, laughing loudly and without care. She watched them, mesmerized. The artful fluttering of one woman's eyelashes, another's leisurely lick of her painted red lips – the men were drawn like bees to honey, like a hummingbird to nectar. Her eyes narrowed, shaking off the urge to laugh at such behavior.

But then, the men were no better. She shuddered as one aged fellow grabbed a woman around the waist, laughing when she squealed in protest. But the protest was farce, for the woman relaxed against the man with a smile full of promise. Another man had no qualms grabbing the breast of an almost bare-chested serving girl. The girl barely glanced at him, intent upon her work.

She had no desire to learn such artifice or tricks.

As her gaze swept the room, she found herself clinging to the column. She could not force herself to move, to let go and venture into the mayhem of this feast.

She chided herself. The time had come to be more than a safely kept Goddess, playing with plants and nonsense. If her mother wanted this marriage, she should do all she could to ensure the match. Her nerves were nonsense.

A man, masked and alone, stood at the back of the hall, standing in the shadows. He was draped in grey, his cloak covering all of him. His grey mask scowled at the room with condemnation.

She stared at the man, sharing his displeasure. She made a rash decision. *If you move, I will move too.*

The man leaned against the wall and turned his head, ever so slowly, to inspect the room. When his eyes found her, he stiffened.

He stared, surprising her. His body tightened as he straightened, and she feared he might leap upon her in his agitation. Instead he pushed away from the wall and swept from the room.

She felt the air escaping from her lungs. Now she had to move.

She squeezed her eyes shut and drew in a deep breath. She was scowling when she stepped around the column and walked directly into the chest of Erysichthon.

She stared up, thankful for her mask for the first time.

The man could not be mortal. Surely he'd descended from the Giants.

"What a tiny flower you are." He stared down at her, the crinkles about his rich brown eyes creasing deeply as he smiled.

She was too startled to find a response. His smile, she supposed, was pleasant enough.

"Can you speak, blossom?" he asked, making those about him laugh.

She felt a flash of irritation. "Pardon my silence, my lord. I've rarely come upon a man with so... commanding a presence."

He laughed.

She smiled, though none knew it behind her mask. He had a sense of humor. That, too, was pleasing.

"You are careful with your words, a sign of superior intelligence." He paused, waving those that followed him away. "Will you join me, mysterious maiden?"

Persephone took the massive hand he offered, oddly relieved to lean upon him as he led her back to his chair. All eyes followed them as they made their way to his throne. He sat on a raised dais, the highest point in the room. This dais was arranged for comfort, covered with reclining benches, each laden with soft tapestries and thick cushions.

She sat with care, propping herself upon the arm without leaning too closely to the giant at her side. It did not escape her that all within the hall were still watching them. It made her uncomfortable to be so examined. She'd no wish to be here, before them, on display.

He sat with a sigh, summoning a servant and taking two cups from the tray. She watched him, no less a mountain of a man at ease. He had no fat on him save the tell-tale thickness associated with drink. His long hair was dark brown, not black, shot through with silver. His eyes were alert, his features even and strong. She supposed he was attractive.

But the only emotion he stirred within her was vague unease.

He offered her drink, smiling.

She shook her head. "I fear my mask will not allow me such pleasures."

He winked. "Then take it off, fair Persephone, and let me look at the woman who would be my queen." He drank the cup down, wiped his mouth with the back of his hand and turned towards her.

Fear churned in Persephone's stomach.

His eyes held something more than humor or curiosity, something troubling. Yet she would not let him discomfit her. She was a Goddess, after all. Even if she was to be his wife, she was an Olympian first.

She drew in a steadying breath, lifted an unsteady hand to remove the mask. She was thankful to be rid of it... until she saw his face. His eyes widened and his smile tightened.

Did she please him?

She swallowed, turning towards the gawking faces before her. They were a sea of strangers, assessing her. They spoke of her, behind raised hands, with tittering whispers and subdued tones. And her uneasiness grew.

She missed her meadow and her flowers ... even the terse companionship of one with midnight locks and haunting blue-black eyes.

Chapter Seven

It was Persephone. The Fates would show him no mercy, then.

Her green eyes held him, round with panic, even while the rest of her face was hidden by the chalky white porcelain mask she wore.

Why was she afraid?

She looked ready to bolt, as if the slightest motion would send her running from this festive hall. She stood straight, but he could see the trembling of her hands, the unsteady rise and fall of her chest. She clung to the swag of fabric, hiding behind her pillar.

It was too much for him.

He would not stay. He'd let Hermes goad him. Let his temper make him careless with his blade. Hermes had made short work of him, laughing in victory. When they'd arrived, Hermes had left him quickly. Well disguised behind a grinning mask, the light-hearted deity went off in search of more enthusiastic companionship.

While he was left alone to stare into her green eyes, eyes that had plagued his dreams and distracted him from his duties... eyes that crinkled when she smiled, or sparkled when she laughed. They seemed greener now. Perhaps it was the bright white mask that made them so brilliant.

Perhaps it was that he'd missed her.

She blinked at him, stirring him from his musing.

By the Fates, he had missed her. And he would suffer for it.

He forced himself from the room, sucking in air that his lungs seemed too shallow to hold. Once outside, he leaned heavily against the wall.

Mortals brushed past him, peering at him with knowing smiles and whispered assumptions. They thought him some inebriated reveler, a mortal fool unsteady from too much wine and merriment. Their titters and laughter served to heighten his irritation.

Why had he come?

He turned back, peering into the room. She was staring up at this man, Erysichthon, her intended. Yet she was no less rigid with fear. Hades' hands fisted, and a fiery flash of anger ran through him.

Did she not want this alliance?

He watched as the king took her small hand in his. Watched as the king's massive hand clasped hers, enveloping her. Erysichthon's brown eyes raked over her, to linger on her curves with distinct fascination.

Hades gripped the door frame, holding himself back. He would gladly smash the head of this lecherous mortal for regarding her so. She was a Goddess. She was worthy of respect and reverence, not lust.

While she ascended onto the king's dais with easy grace, the panic in her bright green eyes told him she felt neither calm nor assured.

Erysichthon whispered something to her and all fell quiet as she drew her mask from her face.

She *was* beauty. Even now, when her discomfort was obvious, she sat with poised dignity. How could he not admire her?

"Hades?" Hermes whispered his name.

His words were harsh. "I must leave before this arrogant fool knows my wrath."

Hermes grabbed Hades' arm, his voice sad as he said, "Come, my friend. I've asked too much of you this night."

Hades followed Hermes without resistance. The night air was chill in the garden, filled with the scents of fresh flowers and earth. Hades drew in a deep breath, easing the fury from his muscles. He pushed the mask from his face, welcoming the fresh air upon his flushed skin.

"You find him ill-suited?" Hermes asked, sliding his mask back as well.

"He looks at her as if she were a... a delicacy for his pleasure. He would be wise to remember that she is..."

"Soon to be his wife?" Hermes spoke without inflection, causing Hades to turn to him.

"Is it agreed upon?"

"Demeter brought Persephone here with the union in mind. I cannot imagine anything would change Demeter's path. But if you spoke with Zeus..."

Hades held up a hand. "Is that why you brought me here? To encourage my... weakness? Do not continue, Hermes. Leave me and enjoy your companions. I will find my way home without you as my guide."

Hermes hesitated, then entered the hall and left Hades alone with his thoughts.

He sat, wearily, beneath an aged oak. It cast long shadows, no doubt intended for lovers in its seclusion. The thought did little to ease him. He leaned against the tree and scowled, lost in his thoughts and anger.

Demeter favored her daughter. All knew it to be true. Why then would she seek to marry Persephone to the likes of ... Erysichthon? The mortal had the look of... Hades swallowed then. That was it. Erysichthon reeked of the same self-importance, greed, and unrestrained hunger as Poseidon.

Or was he too blind to see that this mortal was a good choice for Persephone?

A slight sound reached him and he pulled his mask into place.

Persephone crept, moving on silent feet, down the steps and into the farthest corner of the walled garden. She pressed herself against the wall, touching the leaves and thorns of the rose bush as she stared up at the moon high overhead.

He watched her, in awe of her beauty.

She was troubled, wary.

His hands tightened, fisting in the dirt. Would that he could cheer her. He could do nothing but ensure a future of sadness, offer her nothing. And still he found himself rising to go to her.

Heavy footfalls found them, introducing Erysichthon to their midst.

Erysichthon stared at the girl. He drank heavily from his cup, letting his eyes roam over Persephone in the moonlight. She was lovely, he conceded, perched at the edge of his gardens, ready to take flight.

"Fresh air?" Erysichthon asked softly. "It is warm in the hall."

She turned wide eyes upon him, nodding.

He saw her skittish nervousness and moved slowly, carefully, to the bench amongst his roses. He sat, smiled at Persephone and patted the bench beside him. "Sit with me, then, and tell me of your life."

She stood still, glancing nervously about her.

His gaze raked her from head to toe. Surely he could find some spark of her mother if he looked hard enough? But where Demeter was clearly driven, fair Persephone seemed uncertain. She was timid, uncomfortable. She bristled when he'd tried to tease. Demeter would have sat at his side, fluttered her eyelashes and bent him to her will with ease.

He closed his eyes, feeling the pain that had yet to dull.

Demeter. She enjoyed their battle of wits, as did he. She knew and accepted him as he was. Like his Ione. The pain intensified. He swallowed down the last of his wine and pushed thoughts of his lost daughter aside. He would bring her home, in time.

He turned, smiling broadly at his intended. "Are you familiar with Thessaly, Persephone?" He added, "I would be pleased to take you on a tour."

He watched the slight crease of her brow, the tightening of her mouth. So she was as pleased with this arrangement as he was, then? It was some comfort.

Her voice was tight. "That would be lovely, my lord."

He bit back his laugh. Her tone assured him she saw nothing lovely about the idea. Perhaps they would suit, in time. "There's much to see, I assure you. In time, I hope you will come to love this land as I do, as your mother does."

She turned brilliant green eyes upon him. Curious, he'd never seen such a shade before. Quite unsettling. "Is it safe?" she asked.

He laughed then, throwing back his head. "You are a young thing, aren't you?" He wiped a hand across his mustache and shook his head. "No one threatens my people or property, Goddess. Not even the Persians. If your mother had not selected Thessaly for her precious cypress grove, I would have built a monument to Ares instead. I'm a warrior. You need never fear for your safety while you are with me."

He saw her nod. "My safety has all but consumed my mother, sir. If she feels I am safe in your care, I know that you are a most capable and skilled warrior."

He watched her, the slight smile that wavered on her full lips. He drained his cup of wine. She was pretty, he supposed, in her own way. But he felt no attraction for her.

"You don't look like your mother," he murmured.

She turned round eyes upon him. "Oh?"

"You are fair where she is dark. You are soft where she is," he paused, "less round. I've never seen the likes of your hair, so red. And your eyes are a most peculiar shade of..."

"Green, while hers are a most pleasing brown? Yes, I know, sir. I've lived at her side every day. She is lovely. And while she is my mother, we are, as you see, different women." Her brows rose, waiting for his response.

His gaze wandered over her, leisurely.

She was not her mother, but she was not hard to gaze upon. True, her eyes were odd, but her lips were lush and full. Her skin was sun-kissed, sprinkled with a fine dusting of freckles. His eyes dropped.

He could find no complaint with her bosom. She had delectable breasts, larger than her mother's and firm with youth. "I meant no disrespect, Goddess. You are a fine woman."

When his eyes settled on her face, her skin turned a brilliant shade of red. She blinked rapidly, turning to regard the dimly lit gardens.

"Come, blossom." He stood, offering his arm. "You've had your air, now meet those who will be your vassals." He paused. Would she tease with him, as her mother did? He would find out. "Unless you were hoping to lure me into the gardens? It is not an uncommon practice, I know."

He bit back a smile as she clasped his arm, tugging him towards the hall with surprising force.

He laughed, cupping her cheek. His next words saw her eyes

widen and her mouth fall open in pure astonishment. "If you wish to wait to bless our union, I will not press you otherwise. Though a kiss would serve, for now?"

Her eyes looked ready to pop out, making him chuckle.

She gasped then collected herself. When she spoke, there was bite to her tone. "I have yet to give you such a promise."

Erysichthon threw back his head and laughed. She was not as soft as he'd thought, then. The knowledge cheered him somewhat.

Erysichthon was snoring.

Persephone smiled then poked him, one toe nudging his leg. He didn't move, so she poked him again, not so gently.

He snored harder, his mouth falling open.

She stood, staring down at the man who would be her husband. She tilted her head to regard his slumbering form. Erysichthon did not wake when she moved from his side.

No wonder. He'd emptied the entire skin of rich wine Olympus had delivered to him this very morning. It was a gift, the messenger said, to honor their impending wedding.

He continued to snore, so loudly the tree branches overhead shook. She sighed, relieved.

It was good he was such a sound sleeper. She might enjoy some of this day, for Erysichthon's mood had been most strange. Until today, he'd been a most chivalrous host, respectful if, at times, teasing.

But today, he'd stared at her with new eyes. He seemed more enamored with her each passing second. Perhaps it was the wine? Stronger perhaps than what this mortal king was accustomed to?

All in all, she'd enjoyed their day. A large company of men had accompanied them to the cypress groves, following Erysichthon's orders to surround the grove and give them peace... and privacy. They'd shared a nice meal. He'd eaten quickly, drinking his wine with relish.

"You tell stories?" he'd asked, his eyes lingering on her face.

She'd nodded. "I do. What stories do you prefer? Of adventures or love or battle?"

Erysichthon sighed, leaning back on an elbow. "Any story from your sweet lips will please me."

She glanced at him, a small smile on her lips. He seemed in earnest. His brown eyes were warm, if heavy-lidded, when they met hers.

"Tell me one of your favorites, so that it might become one of my favorites." He tipped the wine skin up, emptying it before he lay back upon the grass.

"Very well," she began. "In the years after Cronus defeated his father Uranus, the Titans prospered. But greed found him, turning Cronus into as great a tyrant as his father before him. He feared that his children might one day seek to overthrow him, as he had done with his father. Children, his own children, were his greatest threat. When his wife Rhea gave birth to their first child, Cronus swallowed it whole. On and on it went, child after child, until Rhea could bear it no more. Great with child, she hid on the isle of Crete and birthed Zeus. She returned to Cronus and fed him a stone, wrapped in a babe's cloths. But Zeus lived and grew strong and able...."

His snores had interrupted her.

She stretched, walking briskly from the slumbering king. When she could no longer hear him, her pace slowed. Alone, amongst her mother's cypress trees, she found peace.

Birdsong assailed her. The wind lifted the tree branches, releasing their soft welcoming whispers. The grass, too, seemed pleased by her visit. She savored such soothing companionship. Her cloak slid about her hips as she wandered through the cypress trees with soft steps, reveling in the quiet.

It had been three days since she'd arrived, and there had been precious little of it so far. Erysichthon was a loud man, as was his household. His servants, even his animals, seemed determined to out-speak the other. So much noise, for naught.

She closed her eyes. The wind slipped through the leaves on the branches overhead, begging for a song. She shook her head, placing her hand on one of the trunks to explain.

"Savor the lark's song this day," she whispered.

The tree grumbled in return, arguing that the bird's simple melody could not compare to her talents.

The bird, unaware of their conversation, hopped from branch to branch, making its melody bounce too.

"I would sing for you all," Persephone promised softly, "on another day. I will see a great deal more of you. Or so it seems."

Her words chilled her, and she wrapped her arms about herself, rubbing her arms for warmth. She turned, angling her face towards the warm and gentle kiss of the sun. It helped, some. She sighed heavily.

❖

Hades heard her words, saw the shiver that touched her. "Tis a fine day for such a walk."

Persephone turned towards him, her astonishment almost comical if not for the slight frown that crossed her face. Her eyes fell from his because of the tongue-lashing he'd issued at their last meeting. He'd done his job too well.

And he suffered for it, knowing he'd hurt her. She had been nothing but honest and kind in their dealings. She'd done nothing to encourage his temper, yet she'd suffered from it. Whatever else he felt, he respected her loyalty to duty. He hoped she could forgive him.

She glanced at him hesitantly. "It is. A lovely day."

"Are you well?" He could not stop his eyes from traveling over her. From head to toe, he let her presence ease him.

"I am." Her voice wavered as their eyes met, a small smile lighting her face. "But I am surprised to see you. Again... here."

He felt the words like a blow. His behavior, his words, had been malicious. If he could explain himself, he would. How could he make her see him as he was? Empty. He had nothing to offer her.

She blinked, her smile warming.

He shook his head, but took a step closer, then another.

The curve of her face glowed in the sunlight. She spoke, watching him with her bright green eyes. "What brings you to the plains of Thessaly?"

He stepped closer still, the pull she had upon him growing stronger. His words were hoarse, "A matter of great import."

She nodded, her smile brilliant now. Even her eyes seemed to smile at him. "Great indeed, to bring you so far from your realm."

Had it only been days since he'd spoken to her so? Days since he'd learned of her betrothal? Her betrothal... he sucked in breath.

He inclined his head. "I suppose I should offer up my congratulations."

"Oh?"

He spoke with care. She need not know that such news affected him. "Are you not to be wed? To Erysichthon, Thessaly's king, no less?"

Her smile faded, replaced by a frown. "I suppose I am. Does that make me Thessaly's next queen?" She shook her head. "Surely not."

He stared at her, at the play of emotions on her gentle features. If he saw even the slightest joy, the slightest flicker of excitement, it would be easy to leave her. It would please him, he told himself, to know she was pleased by the marriage... and her would-be husband. Instead, she looked perplexed.

"My mother has brought me to him with the hopes that wooing will lead to wedding." Her nose wrinkled slightly, drawing attention to the light freckles there. "I fear I've found little promising in his wooing. Yet I know my likes or dislikes will not stop this wedding." She tried to sound cheerful, but it was farce. One look at her face showed him the truth.

He turned from her, saying, "He is most dedicated to your mother, I hear."

"Would that she'd marry him," her answer was swift. He turned to her, saw her eyes go round as she stared at him. "Forgive me. That was impertinent."

"It was," he agreed, nodding. But a smile escaped him. She saw it and answered in kind. Her smile was bright and warm. *Such a smile.* "Do you speak to him this way?"

"No. Only you." She shook her head. "You unleash my tongue and make me babble like a brook. A habit I'm sure you've become painfully aware of. I fear such... honesty would do little to endear me to him."

He watched her, savoring every word, every nuance, of her being.

"Then he is a fool. Honesty is a virtue to be revered." This Erysichthon would have years to learn her expressions, her sighs and smiles, her laughter. "Honesty is but a gift, one your husband is few amongst men to have."

She moved towards him, almost timidly. Her scent hit him, flooding him with each breath he took. He tightened, drawing himself rigid as he looked down at her. Did she see how he unsettled him? He hoped not.

Her voice was a whisper. "Is honesty the virtue you value most, Hades?"

His gaze fell from hers, but he nodded.

"Then you shall always hear it from my lips, I vow."

He lifted his eyes. She stood so close he could touch her. He could stroke one silken copper lock, or cup the smooth softness of her golden cheek. His eyes did what his hands could not, traveling over her hair, her face... her lips. He remembered the cling of her lips all too well.

He closed his eyes, seeking control. It was a memory he favored above all others. But it must remain just that, a memory. He'd come to say good-bye, to apologize to her. And then, he pleaded with the Fates, he would be released from this strange... obsession that plagued him so.

His eyes held hers. "My words, when last we met... I should not have berated you. It was not my place."

She blinked, her lower lip trembling. "You were right to scold me. The grass would grow, the flowers bloom, without me."

He shook his head, self-loathing near choking him. He swallowed, speaking softly. "No. You honor Olympus with your gifts. You fulfill your duties, Persephone. Bring growth and renewal. It is an important task, you are important, to all who live." His throat grew tight as he added. "Forgive my temper. It was misplaced."

He'd never seen such a smile. How she was capable of such emotion, such joy, with such a simple gesture astonished him. He drew in a deep breath, near trembling as her scent filled him once more.

"I forgive you."

It was done. She'd forgiven him and he was free. He could leave her, should leave her. She would be well guarded by this Erysichthon of Thessaly. Demeter was careful with her daughter.

And yet, he would see her happy. He wanted more for her, a marriage beyond that of Zeus and Hera's deceitful and jealous match... beyond his own... In time, she would be happy, surely? "You will marry this mortal?"

She drew in breath. "Of course… As you reminded me, my mother's will demands fealty. I would be a good daughter, and a good wife, and obey."

Her words did not satisfy him. "He is a good man? He will look after you?"

She frowned, shaking her head. "From what little I know of him, yes. He is, by all word and deed, an honorable man. Does it matter?" She paused. "To you?"

He knew what his answer should be. He should tell her that her marriage was a reflection on Olympus, and the Gods. He should tell her that such an alliance would benefit Thessaly. But he did not speak, for fear of the truth slipping out.

Chapter Eight

"And who would you be?" Erysichthon spoke with surprising menace.

Hades spun, standing between Persephone and her betrothed, to regard the man. Erysichthon did not pause, but drew close enough to tower over Hades, bumping him with his broad chest. Hades smiled up at the man, torn between admiration and amusement. The man was brave, or foolish.

Erysichthon scowled in return, his thick brows furrowing deeply while his face turned an alarming shade of red.

"Peace, your majesty," Persephone spoke, her voice soothing. He knew that tone. It was the tone she'd used when healing the tree, in the meadow. Hades longed to push her back behind him. "You speak to..." She came around him, holding her hands out in supplication.

"You will keep your opinions to yourself, woman." Erysichthon interrupted her, grabbing her arm and pulling her behind him. "It's obvious he's here with the intention of stealing you away."

That this mortal manhandled her so was an outrage. Hades could do nothing more than stare at him. The bastard. This... this mortal... Demeter thought *this* man worthy of her daughter? Was she blind?

Persephone was watching him. He saw the surprise upon her face, the worry clouding her eyes. His hands fisted, the freezing heat pricking the skin of his palms. King or no, he would see this man put in his place. She shook her head, ever so slightly.

Erysichthon continued, his finger jabbing Hades' chest. "Are you from Thrace or Sparta?"

"I am neither, mighty King." Hades tore his gaze from Persephone's, offering her no assurance. If this mortal sought only her safe keeping, he would be appeased, a bit. His gaze drifted, narrowing at the sight of Erysichthon's hand tight about Persephone's golden arm.

He glanced at her again. The shake of her head was not so subtle this time.

He drew in a deep breath, willing the fight from his palms. He would test this mortal himself, and see if he was worthy of Persephone's hand. "I'm but a traveler."

"You?" Erysichthon's gaze swept him from head to toe. He snorted, clearly disbelieving. "A traveler? Well, traveler. Be on your way. You trespass on my land."

"I was seeking Demeter's grove. Am I mistaken? Are these not her cypress trees?" Hades' eyes narrowed. "I would pay homage to the Goddess."

Erysichthon laughed, loudly. "All of Thessaly is mine, traveler. If you would commune with the Goddess, you may do so... when I am finished here."

Hades met the man's gaze, at once struck by the hue of his eyes. They glowed, almost imperceptibly.

He glanced at Persephone then, torn. She was clearly horrified by Erysichthon's speech. No mortal, king or no, could claim such dominion over Demeter's grove. And all of Greece knew it. "I had no knowledge of such an arrangement..."

"You know of it now," Erysichthon stooped, his face inches from Hades. "Be gone with you."

Persephone stepped forward, softly pleading, "Your majesty..."

He held his arm up, forcing her behind him. "Hold your tongue, woman."

Hades would kill him. His hands tightened, burning cold. His body tensed, welcoming the challenge before him. He smiled when Erysichthon, too, seemed to tighten and ready.

"Be gone, or I will make you go," Erysichthon bit out.

Hades glanced at her then. She shook her head fiercely, her

eyes round and pleading. She would see no bloodshed. She asked him to spare this man.

He stepped back, though every muscle in his body rebelled.

She sighed, smiling her thanks. She gripped Erysichthon's arm. "Come, my king, let us find our way back to our feast."

Hades would not look at the man, for fear of sending his soul straight to Tartarus.

"You, traveler, will leave. Now," Erysichthon growled at Hades.

Hades watched, fighting his fury as Erysichthon's meaty hand grabbed Persephone's arm. He stared, stunned as the mortal pulled her along behind him.

He could not stand by. He took one step, but she turned back.

"No," she whispered, shaking her head. "Please."

He shook his head, shifting from one foot to the next. He made no effort to keep the anger from his face. He had no restraint left, his jaw tightening as he sucked in breath sharply.

She smiled at him then, before Erysichthon pulled her down a line of cypress trees and out of his sight.

He did not hesitate. He had a long journey ahead of him, and little time to make it. He whistled, leaving Theron to watch over Persephone as he readied for Olympus.

Erysichthon could not ease the grip upon her arm. His fear was too great. He'd awakened, from dreams full of her, only to find her missing. And that man... that man had been with her, speaking to her, walking with her... alone. His anger choked him.

He stopped, turning to regard her.

She was breathing heavily, her cheeks tinged red from the rapid pace he'd set. He moved forward, gripping her shoulders in his hands. She was there, in his hold.

He smiled down at her, savoring the feel of her beneath his hands.

"My lord," she gasped, shrugging against his grip. "I... I demand you release me."

Erysichthon chuckled, admiring her spirit. "You demand?" He shook his head. "We return to my home, Persephone, to wed. I will not have you stolen and ransomed against me by my enemies. There will be no more delaying things."

She was surprised, he could tell. But not displeased. His eyes traveled over her, astounded by how dear she'd become to him. When it had happened, or how, he did not know. She was more dear to him than anything. And he would not lose her to another. He lifted a strand of her hair and wrapped it about his wrist.

She pulled her hair back. "My lord..."

He grabbed her then, lifting her off of her feet. "You would be wise not to tease me, blossom. You've possessed me. Each time I look upon you, I see more clearly that you are mine. And now, I've awoken with a powerful hunger for you. You will not deny me." He spoke the truth. And he would brook no arguments from her. "You are mine," he murmured, pulling her close. He bent his head, his lips descending eagerly upon hers.

She twisted, whispering, "I am not yours. I will not marry a man who has so little respect for me, a Goddess..."

He shook her roughly, startling her into silence. He settled her over his shoulder and smacked her soundly on her rump. "Hush, woman. Or I'll find a way to keep you quiet."

She did not move, but hung limply over his shoulder. He smiled.

He stroked the line of her leg, felt her tremble. She wanted him, too.

He ignored his men, letting them rally behind them, as he made his way to his home. He'd not thought his marriage would give him such joy, but he could not remember a time when he'd been happier.

He swept into the great hall, smiling and nodding at all he passed.

"Make ready for a wedding," he bellowed over his shoulder. "This very eve."

She squirmed then, but he smacked her and she stilled.

They reached her room and he threw open the door. "Do your chambers please you, blossom?"

He lifted her again, setting her on her feet before him. There were tears in her green eyes.

"What is it, my sweet?" His hand cupped her cheek, smiling when she shivered. "If I injured you, I am sorry. Blame my carelessness on my craving for you. I fear I may not make it through the ceremony, my wanting for you is so great."

She blinked, her lower lip quivering in earnest now.

"I'll leave you now." He smiled and patted her cheek. "For but a moment."

He all but ran to his chambers. Never had he felt so giddy, so impatient. He hurried, making himself ready for his bride. Once he had bathed and groomed, he regarded his reflection in the looking glass Ione had left behind. He straightened his braid, using a handful of olive oil to smooth his thick curls. He rubbed a finger over his brows, his mustache and beard. He would make her proud, his Persephone.

Green eyes appeared, haunting him. Strange that he should feel so overcome, the need for her almost sending him back to her chamber.

That he wanted her was a good thing. That the sight of her made him ready to protect her, almost blindly so, was mildly troubling. That she seemed to occupy his every thought and breath, that not having her in his sight was painful, was new and puzzling.

Had he felt so passionately this morning? He could not recall.

"Wine," he murmured to the slave.

His cup was refilled and he drank deeply. It was bitter, stinging his tongue.

"Is this the drought from the Goddess?" he barked.

The slave shook his head, "The skin is empty, my lord. This is your own vintage."

He grunted and drank, missing the heady richness of Olympus gift. But, he supposed, missing wine was better than missing the Goddess herself.

He paused, looking at his reflection. He tried to pull an image of Demeter from his memory, but found only Persephone. She so fully filled his heart there was room for no other. And today he would marry her. He turned, stretching his arms wide to allow the servants to dress him.

He all but trembled with anticipation. How would it feel to have these robes removed by his fair wife's hands? Would she tremble beneath him? Would she fight? Or cry?

He smiled as his slaves stood back. He was a fine man, a man his Persephone would be proud to call husband. He could hardly wait to hear the words tumble from her full lips.

"My lord." The house master entered, his broad face clearly distressed.

"What is it? There will be no grave news on this day." He smiled at the man. "Today I shall hear only joyous news."

The house master opened his mouth then closed it.

Erysichthon laughed. "I should declare such a dictate for every day. Should I not?" He turned, well pleased with his image. "Summon your new mistress and bring her to the gardens. I'm of a most impatient mind."

The man stepped forward, "But, my lord..."

Erysichthon glared at the man. "Go. Fetch her immediately."

The man whispered, "She is gone."

"What?"

"The lady Persephone is not in her chambers... She is nowhere to be found..."

Erysichthon froze. She'd been taken, just as he feared. And now he would bring her back... No matter what, he would bring her home.

A deep roar filled the air, releasing his fury into the morning air.

"Bring me my sword and ready my guard," he bellowed. "Prepare the feast. There will be a wedding this day."

Persephone crept through the woods, her heart hammering.

She'd no choice, she reassured herself. She'd no choice but to leave. Her betrothed had a sickness about him she could not discern. He was bewitched, as he'd claimed, but she'd no hand in the bewitching. Indeed, she'd no wish to have anyone so overcome as he appeared to be.

She stilled, catching her breath. A soft crackle echoed in the underbrush behind her.

Was she being followed? Had he found her already? Her hands dug deep into the earth, but the earth and roots did not see who followed.

She could scarcely afford to turn and search it out. She did not know how much ground she'd covered, remaining hidden as she went. She'd scarcely made it from the walls of Erysichthon's house before she'd heard him cry out. She did not slow or turn back, or pause to decipher his words.

Would he follow her? She shivered. Would he bring men with him and track her, as she suspected?

She pushed herself upright, sliding her hand down a tree trunk for balance. A thorn punctured her hand, sliding deep. She hissed, stilling long enough to tear a strip of cloth from her cloak to wrap the wound tightly.

The tree whispered apologies, saddened by her injury.

"Worry not, friend. It was no fault of yours," she whispered in response, pressing her palm against its bark in comfort.

A snap of a branch, the rustle of leaves, and she saw him, in the shadows.

Her knees weakened with relief as Hades' hound came to her. He pressed against her, leaning heavily.

"I am glad to have you at my side." She knelt, meeting his golden eyes.

He pressed his nose to her injured hand and she nodded, tying a knot and pulling it sharp. Once it was secured, they moved on as silently as possible. The sun rose higher, casting them in thicker shadows, shielding them from discovery. She was thankful to Apollo for his golden orb.

It was the hound that nudged her on, leading her on silent paws. She followed, caring only that he led her away from Erysichthon.

They could hear them, though, the faint cries of many men, carried on the wind.

And while she thought they moved swiftly, it was not her heart that shook her. She realized that it was the earth, beneath her very feet, that trembled. Not from her pounding heart or exhausted lungs, but from man.

She knelt, peering around the edge of a boulder. If they'd been found, Erysichthon and his men must have circled round behind her, for they seemed to travel from the wrong direction.

Men, an army of men, were heading north. But these were not Erysichthon's men... They did not wear the Greek chlamys or hold the round shields of the Hoplite. They carried oblong wicker shields, carved arrows, and serrated swords. They were dressed in black, swathed in layers of fabric that veiled their faces. They were dressed as the men in the meadow... Persians.

Her throat closed, making breathing difficult.

There were so many of them. Her eyes drifted over the amassed troops. For their number, they moved with surprisingly little noise.

Unlike Erysichthon's men. She and the Persians, likely most of Attica, could hear their advance clearly.

How far away or how many men he'd brought were unknown, but Erysichthon and his men would soon arrive. The Persians prepared, lining up in formation with hardly a command uttered. They waited, ready for Erysichthon.

She must do something. She must. Erysichthon would be taken unaware, seeking her, a runaway bride. They would not expect such a force, how could they? And his men...

She'd endangered Erysichthon's men.

She sat back. Could she reach Erysichthon? Could she warn him? If she tried, would the Persians see her? What would they do to her? Hades' warnings filled her ears.

She would never reach Erysichthon in time.

The hound shifted from paw to paw. His ears pricked up and his eyes turned towards the Persians.

She took the hound's head, turning him to look at her. "Go," she whispered. "I need his help. Please go."

The hound whimpered once then ran, a black flash too fast for her to follow.

Chapter Nine

It took only moments for Erysichthon to arrive. Perhaps he'd anticipated a battle after all? While he was outnumbered, he was accompanied by a large troop of soldiers. Erysichthon himself was a daunting sight. Persephone could see the determination on his face, the narrowing of his eyes and the twist of his mouth as he spotted the Persians. But he did not pause. Instead, he smiled, raising his spear with blatant enthusiasm.

Persephone gasped. The Persians were too many. Surely Erysichthon could see that?

"Do not act rashly," Persephone pled. He could not hear her, she knew, but the words slipped out anyway. She leaned forward, causing the ground beneath her to shift. The rocks slid, sending her toppling down the hillside and onto the ground before Erysichthon and his men. She landed sharply, the air knocked from her lungs. She pushed herself up, wincing as the rocks bit into her knees and palms.

She saw Erysichthon then, saw the confusion on his face.

In Persephone's life, she'd had little to fear. Her mother was always close at hand, had seen to it that someone else would protect her daughter in her stead. She'd never faced anger or danger, not really. Until now.

And the look of understanding upon the king's face stole her breath and stilled her heart. "*You.*" The word was harsh. "You've led me to them, blossom. To challenge me? Would you have me prove myself worthy of you?"

She shook her head, terrified. She stood, edging toward the trees. "Never, my lord. Run from this place, I beg of you."

Erysichthon laughed, snapping his chariot's reigns and plowing forward.

The men erupted then, Persians and Greeks alike, running at each other with angry cries and swinging swords. Several dorus flew, the nine-foot long spears skewering the Persians with clean skill.

She turned away, horrified by the sight. But she saw Erysichthon then, saw his chariot bearing down upon her. Erysichthon came for her now, when his men needed his leadership?

She ran for the trees, but slipped and fell again. She gasped, knowing he came, and crawled awkwardly to the trees. She screamed, startled, when his huge hand caught her foot. He pulled her back. The tender flesh of her stomach was cut and bruised, and still he dragged her across the battlefield.

She reached frantically, pulling at the tree roots, the grass, the thorny vines beneath her, begging for help. They could do nothing, she knew. She turned, twisting her body.

Erysichthon's hold did not ease as he skewered a running Persian with his dagger. Once the man fell, he pulled her along. Screams and grunts, the clash of metal, the break in the air as a spear flew true; these sounds surrounded her.

She was trapped, truly trapped now.

How had this happened? She'd left Erysichthon because she feared him, but now her fear seemed foolish.

Another Persian attacked, swinging his serrated blade at Erysichthon. Erysichthon did not release her foot. With one hand, he pierced the foe with his spear, pulling it free as the man went limp. The body fell by her, the man's blood pouring onto the sand at her side. She shuddered, unable to stop her tears.

Erysichthon moved on, pulling her towards his chariot without a backwards glance.

He was forced to stop again, cleaving the head from this new attacker without hesitation. Persephone screamed as the Persian's body fell, barely missing her. The sand beneath her grew sticky with blood, and still Erysichthon held her.

When he was next set upon he had no choice but to release her. Three men, armed and wary, smiled expectantly. Their smiles chilled her. Erysichthon smiled in return. His arms rippled, flexing and tightening as he blocked and jabbed.

She tried to stand, but the sand was slick, causing her to slip back to her knees in the muck. She drew in breath, sobbing uncontrollably as she fell forward, her hands seeking purchase in the sand.

A man's voice, biting and hard, brushed her ear. A hand gripped her hair, pulling her head back and forcing her upright, onto her knees. It was sudden. So sudden she felt the jerk of her body before she felt the pain. She was shoved forward by some unseen force, her head was pinioned back. Pain, swift and sharp, skewered her stomach, spreading with excruciating speed.

The hand released her hair, freeing her to stare down, in shock. A blade protruded from her abdomen, its serrated edges split her from back to front.

The man said something again, but she could not think or feel anything but the pain. She felt his foot against her hip, bracing himself as he pulled the blade free. The blade tore, rending her flesh wider as it went.

She screamed. Bright red blood, her blood, spilled onto the sand, taking her warmth with it. Agony wracked her frame, and coldness... a coldness that chilled her very bones. She shivered, forcing the wound to contract and pull. She cried out again. The wound seemed a living, throbbing thing, intent on her suffering. She clutched at her stomach, pressing against the hole with trembling hands. The pressure from her own hand was too much. She fell to her side, staring blindly as sheer agony pulsed with her every heartbeat.

All about her the ground was red. So much blood – hers, Erysichthon's men and the enemies they fought.

And still the fighting continued. Her ears echoed with the sounds of it, grunts, groans, metal, and death.

She closed her eyes, searching for strength. She must rise, she must flee.

Hades heard her scream, and felt the pain in it. He saw her, saw her fall forward. When the Persian tore his sword free of her, Hades' fury knew no bounds.

He whipped his horses, threatening them. He did not slow, but rode his chariot through the melee. Whether Persian or Thessalian that fell beneath the hooves of his horses as he went, he cared not. He would not slow.

When he was close enough to reach her, he leapt from the chariot and knelt at her side. "Persephone?" he murmured, reaching for her.

A blade grazed his shoulder, but he did not turn. His hounds were on the man in an instant, freeing Hades to concentrate on Persephone.

She lay so still. He could scarce control the terror that threatened to weaken him. He lifted her, ignoring all else about them. "Persephone?"

Her head lolled back against his arm, her eyes blinking weakly. She looked at him with dilated eyes. Confusion lined her blood-smeared face. Her voice was frail, yet she smiled as she asked, "Hades? I am in your realm, then? And you've come to welcome me... How nice."

Her humor rallied him, yet her pathetic attempt at a smile filled him with anguish. He pulled her close. "You cannot die, Persephone."

Her eyes widened then, staring about her in horror. She shivered, turning her face into his chest as she whispered, "You will keep me safe."

He felt her breath upon his skin, unsteady and weak. He *would* keep her safe. "Yes."

"She is mine," Erysichthon screamed at him, mindlessly battling the men before him. "Leave her to me."

Hades did not look at the king as he climbed into his chariot.

"She is mine," Erysichthon insisted. "If you take her, there will be no safe place to hide from me."

Hades cradled Persephone, holding her gently as his eyes sought safe passage. All about them were men, caught in the grip of battle. He saw no easy route to her home, a long and arduous journey.

Erysichthon killed another, but his gaze remained upon Hades and Persephone.

He saw the blood drunk mortal moving towards his chariot, gripping his dripping sword. If not for Persephone, he'd welcome the mortal's advance. Greek or no, he would feel no remorse ripping the king apart. He looked forward to such a battle, once she was safe.

A Persian stopped the king, swinging a red blade and cleaving the king's shoulder armor.

Hades turned, scouring the plains. There was no clear path to freedom, except the way he'd come. Could he risk taking her there? He looked down at her, pale and limp in his arms. He had one choice. He flicked the reins, turning his team towards the Underworld.

"I will find you," Erysichthon's roar echoed above the fighting, but Hades did not turn. "And you will suffer!"

"Run," Hades hissed, urging his chargers faster.

He pressed her closer to him, supporting her as best he could. She still bled heavily, her tunic wet and sticky. She was immortal, yes, but such wounds could be too. If she was not healed, she would suffer its pain forever. Or never wake from its effect, but live on in eternal sleep. Such a fate was worse than death. He spoke to her, repeating soft assurances over and over as they went.

The journey was interminable. With each step, she seemed to fade within his arms. He grew frantic, tearing across the plains of Thessaly, the hills of Larissa and stilling the River of Acheron to ride atop its black waters with ease.

The sight of his mountainous fortress eased him greatly, but he did not pause until he'd carried her inside the safety of his home. Only when he gently laid her upon his bed, when he was free to inspect the grey cast to her skin and the unsteady rise of her chest, did fear defeat him. He knelt, taking her hand in his. "Be brave, Persephone. You must be brave."

She lay so still, too still.

"My lord?" Aeacus was here.

He turned, not bothering to hide his anguish. "Send Theron to find Hermes. Have him bring ambrosia and nectar."

Aeacus nodded. "Shall I send someone to assis–"

"Only Hermes." He turned back to Persephone. "Hurry!"

He did not hear Aeacus go.

He removed her cloak, slitting her peplos up the front and spreading it wide. The wound was angry, gaping wide and seeping blood. Her face was covered in a sheen of sweat. He covered her with clean linen, leaving only the wound exposed.

She stretched, then groaned when the wound gaped and pulled. He winced at the bright red blood running from the jagged hole.

"Hades?" she whispered.

He leaned over her, careful of jostling the bed with his weight. "I am here." He took a deep breath as she turned her head to stare at him.

She looked dazed, disoriented. "Here?"

"My home."

"Oh..." She stared at the fire. Her eyes closed, pinched tightly as her hands flew to her waist. She clasped her wound suddenly, her face twisting. "I fear... I fear I may retch..."

He reached for her, helping her lie on her side. "Your wound is deep. Jarring it will worsen the damage."

She stared at him with glassy eyes, her body shaking. "Those men... those men..."

He could not stop himself from taking her hand in his. He wished he had some words of comfort for her. But his throat was tight and his chest heavy. He had no experience with such words, or emotions. But he sought to soothe her, to reassure her. His voice was hoarse as he offered, "You are safe now."

She smiled slightly, even as she was racked with shudders. Her stomach convulsed, forcing a moan from her parted lips.

He turned her, supporting her chest with his arm. She shook so violently. Then, suddenly, her body tightened as she retched on the floor. Her hands grasped the angry wound in her side and he ached from her suffering.

"Do not fight it," he murmured into her ear.

She tightened, heaving again, as she cried. He could hold her no tighter, for fear of injuring her. But neither could he lessen his hold upon her, for she was too weak to hold herself upright. She went limp against him, gasping.

"Persephone?" He cradled her, gently turning to place her upon the bed.

Her face was grey, her lips white. Her chest rose and fell slowly.

But her eyes were focused intently upon him. They blazed, round pools of luminescent green, in her exhausted face. He glanced at her stomach. The wound oozed, further torn by her sickness. His arm and thigh were smeared with her blood.

Her eyes fluttered, and the shadow of a smile found her. "I am fine."

"You are brave." He could not help but smile. "And more fierce than Athena."

She shook her head once.

"You are." His voice was hard, defiant.

She closed her eyes, the smile fading as she relaxed. He sat, watching the rise and fall of her chest, appeasing his worry... and anger. She dozed, stirring restlessly, unable to find comfort. When she seemed more peaceful, he stood, restless.

He dropped a thick cloak over the sickness on the floor and moved to build up the blue-white fire. Only when the air was smoldering did he drag a chair beside the bed. He poured a goblet of water and returned to her. He held the water to her mouth, tipping the cup slightly. Her eyes were closed, but he whispered in her ear, "Drink, Persephone, and heal."

She turned from the cup, moaning.

He sat beside her on the bed. "Shh," he whispered, hesitantly resting his hand upon her shoulder. She sighed, shuddering heavily, and turned her face into his arm. Her hand came up, loosely anchoring his arm in place. Her touch soothed him as nothing else. If only he might do the same for her. He watched her, exploring her features in the flickering firelight.

She was beauty.

Her brow smoothed, her lips relaxed, her breathing grew deep and even. Her hair seemed to dance in the firelight, casting an ethereal glow about her. She smiled slightly, her lids fluttering in dreams. Sleep, peace, had finally found her.

He drew in a steadying breath, his nostrils filled with her scent. Panic found him anew, and he closed his eyes to fight it. He had never known such fear, never. His hand tightened upon her shoulder as he bent forward to rest his forehead atop hers. He would never feel such suffering again, nor wish it on his deepest enemy...

"Hades?" Hermes stood inside his chamber, staring at them

with wide eyes. "What happened?"

"I've never been so pleased to have you here," Hades spoke softly, too relieved by Hermes' arrival to safeguard his heart. He stood carefully, slipping his arm from her hold and pulling the furs over her. "She was caught on a battlefield, between Persians and Greeks. She was wounded, gravely so. She needs..."

Hermes handed Hades a large cask of nectar and a basket full of ambrosia. "I have it."

Hades nodded. "My thanks."

"She is an Olympian, Hades. And friend to me. Persephone has my protection as well as yours." Hermes' face hardened with anger. "I would see those that did this suffer."

Erysichthon's face rose before him, hard and... crazed. He'd been drunk with bloodlust, more so than any mortal Hades had ever witnessed. "As would I," he agreed.

"Did they? Were they punished? Was justice delivered?" Hermes rarely spoke with such heat.

Hades gazed at Persephone then, explaining. "There was no time for vengeance. She was..." He paused, swallowing back the emotion that choked him. "She was too frail." Hades shook his head, rubbing a hand across his face.

"No... It was wise, to shelter her... But I would go with you when you seek vengeance, when she is well once more."

Hades nodded, worry rising within him once more. He would see her laughing again. Feast upon the sounds of her teasing voice and the sparkle in her green eyes. But she did not stir. Her long lashes rested on pale cheeks. He sighed, feeling useless once more.

"Did Erysichthon not protect her?"

Hades shook his head. "He wanted me to leave her..."

She moaned, her brow furrowing as her hands hovered over her wound.

Hades poured a glass of nectar and knelt beside her, lifting the cup to her lips. "You must drink, Persephone."

She did not stir.

Hermes cleared his throat. "She will heal. She is strong, Hades."

Hades nodded, but his gaze was fixed upon her. He spoke softly, cautioning himself, "Take word to her mother. Assure her that, once Persephone is well enough, I will see her safely home."

"What else do you need of me?" Hermes asked, his face pained.

Hades could not think. Was there anything else? She had the food and drink of the immortals. Time would heal her, if she could be healed. There was nothing else to be done. He shook his head, saying, "I thank you."

Hermes' face was somber as he regarded Hades, but he nodded. "Shall I send Aeacus to you?"

"No. Tell him I am not to be disturbed. He and the judges will earn their keep."

"Surely there are women who might tend to her?" Hermes asked softly.

Hades glanced at Persephone, her pale skin... how still she was. He nodded. "Ask him to send a woman, a servant, one with some knowledge of healing. Aeacus will know who."

Hermes nodded. "You have done all you can."

"She will be well." His voice was hard. "I will see to it."

"Let the woman tend her, Hades. And rest easy."

Hades glared at Hermes. He would not leave her, not yet. How could he? Did Hermes not see her? Did he not see how fragile she was? How could he suggest such a thing? He bit back his tirade, though his tone revealed him. "In time, Hermes."

Hermes' tawny eyes assessed Hades too carefully. Hermes would draw his own conclusions, but Hades had no desire to hear them. Instead he held his arm out, waiting for Hermes to clasp it.

"You've only to send Theron, if you or Persephone have need of me," Hermes offered in parting.

She sighed, drawing Hades' attention back to her. The muscles of her face moved easily in sleep. He resumed his seat by the fire, his eyes never leaving her.

The servant woman arrived soon after, cleaning the floor and removing Persephone's bloodied garments. She warmed a pan of water over the fire to clean Persephone's wounds, but when she reached for the pan, Hades stopped her.

"You may go," he murmured. "Return in the morning." As she left, he went to work sponging the smooth flesh of Persephone's stomach with gentle hands. The wound was dry, the telltale start of a scab forming. He took care not to poke or prod it. But the sight of her, covered in so much blood, was too much for him... It would distress her, should she wake. And he would do all in his power to keep her calm and safe.

Chapter Ten

Erysichthon swayed. He'd yet to stop, to rest, since she'd left. He could not. He could think of nothing else.

She'd suffered. Her screams filled his ears and pressed the air from his lungs.

Where was she? Where?

Who was the bastard that had taken her? Erysichthon's hands fisted, a snarl escaping from him. He would see that man suffer. He would see him suffer as none had suffered before. He would watch the light in his black eyes die out.

His men... He'd none to call upon. He'd left them to the Persians. What else could he do? There were too many of them, too many... And she was being taken from him. He'd no time to call them back, no time to prevent their defeat... their slaughter.

He stilled. So many dead... He could do nothing for them.

Instead, he must find her.

He'd ridden after her but found nothing, though he'd searched long into the night. No tracks from the bastard's chariot, no path from his monstrous chargers, and none that had seen the man who'd taken his Persephone from him.

Two days of searching. Two days of praying to Demeter, demanding her aid.

He offered sacrifices, offerings... Whatever the Goddess sought, he would appease her.

But he was alone, with no clues to guide him. He was

powerless... but his fury was limitless.

An idea formed, one he refused to accept. But the more he prayed, the longer Demeter stayed silent, the more his idea took hold and rooted deeply. If Demeter would not answer him, there was some purpose behind it. In all of his years of fealty, he'd respected her careful actions. She did nothing without deliberation. If she remained silent now, there was a purpose.

Had she had taken Persephone? Was that why she did not answer him? Had she sent *him*? He would know the answers, hear them from her lips. For his mind was too clouded to see the truth.

He stared at the ax in his hands.

He had no patience for games. He knew only this: Demeter had deserted him, deserted her daughter to some... some barbarian.

"Persephone," his voice twisted, his grief choking him. She'd taken the breath from his lungs and the strength of his heart. He felt nothing but agony at the loss of her.

And anger.

This man, whoever he was, had no knowledge of the reckoning Erysichthon would deliver upon him. He would learn who his foe was, he would hunt the man down, and he would see his vengeance appeased. He would bring Persephone home.

And Demeter, Olympus, would learn that a mortal's wrath could rival even Zeus' temper. His face twisted. He had no interest in the Gods, save one. If Demeter would not think of her daughter, then she must have a hand in this. And he would see her suffer as he suffered.

"Hear me," Erysichthon cried out. "You faithless harpy, hear me!" He lifted the ax. "If you no longer feel the need to protect sweet Persephone, if you would take her from me, I no longer feel the need to protect your precious trees."

His arms trembled under the weight of the ax, angering him all the more. There would be no weakness in him. He would not rest until justice was done.

He swung the ax, gritting his teeth as metal met wood. The trees were old, hard, and hearty. This would be no easy feat. The tree shook, the sudden snap and crackle of its breaking trunk pleasing him. He turned to the next tree, his purpose restoring his drive. He would fell the whole grove and build a feasting hall for his wedding.

When Persephone was found, their wedding would be celebrated across all of Thessaly. And she would smile at him, in awe of his daring.

His arms burned, his back cramped, but he set a steady rhythm. Nothing existed but the sound of his ax against Demeter's trees.

The ax struck, piercing the tree's bark with a strange sound. Unlike the hard crack of metal on wood, this was akin to metal on flesh. And when Erysichthon pulled the ax free, the trunk spurted blood. A keening, wailing cry began, sharp and stabbing to his ears. He lifted the ax, striking hard. The blood continued, flowing down the trunk to soak the ground. On the fourth strike the sound stopped. It took longer to see the tree break and fall.

"You kill a wood nymph?" a woman's voice, old and rasping, reached him.

"Do I?" he shrugged. "I'd not meant to." He looked closer, spying the lifeless limbs of the woman hidden inside the tree. He felt a twinge of regret... Did it matter? This wood nymph would be one of Demeter's faithful. His anger rose within him and he swung the ax again.

"What is the purpose of such destruction, sir?" the old woman asked.

Erysichthon barely glanced at her as he hacked away at the tree. "These trees will appease my lady wife, the Goddess Persephone. I shall build the finest feasting hall in all of Greece, to celebrate our union."

"She asked this of you?" the old crone wheezed.

He turned, raising the bloodied ax. "It is a surprise, woman. A gift."

The old woman regarded him with clear brown eyes. "A gift, you say? What of Demeter? Will she give you her daughter after such a deed?"

"Give me? I am king here." He smiled, shaking his head. "And Persephone is mine."

The old woman stepped closer to him, her knobby hand resting upon the ax handle. "Careful, my lord, I entreat you. You've had the favor of Olympus. Such a course, such blasphemy, will see you lose it. And, perhaps, your Persephone too..."

His chest tightened as he bellowed, "You think I fear the Gods?

When I have pleaded for their aid and they have offered none? I have lost her! Persephone, she is gone from me... Taken... And still they do nothing..."

The old woman stood still, her hands trembling and fisted. "She is gone?"

"But I will bring her back. I will wed her. The Gods cannot stop me." He shrugged her hand from his ax and returned to the trees. "And we will celebrate in a hall the likes of which the Olympians will envy. We will dine on the finest foods, my lady and I."

"Your soul is trapped in a dark place, my lord. Where are your wits? What has happened to you?" her voice sounded strange to him, familiar. "You say you are king? But I've heard of Erysichthon's unwavering loyalty to Demeter..."

He glanced at her, laughing. "I am loyal to none who turns from her daughter. Be gone, woman. Your prattling slows my work."

"Stop this desecration, my lord. I beseech you."

He snorted, cutting through the tree with powerful strokes.

"You bring about your own downfall, oh King." The woman pointed one gnarled finger at him, "You shall never satisfy the hunger in your blood, Erysichthon of Thessaly. No matter what you eat or drink, your hunger will demand more and more. Until you've nothing left to feast upon but your own greedy flesh."

He felt a chill down his spine, a queer uneasiness in the pit of his stomach.

Would she continue on? Would she continue to berate and warn him with empty words? He turned, all but snarling, and lifted his ax in warning. But she was gone.

The moon was gone and the sun was high, yet he tried to carry on. He'd no strength left, his body collapsed beneath the last cypress. He sat and stared over the stumps, bleached white in the moonlight. Their broken, jagged remains were a fitting image for his broken soul. Sleep eluded him. He felt nothing but desperation... and hunger. A powerful hunger, rivaled only by his need to find Persephone.

Persephone was cold. Hades piled on furs and linen, stoked the fire and drew closed the windows. And still she was cold.

He took her hand in his. She looked so frail to him, exhausted and defeated.

The moon had risen twice since he'd brought her here, but there'd been no change. Her wound was healed, pink and sealed with no trace of a scar. He'd left her but once, in the care of the woman Aeacus had sent to him.

And still, she did nothing more than shiver. But that, he supposed, was something.

He sat beside her on the bed and leaned forward to smooth the hair from her forehead. He knew it foolish, but he whispered into her ear, "Be brave."

Her eyes opened, and her head turned towards him.

He stiffened, daring to hope. "Persephone?"

She tried to keep her eyes open, but they drooped shut.

Relief found him. He let go of her hand and stood, pouring a small amount of nectar into a cup and returning to her. A movement caught his eyes, drawing his attention to the bed. Her fingers waved weakly and her hand lifted slightly from the furs. He glanced at her hand then took it in his. Her hand relaxed.

He swallowed, looking at their joined hands. Did she find comfort from his touch?

He squeezed her hand then released her to lift her head. "You must drink."

Her eyelids fluttered, but did not open. He lifted the cup and she drank. A small sip only, but it was enough. He set her back upon the furs and smiled broadly, pleased.

Her hand fluttered, and he reached for it. He could not stifle a soft laugh as her hand stilled, clasped warmly in his. He stared at their hands, considering.

She was shivering, her hand like ice in his hold. She felt truly frozen, yet her skin was covered in a light sheen of perspiration. He stood, hesitating only seconds before he lay at her side and pulled the furs over them.

His hands found her first, startled by her temperature. He drew in a tight breath, cursing his weakness as he drew her against the length of him. Fragile as she was, he could not ignore the feel of her–soft against him–or how she affected him.

He froze then, for she moaned and turned into his chest.

He gathered her close. "Shh," he murmured into her hair. He lay back, settling her forehead on his chest and wrapping them tightly in the furs. "Sleep."

He resisted the urge to bury his nose in her hair, to press his lips against the top of her head.

She slept instantly. Her body softened and her shivering ceased. Her hand, pressed against his stomach, twitched in her sleep. That she lay with him, silk and woman, was torture enough. Such movements did little to calm the heat in his blood.

He took her hand in his. Her fingers clasped him in return. It did not escape him that she fit against him perfectly...

"You will be well," he murmured against her head, his passion cooling to be replaced by something else... something infinitely more dangerous.

She sighed in her sleep, causing him to smile as he finally drifted into sleep.

She heard him. He spoke to her in her dreams.

There were times she almost thought them real. But he would never hold her against him, never cradle her hand in his.

Yet she knew his voice, for it was her favorite sound. And he demanded, earnestly, for her to be brave and heal.

She was feeling better. The pain in her side had raged, but now it only ached. And yet, her body felt so weak and tired. She could not bear to open her eyes or speak.

Besides, such dreams kept her pleased with sleep.

"More?" he offered, keeping his face under careful control.

"No, thank you." Her voice was unsteady, but oh, how he loved the sound of it.

He nodded, sitting the ambrosia beside the nectar. He cast another glance at her, watching her as she looked around her with wide eyes.

"How long have I been here... in your home?" she cleared her throat, coughing slightly.

He offered her water, which she drank thirstily. "Three moons."

She froze, staring at him. "So long?"

He nodded. And every night he'd held her close to warm her. "Do you remember nothing of what happened?" He prayed she didn't.

Her face fell, her forehead wrinkling as she concentrated. "I remember running away from Erysichthon."

"Were you?" His throat went dry. She'd been running away? If he'd taken Erysichthon's challenge, so arrogantly issued in Demeter's grove, he would have spared her all of this. She would never have known such suffering.

She nodded. "The rest is unclear."

He nodded, wrestling this newfound guilt. "Perhaps it's better you have no memories of what happened."

Her voice was steadier now. "You brought me here?"

"You were injured."

"Injured?" Her brow furrowed as she regarded him, perplexed. Then her eyes grew wide and her mouth opened. She pushed the furs back and lifted the linen from her skin. The smooth golden expanse of her stomach greeted them.

He swallowed.

"I was..." she whispered. "You were there... And you..." She turned bright eyes upon him, the sheen of unshed tears unmistakable. "You saved me."

He swallowed again, nodding once. She studied him, her eyes traveling over his face, his hair and shoulders.

He stood, moving towards the fire. It was one thing to care for her, to aid her as she healed, when she was unaware of the lengths he went to do such things. It was quite another to have her look at him with such pleasure.

She should not look at him so.

The silence grew, forcing him to turn to her.

She looked into the distance, her hand upon her stomach. No sign of her wound remained. Did she suffer still? He held his place before the fire, gripping the mantle to do so. "Does it pain you?" His voice was harsh.

She blinked, turning to him and shaking her head. "I suspect you took very good care of me. And I thank you, Hades, for ... caring for me."

He said nothing.

She lay back, resting carefully on her side. Her arms were unsteady as she drew the furs higher. "Why?"

He scowled.

She laughed.

He smiled.

"Forgive me the question." She shook her head.

"Does it surprise you that I am capable of such things?" His voice was low.

She glanced up at him, her green eyes sparkling. "No. Not in the least. Why would you ask such a thing?"

He would ignore the lightness in his chest. He would ignore the desire to smile. He turned towards the fire.

Her voice was soft. "I fear I must be a sight. I need to bathe."

Images of her, warm and soft against him in sleep, flooded him. Her sighs, her smells, the feel of her pressed tightly against him, clutched his chest.

He turned. "I will have a bath delivered."

Her eyes held his.

He nodded then left the room.

"The water is warm, Persephone." He was speaking to her, staring down at her with his midnight blue eyes. And she could do nothing more than stare at him. He was so beautiful.

"My thanks," she murmured. Had she fallen asleep? And now a steaming tub waited for her. She smiled in delight.

He cleared his throat. "Shall I leave you?"

Her stomach tightened. No, he should stay. He should climb into the bath with her. If she were her mother, or the nymphs, she'd know how to entice him. But she was not.

"Do you need assistance?" he asked.

She pushed herself from the furs, wobbling a bit as she did. The room spun, so she waited until it stopped, then stood slowly. "I think I can..." Her side pulled sharply, causing her to gasp and cover it.

He lifted her, carrying her to the tub and setting her into the water before she could respond. She blinked at him in surprise, seeing his nostrils flare and the rapid rise and fall of his chest. "My thanks."

He nodded tightly. "I shall wait." He crossed the room and pulled back the thick linens. A stream of pale sunlight spread across the floor, startling her.

She had not expected sun here. Her mother had said it was eternal darkness.

She peered beyond him at, yes; a large balcony. He glanced back at her before going to stand upon it.

She watched him. His back was straight and his head held high. And then he grasped the railing and his shoulders drooped, his head falling forward. He carried too many burdens upon his shoulders. They were broad shoulders, strong and sure. But he did not have to bear all alone.

Was she one of them? She frowned.

It took an effort to untie her peplos. She was weak and the fabric was soaked through. When she managed to remove it, she dropped it over the edge of the tub. It slapped loudly upon the stone floor.

She sighed, resting her head against edge of the tub.

Her mind spun. Long days of sleep and dreams blurred with what she thought were memories. But could they be? Surely not. Such dreams were too sweet to be real. And yet, she could imagine the feel of him pressed against her in sleep. She could smell him and...

Be brave. How many times had he whispered those words to her? He had, she knew it. It was no dream. She leaned forward, glancing at him. How she longed to hear him whisper to her again.

She washed, the soap he'd left smelling of him, spiced richly, musk and earth. She took a deep breath, drawing in the heady scent. She wet her hair, but her arms began to shake. She lathered the soap, but could not manage it alone.

"Hades?" she called, at once timid and excited.

He entered the room, his eyes upon her face.

"Is there someone... someone to help me?" she stammered. "I cannot... manage my hair."

He nodded and crossed the room. She sat forward, drawing her knees up and resting her chin atop them.

She had not expected his hands to sluice through the water, catching her hair. He lathered it gently, kneading her scalp with firm fingers. She moaned, and he stilled.

"You'd make a fine attendant." She sighed in pleasure.

He laughed softly, making her heart swell with happiness, and returned to his work.

She leaned into his hands, letting him tilt her head first to the left, then to the right. His hand rested on the base of her neck, and she felt her body respond. Even now, weak and tired, her body ached for his touch.

He poured water over her hair, twisting it to ring out the soap. His hands cupped her forehead, lightly pressing all the way down the length of her hair until the soap was gone.

"Done." His voice was hoarse.

She turned, looking at him. Could a man be beautiful? She could think of no other word for him. She felt such pleasure, dazzling warmness from deep inside of her. "Thank you."

His jaw clenched as he nodded.

Did she dare stand? Was she brazen enough to use feminine wiles after all? Her eyes searched his. And she stood slowly, wobbling. "Will you..."

His eyes were round, but he moved quickly. He wrapped one of his own chlamys about her and lifted her out, carrying her to the chair before the fire.

His hands returned to her hair, brushing through the locks with a finely toothed comb.

"Is there no one else to tend me?" she asked. Her body was aflame. And his every touch, his hands lifting her hair, his fingers brushing her neck, heightened her awareness of him.

He stilled, and she glanced back at him.

His face was impassive. "I will find someone more pleasing."

"You mistake me, Hades." She shook her head, overwhelmed by his closeness. She swallowed the lump in her throat. "I've no desire to send you away, none. I meant no offense. But I know you've more important matters than smoothing my hair. If you've no such responsibilities to manage, I beg you, stay and continue." Her cheeks grew hot at such an admission. "Your touch is a comfort."

His eyes widened.

She smiled. "I vowed honesty. You shall have it." She'd said too much. And while she would declare her love instantly, she knew he was not ready to learn the truth yet. He would learn, in time, he was hers. She was careful with her next words, teasing, "You are uncommonly gifted as an attendant."

He shook his head. "I shall tell the Fates so that they might release me to serve you so."

She laughed, delighted. More delighted when he smiled in return.

Chapter Eleven

"Each day brings us closer. I think," Persephone said, glancing at Hermes.

Hermes nodded. "You are happy."

"I worry that what I want colors what *is*. I *want* him to be fond of me. I *want* him to enjoy our time together. When we are together, we speak and laugh and walk together. And I want those things to mean something to him."

Hermes patted her hand, resting in the crook of his arm. "He would be a fool not to enjoy such times."

She shook her head. "You've no need to flatter me, Hermes."

"I did not mean to flatter you," he grinned. "You are a most unique woman, Persephone. You speak plainly. It can be quite disconcerting."

"Perhaps too plainly." She glanced up at him. "I fear I lack my mother's art of seduction..."

"Artifice would not suit you," he assured her.

"That's a relief," she admitted.

He laughed.

"What other news? Hades spoke of a great battle, one that might end war with the Persians?"

Hermes nodded. "The war will end soon enough, though man's fickle nature will see another soon enough."

"Is it man's nature alone that's fickle, Hermes?" she teased.

He shook his head.

"And Greece? Athens?" she asked.

"Greece lost many sons, but will recover. Athens was burned and looted, forcing all Athenians to flee. Yet they work tirelessly to rebuild. Even now, Athens rises from the ashes, a white city. Athena will build the grandest temple in all of Greece, or so she's declared, to remind Athens of their victory and survival."

"How did Poseidon take such a proclamation?" She suspected she knew the answer.

"He had no objection," Hermes said with a shrug. "But his mischief sometimes takes some time to reveal itself."

She nodded. "How fares my mother?"

"She misses you." Hermes' face grew pained, but he smiled suddenly. "She will be pleased to see you return to her."

Persephone sighed. "Soon, I would imagine."

"You don't sound pleased?"

She glanced at Hermes, admitting, "I will miss him."

Hermes was silent as they walked across the fields.

"I would stay with him, Hermes. I love him so." She stopped, forcing him to look at her as she asked, "Does he have no affection for me?"

Hermes glanced at her. "You know why he keeps himself from you?"

She looked at him, confused.

"He was married."

Persephone turned to him, her heart in her throat.

"Many years ago, mind you. She was a mortal, I remember little about her. She was cruel to him, refusing to come here, to his realm."

"Why?" How could a woman turn from Hades?

"She cared for another." Hermes grew somber. "You know of Hades'... *fondness* for Poseidon?"

"But... but Hades is his brother." She could hardly speak the words.

"Poseidon is..." Hermes fell silent, shrugging. "Poseidon."

"Poseidon was pardoned?" She stared at Hermes, feeling an angry flush steal over her.

"Hades wanted it forgotten. Their reign was new. He knew the importance of harmony and balance." Hermes shook his head. "He, above all others, holds to his responsibility."

She could not speak. Did she dare to tempt him now? He was wary and cautious of his heart, with good reason. To be rejected by one's love was devastating, but to be betrayed by one's wife and brother?

She forced the words from her lips. It made a difference. "Did he love her?"

Hermes looked at her. "I cannot know. As I said, it was long ago. Surely, his pride was wounded, for his word is a vow. And she broke their vows, in every way possible."

She looked at Hermes, unable to stop the tears from spilling over. "What evil lies in the hearts of some? I cannot fathom it. That his own brother could..." She wiped the tears from her face.

"Rest assured, Persephone, he cares for you," Hermes murmured.

Persephone gaze wandered from Hermes, then beyond him.

Hades approached, the scowl on his face growing when his gaze settled upon her.

She sniffed, wiping the tears from her cheeks. And still they fell. Seeing him, his stern face and formidable presence, her heart broke for him. How she longed to wrap her arms about him, to soothe the torment he surely still endured. His heart, though he might deny he had one, was strong and true. And she would honor him, if he would let her.

He stopped before her, the slightest crease of his brow revealing his concern. "What ails you, Persephone?"

She shook her head, unable to speak.

Hades looked at Hermes, the crease deepening. "Hermes?"

"Her side," Hermes spoke quickly. "She said it pained her."

Persephone glanced at Hermes. How easily he lied. Now Hades would worry over her, something he'd done enough of. But she could not refute Hermes, or share the truth. She feared Hades would set her further from him.

"You need rest." Hades' blue-black eyes swept her face, stirring both her delight and guilt. He moved forward and swung her into his arms.

She swallowed, wrapping her arms about his neck and gazing at him. If she were able, she would right his past and erase such suffering.

"It's too soon to send her back yet, Hades," Hermes said. "Let it be, for now. She's not ready for such a journey. I will take her home soon enough."

Persephone glanced back and forth between them. "Is that why you're here, Hermes? To take me home?" Her voice trembled. She turned tear-filled eyes back to Hades. "Are you so eager to be rid of me?"

Hades face hardened, but he nodded once. "You do not belong here."

She began to cry in earnest, not bothering to cover her face.

Hades set off, carrying her to the house with long strides.

"She is overwrought." Hermes was smiling. Persephone could hear it in his voice. "I will call again soon. Rest easy, Persephone."

She sniffed. Why was Hermes smiling? Why had he assured her that Hades cared for her? He wanted her to leave. She sobbed.

"Shhh," Hades soothed.

She looked up at him, hiccupping.

His words slipped over her, his tone stirring her. "Be brave, Persephone." He glanced down at her, his face stricken.

Perhaps he did care for her, but was it enough? Her tears continued as she stared at him. She loved the line of his jaw, loved the sweep of his brow above his blue-black eyes. Even knowing he meant to send her home, his presence eased her. Oh, how she would miss him, everything about him, when she was sent away.

They reached his room, hers now, and he set her on her feet. She moved from him, leaving the room to stand on the balcony. She wiped her face, wishing the tears away. If he wanted her to leave, she should go. Even if she did not want to go....

Her name was a rough whisper. "Persephone?"

She turned to him, and forgot to breathe.

All of her dreams, smoothing the crease from his brow, crawling into his lap and sweeping his midnight curls from his forehead, would go unfulfilled if he sent her away. And she would never enjoy the feel of his lips upon her, offer him the comfort of her arms, or the love of her body.

"Are you well?" He came to stand before her, his eyes searching hers.

She blinked. "I know not."

His eyes bore into her. She met his gaze.

"What upset you so?" His voice was desperate. "Are you in pain? Suffering?"

"Hermes told me..." She paused. She had no desire to dabble in deception. Yet, she could not tell him. She swallowed, shaking her head.

"What?" His voice was hard, edged with threat.

Persephone remembered her promise to him. She would not break it now, no matter how difficult the truth might be. "He told me of... of your marriage." She watched him closely.

His eyes narrowed, yet his words were a whisper. "And you weep?"

Persephone sniffed. "She was cruel to you..."

"What did Hermes tell you?"

She hesitated, her words falling heavily. "Very little. Only that you were betrayed by your brother... and... her."

Hades face softened, or so it seemed. His eyes searched hers. "And you weep?"

She nodded. "Of course I weep. You are a good man..."

He held up his hand. "A good man? I near killed her. My brother gave her what I could not."

She paused. "I don't... I don't understand."

"No."

"I would hear it from your lips, Hades," she implored.

"Priska, daughter to one of the ruling mortal tribes, was offered to me, newly triumphant over the Titans. Zeus accepted the alliance." He paused. "The lots were drawn amongst the *festivities* of the wedding. She went with me that night, fearful and unhappy."

"But how..."

"She is... was mortal, Persephone." Hades' words stopped her, his eyes going black as he continued, "Think of those men, in the meadow. You saw what I did. What I am capable of. When I reached for her, in our marriage bed, I'd no knowledge of the new power inside of me. My hold went beyond her flesh, as it did with those villains that day. She suffered, as they did, for I had no control of my abilities, knew *nothing* of them... When I saw it was pain, not passion, that I inflicted upon her, I released her... before I'd managed to tear her soul free. But she feared me, and rightly so. I never touched her again."

She shivered. She had no fondness or allegiance for this woman, but felt sympathy for this Priska nonetheless. And Hades. She met his gaze. How had he suffered? He would have felt this woman's pain. Even if she'd managed to forgive him, as she must have done in time, would he have forgiven himself?

"I returned her to her father, determined to make the Titans' caverns, dank and bleak as they were then, something bearable for her. It took time, to build this and to control my... gifts. Too much time for a mortal. Her father worried over the alliance he'd forged with me, with Olympus. So he sought Poseidon's interest in my stead. Whether or not she was willing, I cannot say. But in time, she grew fond of my brother. I know nothing of how he felt or if he cared for her at all. When I returned, intending to bring her home, I learned the whole of it. As did Zeus. Poseidon was punished..."

"The horses?" she whispered. "The team that pulls your chariot?"

Hades nodded. "They were the very first of their kind, magnificent beasts, as wild as the ocean waves my brother modeled them after. They were – are – Poseidon's greatest creation. And not an easy sacrifice to make, Persephone. Zeus knew forfeiting them, to me, would punish him more dearly than anything else." He shrugged. "And Priska was told to return with me."

"Was she pleased by her new home?"

"She never saw the Underworld." His eyes drifted from hers, his face growing hard as he continued, "I do not remember her... But I cannot forget her voice." He paused. "She would not come. She hated me... hated me for the pain I'd inflicted upon her. Because of him, Poseidon. She blamed me for their separation. To her, *I* sent him away."

Persephone's eyes filled with tears, but she said nothing. What could she say?

"Her tribe lived on the cliffs, near where Athens sits today. She threw herself from them. And by taking her own life she ensured she could not cross over." He shrugged again. "Even in death she vowed never to be with me. She succeeded."

Persephone could not breathe. She could not think. His words roared in her head, flooding her with agony and fury.

"She was right. Such... alliances suit my realm poorly." He looked at her then, his features cold and unreadable.

She could listen no more. Of course he would refuse her. How could she expect anything from him now? Knowing what he'd endured. Her heart convulsed. She watched him move to her, his face suddenly concerned.

"Rest easy."

"I don't understand." She wrapped her arms about herself. How could a person inflict such wickedness, willingly, upon another? Persephone felt ill and strangely weak. "She... she..."

"She is gone." His brow furrowed. "Let it go."

"Have you?" She winced as soon as the words were out, hearing his sharp intake of breath. She had no right to ask such a thing. She was angry and hurt, but not with Hades.

Would she not lock her heart away after such an ordeal? If she'd not died from the suffering it unleashed upon her... "I'm sorry. I act as if I'm injured. I've no cause to snap at you. You, who've been gravely wronged. You endured all... You survived it..." She shook her head, a sad smile on her lips. "I am not as strong as you, that much I know."

He regarded her silently, until she feared she would throw herself upon him. She longed to wrap her arms about him, to comfort him.

He spoke softly. "Time heals a great deal."

"Time." She nodded. She needed more time, with him. What happened with Priska, and his vile brother, was far worse than anything she could have imagined.

But what they, she and Hades, might share... it would be wonderful between them. She must convince him that her heart was, and always would be, his. She needed time to show him what their love could be.

He watched her carefully.

She let her gaze wander over his features, adding, "Does time heal loneliness?"

His eyes widened, his jaw tightened. "Have you been lonely?"

"I have not been alone. I have you with me," she smiled as she spoke. "And I am thankful to have you..." She blinked, embarrassed. "I mean... I suppose... I have kept you from your responsibilities too long."

He said nothing, though his eyes bore into hers, burning intensely.

She sucked in a breath, speaking rapidly, "It is selfish of me to stay any longer, I know. But, I *would* stay. Let me stay here, Hades, please. My wound is healed, but I am not strong yet. I, too, will be well... in time. It is peaceful here."

It was the truth. She'd felt such peace only when she was in the meadows or trees, alone with their presence and none other. Being here, with him, was so much more. Yes, she was peaceful, but she felt alive.

Because of him.

She knew he'd brought her here to keep her safe. That he'd had no choice in the matter. And perhaps Hermes' visit indicated he *wanted* her gone. She searched his face, desperate for some sign from him.

She was not ready to give up, not yet. There were times when he yielded to her. In those moments of softness, she saw warmth in his gaze. She suspected it was more than just the desires of the flesh... And yet, if he would not give her his heart, would he give her his body?

She blinked, letting her eyes travel the line of his mouth. It was pressed tight, his lovely lips a hard line. Could she be happy with that? A joining of the flesh, but no more? She blinked, tearing her eyes from his mouth.

He mumbled, "You are welcome here until you wish to leave."

Then you will have to make me leave, for I would stay at your side, as we are now, forever.

Chapter Twelve

Hades leaned against the arched doorframe, too pleased with the sight before him. Persephone slept, the even rise and fall of her chest offering him comfort. Her copper hair spilled over the kline's pillows, blown gently by the evening breeze. He moved to her side, his fingers light upon her cheek. The absence of her, the touch of her skin and sound of her breath, plagued him nightly. And though he knew it was wrong, he did could not stop himself from touching her now.

How soft her skin was. Was she too cool? He turned, heading for his chambers. He would bring some furs to warm her.

"My lord Hades," Aeacus called out, his footsteps heavy in the otherwise silent room.

Hades raised his hand, pointing at Persephone.

Aeacus nodded, pressing his lips together. He placed the scrolls upon the table and tapped them with his fingers.

"Much to report?" Hades asked softly, leading Aeacus into the hall and away from the balcony.

"None of interest," Aeacus said. "The end of war brings a lull to your judges' chambers."

"Enjoy such idle times as you can. Man seems too eager to find their next conquest."

Aeacus nodded, though his eyes returned to Persephone.

"Yes?" Hades asked, following Aeacus' gaze.

"Is she well?"

"She seems to be." Hades could not stop himself from lingering upon her face, relaxed in sleep.

"I have seen you walking together. Something she'd not been capable of when she first arrived here."

Hades nodded. It was too soon to think of what she'd endured without rage and helplessness consuming him. But seeing her as she was, at ease, helped.

He turned, unrolling the scroll and spreading it flat upon the table. His eyes scanned the list.

"My lord Hades?" her voice was soft.

"Within," he answered. He would not go to her, he would not further unman himself before Aeacus.

She joined them, smiling at Aeacus with warmth. As was her way.

"Good evening, Goddess." Aeacus bowed low.

"Is it?" she asked, her brows rising.

To Hades' eyes, she looked fragile, and lovely. He turned back to the scroll as she asked, "Have I slept the day away?"

"Sleep is best," Aeacus offered, "when recovering from illness or injury. Or so my wife believed."

He was aware of her every move. She moved closer to him, to his side. "Was she right?"

"I believe she was. Though I knew better than to praise her too regularly, for fear of increasing her self-importance." Aeacus sighed, sounding amused. "But she was a good wife. A devoted mother."

"And were you a noble husband?" Persephone asked. But Hades saw the panic on her face and the color on her cheeks. She did not wait for Aeacus' answer, asking instead. "And these are your accounting?"

"Every soul's story is recorded." Aeacus paused. "Life's deeds are weighed, each small thing tipping the scales one way or the other. So such records are necessary–"

"I believe you've called them tedious on more than one occasion," Hades interrupted.

"Oh, they are that," Aeacus assured him.

"But necessary," Persephone prompted.

"You were blessed with Olympus' favor," Hades said.

Aeacus nodded.

"Tell me how, Aeacus," Persephone urged. "Please. I'm very fond of stories. I would be delighted, and honored, to hear yours."

Hades saw the indecision upon Aeacus' face. When Aeacus glanced his way, Hades nodded his approval. "It is a good story, Aeacus. One worthy of being told." He was aware of Persephone's eyes upon him, but fixed his attention on the scroll once more. He'd been too unguarded in Aeacus' presence. It was unfitting behavior for the one ruling the Underworld.

"It helps to be one of Zeus' halflings," Aeacus laughed.

Hades smiled. "It did not hurt."

"He is... Zeus is your father?" Persephone asked, startled.

"Mine." Aeacus nodded. "And many others."

Hades glanced at Persephone. She looked surprised by this news. Perhaps Demeter had not revealed all of Olympus' affairs to her young daughter. And yet, he knew Demeter had no qualms painting Poseidon a villain. For that, he was grateful.

"My mother was briefly favored by Zeus," Aeacus began. "In that time, I was born. Hoping to see me safe from Hera's fits of jealousy, I was placed on an island. Zeus named it after my mother..."

"Aegina?" Persephone asked.

Aeacus nodded. "And my father... Zeus, gave me people to govern. And companionship. It was a blessed time. I had a wise wife at my side and three able sons to help my rule. But they were restless boys, frequently given to pointless rivalries and competition. My youngest, Phocus, was the peacemaker."

Hades watched her face. With each word, she grew more entranced by Aeacus' tale. He moved to her side, knowing this story was not one of good fortune alone.

"He was not only a skilled negotiator, he was an athlete as well." Aeacus shook his head. "And his brothers could not bear the sight of him. The more capable Phocus became, the more bitter his brothers grew. Until they could stand it no more."

Persephone leaned forward, her eyes round. "But Aeacus, surely..."

"But they did, my lady," he mumbled, the ancient hurt still evident. "They killed their brother without thought to the consequences."

Persephone shook her head, "You... you... I'm so sorry."

Aeacus' smile was genuine. "It was long ago, Goddess. The pain is but a dim memory now." He nodded at the scroll on the table. "A memory likely forgotten if not for the scrolls Hades keeps."

"But that is not the end of your story," Hades encouraged.

"I banished them," Aeacus went on.

"Your other sons?" Persephone asked.

Aeacus nodded. "Peleus and Telamon. I could not ignore the heinous crime they'd committed. Whether or not they were my sons, they would face justice."

She nodded. "A thing easier said than done."

Hades bit back a smile. She was quick to grasp Aeacus' strength. "And yet, Aeacus prized justice above all else. And when he died, I hoped he would aid me in the governing of this realm. He carries the keys to the Underworld." He pointed to the brass circlet tied to Aeacus' belt. "They unlock not just Tartarus' gate, but the records room as well. We must preserve our past to–"

"Remember our mistakes," Persephone finished for him. "If we forget, we learn nothing. And these scrolls?" She stood, moving to the table and studying the parchment. "They hold the stories of all who live here?"

"They do," Hades affirmed.

"Such stories." Her voice was soft.

"Some are too tragic to read," Aeacus assured her.

She made a soft noise of agreement, then said, "But you do honor to them, to remember. For every story has merit, every life purpose, surely?"

Hades drew in a slow breath as her bright green eyes rested upon him. He nodded.

Aeacus cleared his throat, glancing first at him, then at Persephone. "I shall leave you."

Persephone smiled at him. "Thank you for sharing your story with me, Aeacus. Hades, and those within his realm, are fortunate to have your loyalty."

Aeacus bowed and then left.

Persephone watched Aeacus depart, her face thoughtful. "Has he been here long?" She glanced at Hades.

He nodded. "He arrived after I'd begun work on the three levels of the Underworld."

Her green eyes went round. "How many were here when you took charge?"

"One." He paused, watching astonishment cross her face. "The titans had no interest in honoring the dead. Death was simply the end."

She blinked, shaking her head. "So you...you created Tartarus–"

"That was here, Persephone. I created Asphodel and Elysium."

She shuddered, rubbing her arms. "All were sent to Tartarus... No wonder death was so reviled. But now, death need not be feared." She paused, looking thoughtful. "May I ask why three levels?"

How lovely she looked in the fading sunlight spilling into the room. Watching her, each graceful gesture, provided him endless fascination.

She stared at him now, waiting.

"Not all mortals live a truly honorable life. There are heroes, martyrs, noble leaders, and the like. Mortals are born with both good and evil within – they're tempted daily. Too often mortal man succumbs to weakness. It is in their nature and, most of the time, not worthy of condemning them to Tartarus. Nor does it grant them an afterlife of abundance and pleasure, as Elysium offers. So Asphodel was created, for those in-between."

She nodded, her gaze wandering to the parchment before her.

Hades sat at the other end of the table, his gaze returning to the top of her copper head, bent to regard the open scroll.

She sat, her eyes never leaving the parchment. And as she read, her face changed and moved, reacting to the words before her. Such a face, such emotions. How would he manage when she left?

*

She hopped then ran a few steps to keep up with him. He glanced at her. She smiled brightly at him. His mouth twitched, but he did not smile.

"You need not run, Persephone," he sighed, slowing his pace.

She shrugged. "I've missed running."

She saw him smile then, though he was quick to erase it.

"What a glorious day." Her every word revealed her happiness.

He nodded, his eyes wandering to her once more.

She let her hands trail, listening closely to the strange words. In time, she'd learn their language. It was not so different from that of the oldest trees. Yet some words made no sense to her; not yet.

They, however, had no trouble understanding her. She delighted in the abundance of the grass, the bloom of the bushes and ripening of Asphodel's abundant wheat.

Every day they walked further, crossing the waving sea of Asphodel's grasses. She was surprised they'd not reached any boundaries, but Hades' realm seemed to stretch on and on, never ending. Her eyes searched the golden grass.

He skirted the shoreline, avoiding the rippling blue waters that separated Asphodel from Elysium, but she gazed across the water. Elysium lay, a green gem of an island in the distance. The sun seemed brighter there, bathing the land with the promise of warmth. Here, in Asphodel, there was always a hint of chill in the air.

"It looks a fertile land," she murmured.

He turned to the water as he spoke, "It is always green, without being tended or worked. Fitting spoils for heroes and the like, is it not?"

"Can one enjoy an existence without *some* vocation?" She shook her head, glancing at him. "One would grow idle and bored, I think."

Once more his mouth tightened, and he turned from her. She smiled, a slight sigh escaping her. Why did he still resist her? She knew he turned from her to hide his smiles.

Or perhaps her presence annoyed him? She did not like the doubt that flared within her Did he wish her gone? Was he enduring her presence?

She walked on, such thoughts more than unpleasant to her. She glanced back at him, wishing his features weren't so fixed, that his control wasn't so absolute.

His attention was elsewhere, so she followed his gaze. A black shadow, graceful and large, stood amongst the waving grasses. She narrowed her eyes, surprised to see one of Hades' chargers grazing. "Oh." She ran toward the horse.

"Be careful," he called after her.

She laughed, slowing once the massive black head lifted. Coal eyes stared at her, but showed no signs of agitation. The beast flicked his ears twice then walked to her.

"It's good to see you again," she murmured. "I'd offer you an apple, if I had one. Alas, I fear you'll gain nothing from me but a gentle touch." She reached up, running her hand along the horse's thickly muscled neck.

The horse stared down at her, his great nose blowing her hair as he investigated her thoroughly. She laughed.

Hades arrived, sighing loudly. "He's normally a ferocious brute."

She laughed again, stroking the animal's powerful shoulders with both hands. "You sound disappointed. Do you want him to bite me?"

Hades shook his head, rubbing a hand over his face. "I do not. It had not occurred to me that he'd sit so easily under your touch, either."

"Mighty Orphnaeus," she murmured. "Your master is astounded that one might enjoy my companionship. Should I be offended?"

The horse lifted his head to regard Hades.

She looked too, her smile faltering at the grave expression he wore.

"You're a most pleasant companion, Persephone." His words were soft.

She blinked at him. "Am I?"

Orphnaeus moved behind her, pushing between her shoulders with his broad nose.

She giggled. "What is it?"

Hades moved forward, a frown on his face. "He wants you to ride."

She glanced at him, surprised. "Can you understand him? Talk to him?"

"Not as you talk to your plants and trees, no. But we understand enough."

She looked at the horse, then at Hades. "Enough? And the hounds?"

Hades' frown grew. "All creatures of the night, those that move in shadow. They are loyal to me, my... ghosts."

Persephone nodded. "To earn such loyalty, they must respect you."

"Or fear me." His face hardened then.

She shook her head, "Fear you? Animals, like the plants, know the worth of a soul."

Hades looked away from her. She saw the muscle in his cheek tighten, but he said no more.

The horse snorted, blowing hard. His breath lifted her hair, sending her curls over her shoulder. She laughed and stroked the animal. "Such a beautiful creature."

Again, the horse pushed against her.

She looked at Hades. "Can I ride him?"

He closed his eyes, a crease appearing between his inky brows. "I see no objection from the animal."

"But you object?"

"He's a charger, Persephone. A war horse. He's not ridden for pleasure, only purpose." His words were uttered without inflection, "I worry over your injury."

To hear those words spoken with feeling... she could only imagine such delight. Instead she said, "Then I will not."

He stared at her, the crease returned to his brow, drawing a smile to her lips.

The horse nudged her.

She laughed, stroking the horses soft nuzzle. "Shh, another time."

She watched Hades. Bewilderment crossed his face as he looked from the horse to her.

"Where are the others?" she asked him.

His eyes narrowed as he searched. "Close. Rarely do they part company."

She nodded. "And the hounds?"

"Guard the entrance to the Underworld. A rest after so long at Thanatos' command."

"Thanatos?" She shivered. She had yet to see the specter of death.

Hades moved on, his voice flat. "He hunts only those for Tartarus. You'll not find him here."

She nodded, relieved, and stepped forward, with Orphnaeus at her heels. She whispered to the horse, delighted by her new companion. "Shall I find you a treat?"

"There are orchards." Hades pointed.

She glanced at him, surprised. "Truly? Did you hear that, Orphnaeus? Shall we find you an apple?"

The horse whinnied, ears pricking forth.

She laughed. "I think he agrees?" she asked Hades a bit breathlessly.

Hades moved quickly, gripping her about the waist and setting her atop the horse before she could react. But her skin tingled from the slight contact, making her heart pick up and her lungs empty. He surprised her further when he swung up behind her, his arms enfolding her and pulling her against his chest.

Hades hissed, his knees pressing against the horse's sides. The horse responded instantly, tearing forward with such force that Persephone feared she'd slip off. But Hades' arms anchored her, one hand pressed against her belly. She drew in an unsteady breath, the heat of his fingers branding her.

The horse slowed almost as soon as they had started, easing from a rolling gallop to an easy trot. Hades' knees guided the animal, the flex of each muscle having the most alarming effect on her.

"Apples," he offered, easing Orphnaeus beneath the drooping limbs of the fruit tree.

She knew better than to speak; her heart was surely lodged within her throat. So she reached up, hoping the tremor of her arm was lost upon him.

Her fingers grasped the satin red skin of the apple, twisting the stem until the tree released its fruit. She stared at the fruit, while her body seemed to hum – attuned only to him. His hand moved slightly, his thumb pressing in against the skin beneath her breast. Then he slipped from the horse and reached for her.

She blinked. His deep blue eyes waited beneath the furrow of his brow.

"Persephone?" he asked.

She nodded, placing her hand upon his shoulder and allowing him to lift her. Her feet reached the ground, but she did not want to release him. His hands remained, steadying her.

It would take no effort to kiss him. He held her already. All she need do was raise up on her tiptoe–

Orphnaeus' head descended between them, his nose butting against Hades' chest to reach the apple pressed between them. His teeth plucked the red apple from her hand, piercing its skin and crushing it in seconds. Juice spattered her hand and arm, making her burst into laughter.

Hades laughed too, his fingers brushing the fruit pulp from her arm and cheek.

"He is a brute after all," she said, shaking the bits of apple from her fingers.

Hades smoothed a curl from her shoulder, his face growing remote once more. He lifted his hand and she drew in breath. She knew he would kiss her. He would draw her close, he wanted too. She could see it in his eyes, in the rigid set of his jaw–

Orphanaeus butted her between the shoulders, snorting.

"One is not enough." Hades stepped back, reaching for another apple and plucking it with ease. She offered it to the horse, who gobbled it down and snorted indignantly into her empty hand.

Hades picked more, and the two fed the horse in companionable silence. Yet all the while, Persephone savored the memory of his thighs pressed against hers, the strength of his chest against her back... And quivered with some nameless sensation.

He offered her another apple, but Orphnaeus seemed content.

She brought the bright skinned fruit to her lips. "It should not go to waste."

The strangest expression settled over him. His eyes widened, then narrowed. His mouth opened, then pressed tightly closed. When the skin of the fruit met her lips, he knocked it free.

The fruit tumbled to the ground and Orphnaeus devoured it.

Persephone stared at Hades. "Hades–"

"You cannot eat the food of the Underworld," Hades snapped, running a hand through his thick black hair. His eyes flashed as he glared down at her. "Never. Do you understand?"

She nodded, her mind reeling with confusion. "But–"

"No," he shook his head, his hands clasping her upper arms. "You must not. I fear the consequences of such a thing."

"'Tis an apple," she protested.

His mouth twitched, but his fingers tightened about her arms. "An apple grown here, in the realm of the Dead. It is by the Fates' decree..."

She touched his cheek. "Peace, Hades. I will not eat. I need no more explanation than that."

But she wondered over the wariness upon his face as he urged them to return to his home.

"I cannot, Father." Ione grasped his hands, kneeling in front of Erysichthon. "Please, please do not make me do this."

"Make you?" His words were hard. "Where is the dutiful daughter I raised? After what I have done for you... Need I remind you of my generosity, child? Remind you that I took you in when your husband discarded you?"

"He discarded me for fear of incurring Olympus' wrath. After you cut Demeter's trees he had no choice–"

"So you blame me for his weakness?" He pulled his hands from hers and stood. Was no one faithful anymore? Did none value fealty? "You would desert me too?" Erysichthon did not look at her. "My own daughter?"

His eyes swept the room. Leaves blew across the unkempt marble floor. The candles had long since burned down, leaving the room in shadows, but no servants remained to change them. No one was left to serve him. Those soldiers that had returned he'd sent searching, always searching...

He winced as his empty belly clenched. He turned, staring at the weariness on his once beloved child's face.

"I'm... I'm sorry, Father." She stood, coming to his side. Her face was thinner, her eyes shadowed. "I've done all that you've asked of me, have I not?"

He nodded, his hand cupping her cheek. "You are a good daughter, Ione, when you choose to be."

Her lower lip wavered then, reminding him of Persephone. Could he find no reprieve from her memory? He shook his head, groaning as his bowels twisted within him.

"I am a good daughter. Your daughter," she cried, her voice hitching. "Flesh of your flesh, your only child... and you sell me... for... for bread and wine..."

"I must keep my strength and wits about me." He scowled at her.

"There must be another way–"

"I've never sold you for whoring, Ione, only as servant. You've no need to act so affronted. You should be pleased. I never thought you capable of finding a champion in Poseidon..." He broke off, the ache in his stomach overwhelming him.

"He is no *champion*." Her voice was bitter. "He demands payment, I assure you." She grabbed his arm, steadying him as he bent low from the spasms.

He smiled, amused. "You are... a comely woman, Ione. If Poseidon wants you–"

Her voice trembled. "He did, when first we met. He had certain... expectations of me once he'd helped me leave that brutal fisherman's wife. But when he knew who I was, whose daughter I was..." She shook her head. "It troubled him to look at me."

"And yet, he helps you still." Erysichthon sighed, growing annoyed with his daughter's complaints.

"And each time his patience thins; I see it. Three times he's returned me to you... I'd almost welcome his advances if it replaced the anger within him–"

"Then you must try harder. Soothe him. Woo him, entice him, seduce him, child. He will help you again." Erysichthon cut her off, pulling his arm from her hold. "One last time, for I know where Persephone is."

Ione froze. "Truly?"

He nodded, smiling. "This will be the last time, I promise. Once she is returned, all will be well. You will see."

The sympathy in his daughter's eyes irked him. He needed no pity.

"Persephone will speak to her mother?" Ione asked doubtfully. "See the curse removed?"

"She will." He spat out the words, scowling at her. "Why do you question me so, child? When have I ever failed you? When? Never. Even now, when times are... troubled, have you not returned to me each time, in good health?"

She nodded.

"Then give me thanks. Honor me. It is through my *suffering* that you've found a lover in the God of the Seas himself. My daughter, favored by the great Poseidon."

She shook her head. "As I said, he does not favor me... He said he must help me to ease his part in this matter..."

"What matter?"

"He did not say. And I dare not question him, not when he has come to my aid." Her lovely face looked haggard. "I dare not rouse the fury I see within his pale gaze, Father. He frightens me—"

"Frightens you? A robust lover, then?" He smiled, patting her cheek. "He favors you or he would not continue to help you." He nodded, regarding his daughter with narrowed eyes. "And you would be wise submit to him again and hold his interest as long as you can." His hands pressed against his stomach, the pain forcing another groan from him.

She stared at him with wide eyes. "Look at you, Father. Look at what has become of us. Of your people... Our home. Thessaly is ravaged, as is your body... and mind. I have lost my husband through your blasphemy." Her tone was pleading. "I have lost my pride, sold into servitude three times, and... used by Poseidon to appease your hunger. And now you would encourage me to sacrifice my dignity again... For what?"

"You complain like an old woman. It's unlike you. And will not help you keep your Poseidon." He clasped her shoulders. "You shall have your God and I shall have my Goddess, soon."

She shook her head. "Where is she, then? Where is your precious Persephone? And why haven't you gone to get her yet?"

He ignored her disbelief and patted her cheek. "She is with Hades. It was he that took her from me on the battlefield."

She stared at him. "Hades? You cannot go... How will you bring her home?"

He smiled, rubbing his hands together. "Find me food, Ione, and I will tell you my plan."

"I am victor." Persephone beamed at Hades.

He'd not let her win, this time. She was quick, grasping the game and trouncing him gleefully. He sat back with a smile. "You are."

She sat forward, setting her elbow on the table and resting her chin in her hand. She moved the small carved gray pieces back into place. Her braid fell forward, brushing his hand on the game board before she looked up at him. "Shall we play again?"

His hand burned. He shook his head. "Enough Tavli."

"Shall we walk?"

It infuriated him to know he would be happy to sit here, staring into her green eyes. How easily she'd come to be the most important part of his day... He leaned into the side of his chair, watching her fingers move over the game pieces. She was the reason he woke, full of anticipation, each morning. He was too eager to spend time with her. He savored their walks or their quiet companionship. Everything about her pleased him. Her presence eased some ache within him, an ache that he'd always known, causing him much bewilderment... and exhilaration.

"Shall I sing for you?" She placed the last piece then sat back, tucking her knees under her.

He cocked his head. "What would you sing of?"

She tapped her finger to her lips as she thought, drawing his gaze to her full mouth.

"I know." Her face grew animated as she spoke, "The song of the trees."

"The trees sing?" he asked.

She shook her head, sighing. "Of course they do. Though the language might be too old for even your ears."

He laughed as she stood to retrieve the lyre Hermes had delivered. She could play well enough, but her voice... her voice wrapped about him more sweetly than any binding.

She opened her mouth, the words washing over him. She was wrong, he knew this song. He bit back his smile. He smiled too much in her presence.

He sat back, allowing himself the pleasure of watching her. Her eyes closed, as they always did when she sang, and her brows lifted. The higher the note, the higher her brows went. Her braid slipped from her shoulder, pushing the fabric with it. Her golden skin begged for his touch, he felt the pull of it upon his fingers...

His eyes met hers. The song was over.

He cleared his throat.

"A story?" she asked.

He lifted a brow, nodding slightly. "You owe me a story."

He saw her hesitate, her eyes flashing at his. She shook her head then, smiling at him with unconcealed merriment. "I do. Well then, what will you hear? Would you hear of Gaia and her children? How mortal man came about?" She tilted her head as she spoke, waiting for his answer.

"Mortals hold little interest for me."

She nodded, sitting up. "It is said that before order was found, chaos reigned. In it, all was knotted together. The elements of life, earth, sea, and sky ran seamlessly with no beginning or end. But chaos gave way to creation, for the elements' need for order would not be denied. And from their seed the land took shape. Soil turned thick and rich, birthing all things green and clean. It rose and fell, etching valleys and jutting high above as the peaks of great mountains. The seas filled with water, overflowing into the lakes, rivers, and marshes and feeding the soil and its children. The sky, struck by such beauty, stretched as wide as it could... drawing the earth and seas into an encompassing embrace. It rained when the seas ran shallow, it shone when the earth was too wet, and it thundered when the earth's children should be scolded."

He listened, hearing the words with new ears. She painted their history with such a gentle brush. "What of the stars?" he asked softly.

She reached up, unbraiding her hair and running her fingers through its silken locks as she continued. "The sky could not bear to lose sight of the earth or the seas. The sky drew the stars forth, to light the skies and ease the fear of night's darkness. Well pleased, the three wanted to share their bounty. Fish found water, birds found the sky and the beast of the field were content upon the earth."

Hades looked at her. Her copper hair hung free, falling about her shoulders in the fading sunlight. She gazed off into the distance, lost in thought. Her shoulder, smooth and gold, caught his eye again. The moon had come and gone since he'd last touched her. And yet he could still feel her beneath his hand. He fisted his hand, tearing his gaze from her.

"Is that how you imagine it?" he asked her.

She turned to him, brows raised in consideration. He could tell her thoughts without her words, her face hid nothing. If he was uncertain, her eyes told the rest.

"Why not? It is a peaceful tale." She smiled. "I am fond of peace."

He nodded. "As am I. Even the mortals seem eager for it. I only hope it will hold."

"Is there news? I know Hermes has come and gone since last I saw him. I see the boats passing by and know their purpose. How fares Greece?"

He sighed. "It is over. Persia met defeat at Salamis. The enemy flees, but they leave true destruction in their wake."

"It is some comfort that they *do* go?"

He nodded.

Hermes carried news that disturbed him. The champion Ariston was soon to meet an ill fate, if Olympus did not intercede. And he knew better than to hope for such benevolence. Greece was done with the soldier, soon Olympus would be too. It was the loss of his wife, so ill used and cast aside, that concerned him most.

"What troubles you?" she asked.

He shook his head. "I pity them."

"Mortals?"

He nodded. "Their lives are not their own."

She pulled her legs into her chair, resting her chin on her knees. "No?"

His eyes found hers. "Olympus interferes. Too many souls cross over because they've lost favor with the Gods."

"You see gaining the Gods' favor as unfortunate as losing favor?" Her brow furrowed at his words.

"I am too jaded to answer well." He paused, considering. "If I likened those on Olympus to those toiling aimlessly in Tartarus, you'd think ill of me. But there are times I see that idleness about them. Mortals are but a piece of the game." He clasped the Tavli dice, tossing it in his hand. "Such is the case with the mortal I returned."

"The soldier? The hero of Greece? But Olympus was well pleased with your decision. Hermes and my mother spoke of your ... reward for such action."

Hades stared at her, wondering if she knew he'd rejected his *reward*. He hoped she did. "He's served his purpose. And now he will return to me, more broken that he was before. He will lose his beloved wife not once, but twice, at the hands of our brethren. And his lady wife, sacrificing all to keep her husband safe, will be lost forever in Tartarus..." He heard her sharp intake of breath at the mortal woman's fate. "This honorable man will never find the peace we speak of."

He could feel the unflinching weight of her eyes upon him. He'd said too much, revealed too much.

"Oh, Hades." Her voice was unsteady and she shook her head.

When he looked at her, he was startled by the tears sparkling in her eyes. "Such an end, after enduring so much? I share in your grief."

He shrugged, not daring to say more. It was a puzzle he'd not yet answered, but he would find a way to appease the Gods, the Fates and himself.

Persephone watched him, her lovely face lined with worry. "Such sadness." Her whispered words were anguished. "I do not envy you such matters. But I am in awe of your sense of justice. A lesser being might use the wealth you mine, the shades you govern, for selfish purposes."

"I have no interest in power, Persephone. My only interest is order. I have order in my realm and I do what I must to maintain it." But her praise warmed him, deeply.

"'Tis a shame such order cannot be taught to those in the Land of the Living. Or Olympus." She smiled at him, then looked down at the Tavli board, her voice lowering, "We must hope that Greece will find some time for peace. In peace, one might find the time to establish order."

He swallowed. "Will you go, then?" He knew she would. He'd kept her too long already. He tossed the dice onto the board and sat back. He did not care for the tightening in his chest. He'd expected Demeter to come for her long before now.

Persephone did not look at him, but picked up the Tavli dice he'd discarded and studied them. "I suppose I have little choice. My mother has undoubtedly found me a new husband to wed."

He said nothing. Her words cut deeply, for they were the truth.

She put the dice down and stood. "Though why she insists on such a course of action, I cannot fathom," she mused, glancing at him over her shoulder.

He stood too, coming to her side. "She would protect you."

"I am an Olympian."

"One who does not reside on Olympus."

"Yet she would see me married to Hermes."

He glanced at her. "Hermes is the best of them. He is a wise match."

"But he refused me. And no other will have me, so it seems. And she sent me to Erysichthon." She drew in a deep breath.

"Who was, by all accounts, a good and capable man–"

"Until he went mad, you mean?" She glanced at him with arched eyebrows.

He bit back a smile, shrugging. She had a sharp wit, a good mind. He enjoyed their talks, for she did not shy away from plain speaking.

Persephone waved her hand, dismissing her question. "I know she longs to see me safe. But I hunger for more. Surely there is someone who might care for *me*? Not the power I bring, as an Olympian and Goddess." She looked at him, sincerely asking, "Is it foolish to wish for such things? Is it foolish for me to want to look upon my husband with fondness?"

Her words pressed heavily upon him. She deserved such a husband, if he existed. He met her gaze, unable to offer her the assurance she sought. "Tis a good dream, Persephone."

"A dream?" She looked crestfallen. "Only a dream? So I should go home and accept whomever my mother has found for me. Is that what you think?"

He held his breath. Her words were soft, but each struck him. He did not want her to go. He would have her stay here with him, play Tavli, share stories, walk his realm, and laugh over shared meals. But he knew better.

He nodded.

She scowled at him. "Then summon Hermes, I implore you. I bid you good night."

He watched her go, admiring her graceful movement and the sway of her fiery hair. He waited until she'd left, then sank into his chair and let his head fall into his hands. He must prepare himself. It had been too long since he'd felt anything. And yet she'd given him no choice.

The pain of her leaving would be near unbearable.

Chapter Thirteen

Persephone had not slept at all. Each time she closed her eyes, she'd imagined him coming to her. Words of love had been on his lips while his body had been most eager to show her his ardor.

"More dreams," she muttered to the empty room, pushing the furs from her legs angrily.

She draped her tunic about her, tying it once, and combed her hair. Her head ached mildly, so she left it loose and headed to the hall. They took their breakfast on the balcony, enjoying the warm sun and pale blue sky.

"Good morning," she greeted him, taking an ambrosia cake.

He nodded at her, his face almost hostile.

She blinked, startled by the ferocity of his gaze.

"I'm needed elsewhere," he murmured as he left her.

The cake she had chewed seemed to stick in her throat. She watched his progress from the rail as he crossed the heavy stone bridge and made his way across Asphodel. Her frustration rose up, demanding she call out to him. But she knew better.

He stopped suddenly, and turned back.

She hesitated, taking in his posture rigid with apprehension, before raising her hand. She felt close to tears, but forced a smile to her lips.

He turned away and disappeared behind the boulders around Tartarus' entrance.

She sighed. Her words had been rash but she'd been angry. She

147

was still angry.

A bark caught her attention. The hounds ran in the fields, their long bodies flexing as they covered the ground with broad sweeping leaps. She smiled, watching the eldest trip the youngest. They tumbled in the grass, circling each other and running again.

Persephone grabbed her cloak and headed out, running from the house and across the bridge to the fields.

The youngest greeted her, panting heavily and wagging his thin black tail.

"Good morning," she murmured, rubbing its broad head.

It felt good to stretch her legs. Before she knew it, she was running with the hounds. They were much faster than she was, but they circled back, racing circles around her when she'd slow.

She eventually collapsed, letting herself fall back on the soft, thick grasses of Asphodel.

Why was he making this so difficult?

She'd hoped that his control would falter, that he would finally accept their fate as she had. But it was not to be. He rejected that their fates were intertwined together, forever.

The clouds grew grey, thickening strangely as she watched.

"I'm like that cloud," she whispered to the hound at her side. He turned his head and looked at her, ears cocked. "Whatever is inside of me is building and growing until I fear I'll burst from it."

The hound lay down again, but she sat up.

She knew the truth of it. Her mind and body ached for him, consumed by some sort of throbbing fever. She would tell Hades the truth, what was in her heart. She stood, heading towards the fortress with renewed purpose. The sky grew ever darker as she crossed the bridge, and she glanced up. The clouds thickened, rolling in strange patterns overhead.

She headed to the hall. Mayhap it wasn't too late? If he had not sent for Hermes she might be able to stay. And she would be thankful for every day she had with him. She turned into the hall, ever hopeful.

"Can he save her?" A woman's voice brought her up short. A woman? She did not care for the twist of her stomach or the flash of anger tightening her throat.

In her time here, Hermes had been the only guest. Only shades and ghosts roamed the Underworld, and they never entered into Hades' home. She moved forward, her bare feet silent on the cold stone floor, to peer around the doorway. But seeing the creature that spoke offered little comforted.

This woman was true perfection.

"Is there nothing else to be done for him?" The woman's massive blue eyes were fixed upon Hades.

Even her voice was lovely.

Persephone watched, unable to tear her eyes away from Hades. He said nothing. His face, his beautiful face, remained impassive. It was an expression she was all too familiar with. He was hiding something. But what?

The woman whispered, "You would deprive him of her?"

"No..." Hades' voice was hard. "I control all within my realm."

The woman's long blond locks swayed, emphasizing the shake of her head as she spoke again. It was the woman's words, not her voice or face or curves that held Persephone's attention now. "No... you would tamper with the firestorm. You would ensure he catches her when she falls...You champion them still. Hades, had I known you to be so merciful..." the woman sounded close to tears.

He championed who? A man... and his woman?

"It matters not, Aphrodite," he spoke quickly, his tone even and strong.

Aphrodite? The Goddess of Love? *She* saw the good in Hades... Persephone's heart tightened at his words. Perhaps his heart was not so untouched?

"It matters a great deal." Aphrodite moved forward, placing her small hand upon his arm. Persephone felt jealousy churn hot in her stomach. "To Ariston and his Medusa. They've been sorely abused. But you...."

Persephone smiled. He had championed his soldier and his lady wife. Her heart swelled in her chest, pressing against her lungs and throat.

Of course he had.

"They will never know of it." His words were a command. "And neither will those on Olympus. I demand your vow on this, Aphrodite."

He was merciful, though none would suspect it. His modesty

astounded her. He seemed well pleased to let the worst be thought of him. It was an injustice, for this god was worthy of tributes and fealty. She shook her head. He was worthy of that and much more. But he needed, wanted, none of that.

Hades' hooded eyes bore into those of the Goddess, waiting.

"You have it." Aphrodite's words eased her.

Persephone watched as he nodded and then moved towards the fire. He stared into it, as if mesmerized, standing rigid... anxious.

How she longed to go to him.

"You've fulfilled your purpose for visiting my realm, Aphrodite. You've bestowed Olympus' gift upon the soldier. I doubt you find any more pleasure in the Underworld than I do on Olympus." He was dismissing her, sending her away. And Persephone was glad.

"I leave you then." Aphrodite sighed. "And will recount only Ariston's part in this."

"Fare thee well." He did not turn as he spoke.

"Your heart should not be left in this place," the goddess said in parting. "It is too full, too warm for such a lonely and dismal existence."

He is not alone. He will never be lonely.

She waited until Aphrodite was gone before she stepped into the room. But then he did something that stopped her.

He stared at a white flower... It was the lily she'd given him in the meadow, resting atop the mantle. Her heart tightened. He'd kept it? He reached up, tracing one petal with an unsteady finger. The tremor of his hand, the look on his face, made her rejoice.

He turned abruptly from the fire to his chair and sat heavily. He leaned forward to cover his face with his hands, his breath unsteady and ragged.

She could bear it no longer. He suffered. She suffered.

For what purpose?

She ignored the wild beating of her heart. Warmth coursed through her, burning low and hot in the pit of her stomach. She wanted him, all of him. And she would make certain he knew as much.

Her feet carried her to him, each step more daunting than the last.

Be brave, Persephone. His words echoed in her head.

"My lord." Her voice was too soft. Had he heard her?

He lifted his head from his hands, surprised by her presence. He recovered quickly, straightening rigidly. The haunted look she glimpsed was shuttered away and replaced by his careful mask of indifference. Oh how she longed to touch his face, to cup his cheek and hold him close to her. He had no need to withhold himself from her, no need to be careful with her.

"Persephone."

She was not deterred by his coolness. Her steps were cautious, but she made her way to him. She would not stop now. Her voice was steadier. "Aphrodite?"

His eyes narrowed, briefly. "Aphrodite is gone."

She drew in a slow breath. "I thought as much." Finally, she stood before him. Surely he could sense her agitation? Surely he could hear her heart? Her tunic, the front of her peplos, seemed to quiver in time with its frantic beating.

He clutched the arms of his throne. The line of his jaw grew tight. Tension rolled from him, making her swallow. How to begin?

"I've not asked you for anything in my time here." She paused. "Have I?"

He shook his head once, all the while his deep blue eyes boring into hers.

I must tell him I love him, tell him I need him, as my love... or my husband. But his gaze unnerved her. The words that poured from her lips were not what she planned, "Nor would I trouble you now, if my need were not so great." Her voice was no steadier than her pulse. She was making no sense.

He swallowed, then asked harshly, "What is it?"

His tone almost made her wince, but she forced herself to meet his gaze – so he would know her intent. Her mind raced, searching for the words she needed, as she sank to her knees before him. His hands were taut, his fingers white as he clenched the arms of his throne. She reached up and covered his hands with hers.

It felt better then. She felt better. She could go on.

Yet he no longer looked at her face. His eyes stared at her hands on his. His chest rose and fell. The muscle in his jaw bulged.

She drew in another deep breath. "Show me mercy. Show me the same mercy you've bestowed upon your mortal... the soldier

Ariston." Her hands clung to his.

He glanced at her, his hands gripping the throne harder.

"Have I been cruel? That you feel the need to beg for anything from me?" His voice was low. She shook her head, and he continued, "Then why do you kneel before me?" His words were a harsh whisper, testing her resolve.

"It is a selfish request, one that may turn you from solicitous to ... sickened." Words failed her. His hostility was quickly stealing her determination. She glanced at him, but his eyes were fixed upon her hands, wrapped about his. The slight crease settled on his brow. She stared at his brow, knowing she was failing miserably to explain the necessity of their union.

"Ask me," he murmured, huskily.

"My lover... Release him." Her eyes burned, the well of unshed tears surprising her. "Release the man who loves me, please." There, she'd said it. But he tensed, his eyes closed.

What had she said?

When he looked at her, pain filled his deep blue eyes. Pain the depths of which she'd not expected. He did not conceal it from her. For one brief moment, he looked a broken man. And she could not bear such a sight. Her hands tightened about his, pulling them from the arm rails.

"Who is this man? What...what mortal... who is it?" He spoke, a rasping, anguished whisper.

She frowned. She'd made a mess of things. "No... no..."

Hades' home shook, the very mountain it was carved into trembling. Thunder, louder than any she'd ever heard, set the very air vibrating. "What is happening?" Another tremor rattled the mountain, sending her reeling. He caught her, the strength of his arms easing her panic.

"A firestorm," he spoke softly.

"A firestorm?" she asked. His hands held her shoulders, distracting her.

His hands slipped from her shoulders as the room stilled.

"Is it done?" She waited, wondering what would happen next.

"No. Not yet." He did not look at her as he hurried to the balcony.

She ran after him, frustration and curiosity warring within her. She stepped onto the balcony, eager to express herself. But the sight that greeted stunned her into silence. The murky skies of the Underworld were full black. Strange clouds, churning and twisting, hovered over the fields of Asphodel. The wind roared, bowing the grasses flat before sending the tree limbs sharply upward.

She gasped. Within the clouds, pockets of red and orange leapt and fell. Fire. She glanced at Hades, looking for reassurance. But he stood, staring into the fields before them. His hands gripped the stone of the balcony, his stance at the ready.

But ready for what? She moved to his side, growing ever concerned by the roar of the wind, the flashes of strange fire and lightening. His attention did not waver. She shielded her face from the winds and followed his gaze. The fields were empty, save one.

A man stood, peering up.

Another tremor shook them. But Persephone's eyes remained fixed upon the man. The sky snapped, thunder boomed, and a large hole appeared at his feet. He slipped, one foot sliding forward, before he jumped back from the edge. It gaped angrily, casting a red glow on the grasses lining the sudden gash.

Persephone moved forward, gripping the railing of the banister at Hades' side.

Fire rose from below, lightening forced from above, both caught in the spiraling winds. The man braced himself as the gust of fire wrapped and twisted about him. Orange flames seared, lightening licked and pricked, yet he did not move. The wind picked up, the flames rising with it. His wheaten curls lifted and fell, but the billowing folds of his exomie burned away. And still his gaze remained constant on the clouds above.

The clouds split, unleashing ice and rain upon him.

"Why does he not seek shelter?" she whispered, vaguely aware that Hades stood beside her.

His voice was low. "He is waiting."

"For what?"

But Persephone saw her then. A woman fell, tumbling from the angry black clouds. Skeins of long honey hair streamed up, shielding her face from view. The man in the field leaned forward, teetering precariously on the edge of the open hole. His feet and legs were red, slipping closer to the entrance. His every muscle tightened, readying.

The wind fell still.

She gripped Hades' arm. "He will fall..."

"They will not." Hades lifted his hand, his fingers rippling slowly, forcefully, pulling towards himself in one undulating wave.

A sudden gust caught the woman, casting her safely into the man's arms. Hades scooped his hand sharply, pulling his arm towards his chest. The wind echoed his motion, lifting and carrying the pair far from the gaping hole. Hades exhaled. His hand opened, falling back to the railing, and releasing the couple upon the thick grasses of Asphodel.

The sky cleared, the clouds rolling back with a startling speed. The roaring wind softened. And the hole vanished, leaving the field whole, its grasses waving calmly in the ever present breeze.

But Persephone could not tear her eyes from the couple. The man sat up, cradling the woman with an almost reverent tenderness. He swept the hair from the woman's face, cupping her cheek. His smile was blinding as he pulled her limp form to him.

"This is him? Ariston?" Persephone did not care that tears rolled down her cheek.

"It is." Hades' voice was husky.

Ariston was gazing at the woman, speaking to her. The woman moved then, touching his lips and stroking his cheek. She pressed her lips to Ariston's, wrapping her arms about him fiercely.

Persephone turned from them, wiping the tears from her cheeks. "Such a bittersweet reunion."

"There is no sadness there," he murmured. "There is only joy."

She looked back to find the pair. The woman stood, pulling Ariston up. She wrapped her arms about him and leaned into him as he kissed her soundly. Persephone heard the woman laugh, and smiled as the two headed to the shore. A boat waited.

"Elysium?" she asked, turning her still wet eyes to him.

He barely glanced at her as he made his way back inside the hall. "Yes."

She watched them. They held tightly to each other, climbing into the boat and sailing to the end of their journey. Hades was right; there was no sadness there. Such pleasure, such joy... she envied them a little. They would never be parted.

"You'd come to me for aid with your love," Hades said, his

words clipped.

She took a deep breath, watching the couple a moment longer. She turned, joining him in the hall. "Hades," she murmured, unable to stop the quiver in her voice. She had no time to delay. He would send her away soon. And she knew, somehow, he'd take pains to avoid ever seeing her again.

He glanced at her, resting one hard arm across the polished black mantle. He turned, ill at ease. He pushed off the mantle, paced the room and sat in his chair. His every muscle tensed as he turned his gaze upon her. She shook her head, coming to stand before him.

"It is you, Hades," she whispered, placing her hand over her chest. Her heart seemed to stop as she waited for some sign, some reaction, to her clumsy confession. "It is you."

His face revealed all.

Gone was the blank mask he wore. His pain and anger vanished, replaced by doubt and disbelief. His eyes widened, the crease marring his brow deepening as he searched her face. His inspection was wary, until his eyes fastened on her lips. The muscles in his throat and jaw flexed, his nostrils flared slightly.

She saw it, knew it for what it was. His mind might resist her, but his body did not. It was a start...

Ignoring the nervousness that tightened her stomach and squeezed her lungs, she moved forward, sliding onto his lap. He stiffened, but she did not hesitate. She faced him, her legs resting on either side of his thighs. He was very warm. He could toss her onto the floor, order her to leave, curse her... but she would not make it easy for him.

Her eyes met his, trembling from the hunger that gripped her. Did he feel it too?

She placed her hands on his shoulders and met his gaze. "I beg of you," she whispered, leaning so close that her breath mingled with his. Dizziness swept through her, the heat in her belly making her light-headed. "Fight me no more."

His eyes strayed to her lips again. She felt his hands twist in the fabric of her peplos, pressing against her hip. Whether he meant to set her away from him or draw her close, she could not tell. Mayhap he didn't know either. She would help him decide.

Her hand lifted, brushing the midnight hair from his forehead and trailing down the side of his face. His eyes closed when her thumb grazed the slope of his cheek and nose. Her skin tingled at the contact.

Such fine features, so strong and handsome.

She exhaled slowly, the sound echoing in the still chamber. Her eyes dropped, tracing his lips, and her hand followed.

His hand caught her wrist, stilling her. His eyes were dark, almost black, as they bore into hers. But his hand trembled about her wrist, and her heart ached for him. She drew his hand to her lips, pressing a kiss on each of his knuckles and cradling his hand to her chest.

She heard his sharp intake of breath, but did not stop. She placed his hand against her cheek, holding it in place as she leaned forward to kiss him.

Once her lips found his, any hesitancy left her. Her fingers tangled in his hair, pulling him closer, yet not close enough. Her mouth clung desperately, breathing in his breath as his lips parted beneath hers.

His hand slid from her cheek, and she tensed, waiting for him to set her away from him. But he freed her hair, spreading the heavy locks about her shoulders.

He pulled back, staring at her, her face, her eyes, and her lips. His eyes were not so guarded, his desire warred with fear. "Persephone..."

"I will not leave you, Hades. Not tonight, nor tomorrow, never of *my* choosing. I swear it..." She spoke desperately. "I love you. You have my heart. Please... take the rest of me too."

Chapter Fourteen

She was pressed against him, not in sleep or from illness. But because she chose to do so. It was the sweetest torture. Her every curve invited him. Her every breath mixed with his, and her words... She'd spoken them without hesitation.

She loved him. She would stay with him. Her words warmed him, melting the shards of ice from around his ill-used heart.

Her hair surrounded him. Her scent, flowers and earth and woman, tempted him sorely. Everything about her bid him welcome, tempting him to rise against her and make her his.

He could not think... Such feelings overtook his reason and will.

Her lips caressed his forehead, his cheek, the tip of his nose, the corner of his mouth... He breathed raggedly. Her lips were feather light upon his. She teased him, tugging upon his lower lip in earnest.

He gave in with a growl, turning into her kiss, mindless. His mouth parted beneath hers and his tongue invaded the hot wetness of her mouth with dizzying effect. Her hands tightened upon him, willing him to her. He caught her strangled cry with his mouth, his lips sealed to hers.

She wanted him.

His grip on her peplos loosened, but the satin skin of her thigh demanded his touch. She gasped as his palm caressed her flesh, sliding high beneath her tunic. She broke free from their kiss, her hands kneading his shoulders as his fingers gripped her hip.

His lips left hers. This was wrong. This was madness.

Her face was perplexed, startled by these new sensations perhaps? Her eyes were lustrous, sparkling as they regarded him. A joyful smile tugged at her mouth, weakening his resolve. Her hands wound through his hair, pulling him to her, eager for another kiss.... He could not deny her. His hands anchored in the thickness of her locks, giving him leverage to greedily deepen his kiss and admit defeat.

For make no mistake about it, she had defeated him.

She whimpered against his mouth, grabbing at his tunic and neck. He pulled her closer to him, fearing he might crush her by doing so. Yet she moved against him frantically, building the fire in his blood. Her lips moved over his...

How he wanted her. And she wanted him, desperately.

His hand slid to her neck, cupping it gently as his thumb grazed her lower lip once more. He was rewarded with her shudder and gasp.

"Please," she whispered.

She pushed the tunic from his shoulder and ran her hands over his chest, making a soft groaning sound as she did so. He watched, in awe of her uninhibited desire. There was no shame in her sensuality. Her gaze followed the path of her hands, possessed by such a fever of need that he had to appease her. He could not stop his stomach from quivering, contracting, beneath her touch. Or the hot throbbing of his loins. Her lips returned to him, clinging to his ear, nuzzling his neck and the base of his throat. It was hard to breathe, his desire scarcely restrained.

She held such power over him, her lips and hands demanding his response.

"Please," the word brushed across his lips.

His hands were rough upon her, grabbing her hair and pulling her face to him. His lips clung, his tongue invaded... but it wasn't enough. He would have all of her. He grasped the shoulders of her tunic, craving the feel of her flesh. He felt the fever of need in her blood, shared it. But her tunic was trapped, pulled tightly beneath them, denying and inflaming him all the more.

Too frenzied to pause, he stood.

She wrapped her legs about him. Out of instinct, he knew, but it was torture. He'd felt desire, faint memories now, but never like this. Nothing in his life compared to this.

He lifted her in his arms, carrying her from the hall as her lips devoured him. His mouth, his cheek, his ear, his shoulder... He trembled, turning into her kiss when her lips sought his. How they reached his chamber, he didn't know. But they reached his bed quickly. He stooped, set her gently upon the bed, and paused.

The sight of her, her copper hair spread across his furs, was something he would treasure on the dark nights ahead. He swallowed, drinking in each detail. She was a gift. One he'd no right to accept.

His thoughts sobered him, a knot of coldness settling in his stomach. She *would* leave. He did not doubt it, she was right, *he* would send her away. He had to...

She was unaware of his stillness. She sat up, tugging the ties of her tunic and letting the linen slip free. He swallowed as the cloth fell, caressing the curves of her body, to pool about her knees on his bed.

He lifted a hand, but caught himself. He fisted his hands, holding his arms to his side.

She moved closer, her eyes fixed upon him as she waited.

The pain was physical, as if his heart would willingly tear itself from his chest. But he would not take what she offered. He must end this, sever this unnatural connection between them. For her own good. He would find the strength to end this, he must.

"Persephone." His voice was hard, startling her. He bent, lifting her discarded tunic and covering her. "Enough."

She stared at him, blinking in confusion.

"Forgive me." He glanced at her and stepped back.

She sank slowly onto the bed, clutching her tunic in bewilderment. She wrapped her arms about her. "Forgive you?"

It was a hard thing not to fall to his knees, not to pull her back to him. Instead he stood, every muscle taut with restraint. "Your words... Your enthusiasm. I've no excuse for my behavior."

She stared up at him.

The look in her eyes tore at him. He'd hurt her too many times. And now, when she'd done nothing but offer him love, he would hurt her again.

"But you..." her voice broke. "You love me. As I love you."

He swallowed. Was he capable of love? Did she truly believe he could? "I fear you've confused lust with love, Persephone."

Her green eyes narrowed and she stood, charging him in a fury. "Lust? I would not deny that my body aches for you. But it is my heart that would have you... join with me... You and no other..." Her voice grew husky as she placed her hand on his chest. "Your heart answers mine..."

He pushed her hand from him, shuddering from her touch and her words. His words were low, hard and biting. "What do you know of love?"

She moved closer. "I know of no one who feels as strongly for another as I feel for you, Hades. What else could it be?"

He had no answer for her. Because he wanted it to be true. He scowled.

Her words were angry. "Tell me why it is your smile and your voice that I listen for, for the sound of it is sweeter than anything else all. Tell me why my mind and body ease from your scent to your touch. Tell me why my body aches and warms in places I'd not known existed until I felt the brush of your lips..."

"Stop!" He held up his hand. He could not listen. He could not breathe.

She stepped closer, her eyes aflame. "Why?"

He fell silent. He tore his gaze from her, searching for some distraction. Her fingers released her tunic and exposed her fully to him. He could feel the heat of her, for her curves nearly brushed against him. He swallowed, damning the longing that curled his fingers.

Sadness tinged her voice when she spoke. "You are not mine, I know that. But I would make you mine. In my heart, my soul, we are joined."

"I cannot give you what you want," he whispered, hating the desperation that colored every word.

She touched his cheek, shaking her head and moving one step closer. "I want you, Hades. Whatever you would give to me, I will take."

He was lost then, he knew it. As did she. Her breasts throbbed in time with her rapid pulse, grazing his chest rhythmically. He felt his response. As did she.

He denied himself no longer, grabbing her to him, frantic in his need. His nose trailed down her neck and across her shoulder, inhaling deeply. Her body pressed against him, breast to chest, mouth to mouth. It was heady and hot, tender and right. She shook, a soft groan escaping her. She felt it too, this craving. A hunger he roused within her.

He pressed his lips to her throat and heard her whimper. He lifted her, carrying her back to his bed and laying her upon the furs once more. He did not hesitate this time, but let his mouth claim hers. His hands stroked the length of her, from neck to hip. Wherever he touched her, she trembled and sighed. He smiled against her lips, startled by this newfound power. She should be his, like this, for all time. She was made for him.

He rested, propped on one elbow, to watch. The vision, his hand upon her so, made him hunger for more. He caressed her side, his fingers trailing across her collar bone to cup her breast. She filled his hand and drove him mad with wanting. His thumb grazed her nipple, plucking it gently between forefinger and thumb until it pebbled hard from his touch. His lips followed, licking and nipping until she was writhing beneath him. The taste of her, the feel of her... how could he feel such tenderness and such crippling hunger for this woman?

Never had he felt so engorged with heat. His need bordered pain. When she parted her legs, he did not hesitate.

She wrapped her arms about him, kissing him deeply. His eyes sought hers, her hand found his. She stared up at him. He moved, pressing the throbbing tip of himself against her. Her heat startled him, warming him as he entered her. He did not stifle the groan that ripped from his throat as he breached her untried flesh. When it was done, he stilled, finding some thread of control to cling to. She was hot, her muscles cradling and clenching about him.

He stared down at her, knowing... and accepting that she had changed him forever. She was his, his and only his... No, she was his *now*, he cautioned himself. He did not care for the rage that swept through him at such a thought. Or the pain that swiftly followed.

"Hades." Her hands cupped his face, smiling up at him. "Now you have all of me." Her words inflamed him.

"Do I?" his words were strangled. His body demanded more. Was it only his body that demanded more? His heart ached...

He kissed her, ashamed of his selfishness, exhilarated by her love. He moved, unable to fully leave her before sliding deep once more. She gasped, but did not look away.

He groaned, the spasm of pleasure on her face affecting him to his core. She moved beneath him, each stroke deeper than the last. He gritted his teeth against the sharpening of his pleasure. She clung to him, her breathing labored. Her hands slid, holding tightly to his hips, and the fire in his blood roared. His rhythm changed, unleashed by the feel of her quivering about him. Each thrust was primal, hard and fast. He pushed into her, deeply, reveling into her every shudder.

Her cries grew ragged, breathless and raw. He watched her body flush, watched her nipples peak tightly and her body stiffen about him. Deep inside of her he felt her climax, her long, slow contractions driving him harder. She cried out. Her nails pierced his skin, clawing his back. He could not stifle the throaty groan that ripped from him as his release, wave upon wave, followed hers.

Such passion was new to him, giving him both exquisite satisfaction and bone wrenching grief.

He rested his head upon her chest, fighting panic. He'd held her at bay for a reason. Releasing her without this intimacy would have been painful enough. But now... he swallowed, closing his eyes. He drew in long, slow deep breaths, listening to the rapid thrum of her heart. Her soft skin beneath him, the light press of her hands upon his back eased him.

He would not think of the days ahead.

He would savor what magic they'd shared. He lay, propped on top of her, with no desire to leave her. In the seconds afterward, his chest grew heavy and languid. He savored the sound of her heart, the rhythm of her breathing. Her hands moved slowly, tracing his back with her fingertips. The feel of her hands on him eased him all the more.

But how did she fare? Panic rose within him, but he forced himself to move, rising above her on his elbows.

She smiled, rosy and delighted. "Oh, Hades. That was... that was just as I knew it would be."

He could do nothing but smile back, albeit reluctantly. "Was it?"

She shook her head quickly. "No, not at all. How could I have imagined such... such..." She laughed, cupping his face. "Kiss me."

He laughed too, all too eager to kiss her. And though he'd meant to give her a chaste kiss, it quickly gave way to more. His body was not done with her. And so he kissed her, and reveled in the catch of her breath and the silk of her skin beneath him.

The fire burned low in the grate, casting leading shadows onto the ground. Erisychthon stared straight ahead, unable to make out the flames or the contents of the room. His eyes clouded and burned. He would move, he would leave this room with its smells of sickness and wasting. Yet, he could not. He'd not the strength to move. So he stared, unseeing, into the dying fire.

He would starve. There was no hope for it.

Ione had gone, her eyes alight with renewed hope. She loved him still... She would do as he asked. She worried over him, but believed that Persephone might help him gain favor with Olympus once more. He held on to no such hope, but had not said as much to her. He'd been too hungry, too desperate to fill his own stomach.

Yet she had been gone too long. No message had come, no news as to her whereabouts. He'd sent his men, those few that remained, to find her. But she'd vanished.

Had she spoken the truth? Had Poseidon wearied of coming to her aid?

Did it matter?

He sighed, the slight motion forcing pure agony through his entire body.

"My lord," Kadmos spoke, his words startling Erysichthon. It would be all too easy for one of his enemies to defeat him now. If he cared.

Erysichthon stared in the direction of the man's voice. He blinked, narrowing his eyes in an attempt to focus. Kadmos, a large dark figure, bobbed then faded before Erysichthon. He sighed, blinking again and again. "Did you bring it?"

Kadmos' voice was low. "I did, but..."

Sasha Summers

"Give it to me." He reached out, taking the metal handle with an unsteady hand. "You do me honor by staying with me, Kadmos. You and Barak are the best of men. Go now, and do not return. I command it."

Barak's voice boomed, "We will stay with you."

He shook his head. "You will do as I demand. Find Ione. Keep her safe. She will need looking after."

There was silence then, one he hoped meant their acquiescence.

"Go," he murmured. "Go and do my bidding this last time."

He blinked, his vision clearing long enough to see their dark shapes moving further from him. He had no hope of seeing her again, but he would give her all he had. Kadmos and Barak were all that remained of his vast court. How quickly his people had turned from him. Did they think he'd meant to leave his men untended on the battlefield? His hate knew no bounds. Those men, loyal to him, had been left to rot. None had funeral rites, none given passage to the Underworld. Because of Hades... Because of Demeter. He was no less a victim than those who fell to the Persians.

But no more.

He sat, gripping the knife's handle, willing the strength to do what must be done.

The fire snapped, echoing in the empty hall.

His stomach growled, forcing him to his knees as the pain rolled over him again and again.

"I curse you, Goddess," he hissed to the empty room. "I curse you to an eternity of suffering." He sat heavily, too weary to try to stand. "As you have cursed me."

Demeter... It was her fault. She'd done this to him, made him too weak to search for Persephone. She'd crippled him so. He could not take more than a few steps before his own bile rose up to choke him. Such spasms made him retch violently or his bowels empty uncontrollably. He could not seek revenge. Not in this body.

But without it.

He smiled, taking the handle in both hands.

Cutting his leg was easy. He no longer feared pain. He knew what he must do; Demeter had told him as much. She would see him die at his own hand, feasting on his own flesh. He saw no reason to delay such an end. The strip of flesh he sliced from his thigh felt

164

no different from any other cut of meat. True it was not braised in onions, or charred on a spit over a fire to roast. But it was meat nonetheless. Meat that his body craved above all things.

He blinked, but his vision did not clear.

Perhaps it was easier this way. Not seeing it, not knowing what he bit into. But once his teeth tore into the flesh, he did not care. The taste was too much, more potent and delicious than any meal he'd partaken. He gobbled it down, cutting more, larger and deeper than the first.

He felt the warmth of his own blood pooling on the floor beneath him. A chill touched him.

"You will never rest easy, Demeter. For my death frees me from your curse. But you..." He swayed, feeling lightheaded as he hacked into his other leg. "You will never be free of me."

He rested, listing to his side and propping himself upon his elbow. He ate quickly, his hunger consuming him anew.

But he did not have the strength to cut again, his arms were too heavy. His lungs seemed to shrink, drawing in a breath too shallow. He gasped, but could draw nothing in.

"I will never give her up. Never. Persephone is mine..." He cried out, emptying his lungs. He fell back, fighting. His heart thrashed, pumping erratically, searching escape from his chest. He could not lift his hands, he could only lay still. His breath was gone, his eyes feeling tight, his skin heavy. Panic rose, fear gripped him. And the cold... If he'd had the strength, he would shiver. He could not escape... He lay, feeling the darkness pressing more heavily upon him.

And then there was nothing.

The room was quiet, save the crackling of the fire.

How much time passed, how long it took for the spirit to separate from his flesh, he did not know. Gone was the weakness. Gone was the hunger.

He stood, fluid and quick, to stare into the lifeless eyes of his own body. Blood covered the floor, spilled from the gaping holes he'd carved into his legs. He shook his head, the sensation light and insubstantial. He stared at his hands as he stretched his fingers toward the firelight.

In the fading light, he seemed to fade and thin – a vaporous shade. But in the shadows, he felt alive and strong once more. He stepped back, beyond the glow of the dying embers, and welcomed the weight of the shadows. His hands fisted as he peered around what had once been a lavish and abundant home. Now, it was his tomb.

He had no time for such thoughts, for such idle bitterness. He had precious little time. He was free, for now. But Thanatos would come for him, soon.

And he would lead Hades' messenger on a long and merry chase while he exacted his revenge upon Demeter... Olympus... all who would stop him from claiming his love, his Persephone.

Chapter Fifteen

Hades stirred at Persephone's side, but the gentle rhythm of his breath and heaviness of his body assured her he slept still. He was tired, as he should be... as she should be. But she was not, not in the least.

She could not ignore the nervousness that threatened her happiness. She had seduced him... most thoroughly. In truth, she'd seduced him first but what followed had been of mutual accord. It had been a night like no other. And her body ached deliciously. She felt fulfilled, yet swollen and needy.

Looking at him now, she knew she'd always crave him this way.

Morning was finally upon them, the start of a new day for them both. And now that she knew who he was, what he was to her, she would not lose him. She'd simply thought she loved him before. In truth, she had no idea. He completed her, her heart, soul and body, everything about him, his goodness, his loyalty, his duty, his humor... and now this blissful physical joining.

She would not give him up. She could not.

She whispered, "Are you awake?"

His eyes fluttered open, confused, then troubled. She sighed, watching his face stiffen and his body tighten as he woke fully. Gone was the smiling face and freedom of their night.

She shook her head, pressing a kiss to his forehead. "Is it so miserable to find me in your bed?" The rise and fall of his chest was unsteady, she noted. It was something.

He whispered, "No."

She smiled brightly at him, delighted by his quick answer. "Then I bid you good morning."

He shook his head but a small smile found his lips. "Kalimera to you, Persephone."

She let her eyes fall to his lips, his slight smile widening beneath her gaze. She met his eyes then leaned closer to press her lips to his.

His hand caught her hair, stilling her. She leaned into his touch and met his eyes. That furrow, so slight it was almost invisible, marred his forehead. She placed her hand upon his chest, the throb of his rapid heartbeat palpable beneath her palm. Her fingers stroked him, before splaying to lay her hand flat upon his chest. His nostrils flared and his hand tightened in her hair. He did not push her away, or pull her close. He did not release her.

The beat of his heart accelerated, emboldening her to whisper, "You love me."

His eyes widened as he looked up at her. "You should not say such things."

"No? Fine then, I know the truth of it whether or not you speak the words aloud." She touched his cheek, meeting his blue-black eyes without flinching.

His hold eased. "I cannot."

She leaned down and kissed him, a soft quick kiss. "You can, Hades. Your heart will be well treasured by me."

He took a breath, speaking more firmly. "Such words... such feelings are fleeting..."

"If they fade, it was never love."

He sighed. "You've much to say for one with such slight experience."

She knew he was right. But she could not stop herself from defending what was in her heart. "Yet you would malign us, the goodness that is happening here, by your previous... alliance."

His brow arched and his smile grew mocking. "Alliance?"

She felt her cheeks grow hot. "Your..."

"My marriage... You refer to my marriage?"

She answered him quickly. "It was most... unfortunate."

His sudden burst of laughter startled her, and relieved her. Her words were thoughtless, he had every right to be offended. And yet he laughed. Such a laugh, beautiful and rich.

"It was, indeed." His smile transformed him, making him even more handsome to her delighted eyes. "But I was married, Persephone."

She took her time, soaking in the warmth of his smile. "I'm not so naïve as you think. I know love is a rare exception, even in marriage." She smoothed a midnight lock from his forehead, finding the courage to go on. "I know she didn't love you as I do. She didn't love you as you deserve."

Hades swallowed, pleasing her with his flustered expression and rising color.

"I did little to encourage her affections, withholding my time and attention..."

"Your time? Attention? What of your love?" She wanted to know. Had he loved her? Or was it as Hermes said? Had it been his pride, and not his heart, that had been so devastated? She didn't know which would be worse, for him... and for her.

He said nothing, but his eyes bore into hers before slipping to her mouth.

She smiled.

He reached up to cup her cheek, shaking his head slightly. "I know nothing of love, Persephone."

His words sliced through her. She did not worry that she could teach him love. That would be a joyous task. But she was sad that such a task was hers. He'd lived too long without knowing the blessings and comfort of love, even that of brotherly love, and she ached for his solitude. She placed her palm on his chest, looking at her sun-kissed hand upon his alabaster skin. His heart raced beneath her hand, giving her hope. They may have a chasm of differences between them, but it was not enough to stop her. She wanted him to be hers, irrefutably and for all times.

"Then let us learn of it together."

"I cannot," he repeated, gruff.

"Shh. In time, you might." She placed a finger over his lips, shuddering as his lips kissed her fingertip. She removed her hand, placing it upon his chest once more. His heart thumped all the more. "Your heart tells me all I need to know."

"When you...tire of me, of *this*, you are free to go." His words were soft. "You owe me nothing, nor I you."

She scowled at him, irritated at his quick dismissal.

And he laughed again, the sound of it filling his chamber and her heart.

She slid from his hold, stretching as she stood. She wondered if she looked changed. She felt it. And she savored every ache, every surprising tug and soreness. He had left his mark upon her, and she was pleased by it. Did he look upon her? She grew nervous. Was he pleased by the sight of her nakedness? She'd been told she was lovely; she wanted him to think so.

"I'm hungry, my lord." She glanced at him. He was watching her, most intently. *Good.*

His voice wavered, "Are you?"

She nodded, thrilled by the tightness of his mouth and the rigid line of his jaw. "And a bath? Better yet, is there a lake suitable for such things? A swim would be most welcome."

His eyes traveled the length of her, making her body tighten and rise in welcome. She heard his sudden intake of breath and wondered at it. She had no wish to keep her heart's desire from him. Her body, it seemed, felt the same. Should she? Was her behavior wanton? Anxiety rose, forcing her to seek out her discarded peplos. She found it, a forgotten heap, in the corner. She stooped, grasping the linen in her hand and shaking it out.

When she turned, she jumped. He was there.

He pulled the peplos from her hands and reached for her. His body and face were rigid, fraught with need. Smiling, she pressed herself against his bare form. He stared at her, his mouth finding and parting her lips without mercy. She swayed against him, stunned by his hunger for her. And her need for him. The desperation to join, to embrace him with her body, was sudden. His hands lifted her and she wrapped her legs about his waist.

The cool stone of the wall pressed into her back, while his hands tightly gripped her thighs.

She'd no breath in her lungs when he thrust up and into her. She whimpered as he entered her, her legs tightening about him. Her eyes met his and held. Between the cold marble at her back and the heat of his chest, the depth of his invasion, she could only feel. She held on to him, his every movement racking her with pure sensation.

His hands cupped her hips, his fingers digging into her flesh. She sucked in breath, his hands, his body, their rhythm, bringing her to a violent climax. She cried out as his body stiffened against her. He pressed his face against her throat, groaning brokenly.

Little was said afterward.

She was too stunned, her body so drained she feared she would not manage to stand. He was equally dazed, though his hands held her close. Her legs spasmed, forcing her to lean into him. He turned, pressing a kiss to her forehead as he stepped away from the wall.

Her heart still raced. Her lungs still ached. She throbbed... pleasantly. She smiled as he held her, letting her find her footing before he released her. He held her, ever so lightly, about her waist.

"Which is greater? Your hunger or the want of a bath?" He regarded her with an unreadable expression.

She arched one eyebrow pointedly. "My appetite is appeased... A bath is all I require."

A small smile pulled up the corner of his lips and he shook his head. It was an expression she was becoming infinitely familiar with. And extremely fond of.

He shook out the peplos before handing it to her. "There's a hot spring on the mountain." She took the peplos, watching him knot the fabric of his chlamys about his waist. The line of his back, the breadth of his shoulders, the slight curl of his raven curls at the base of his skull, a fine sight to be sure.

It took her some time to wrap her own peplos. She pulled and tucked to the best of her ability, but the seams were ripped. When she was covered, she took his free hand in hers, staring at him with a joyful smile. He glanced at their hands, but did not loose himself from her hold. She squeezed his hand, making him smile reluctantly.

She followed him down the tunnels, through several cavernous chambers, into the main hall and out the front doors. He gave her no time to pause, but turned back towards the mountain and set off along the narrow path that hugged the steep mountain face.

When they reached the top, she stared out over his home. She'd never expected the Land of the Dead to be so tranquil, or so very lovely. But then, she'd never thought she would love the Lord of the Dead as dearly as she did.

"It is not how I imagined the Underworld, you know." Persephone lay on her stomach while her eyes peered across the far-reaching recesses of his realm.

"There is a bleaker, darker side to my realm, Persephone." Hades' eyes moved down the length of her back, tracing the curve of her buttock and the firm strength of her thighs. For a man so recently sated, he felt the fire of passion warm his blood rather quickly.

She turned to him, drawing his attention to the delights of her face. "Is it horrid? Tartarus?"

He studied her, absorbing her features. Her green eyes waited, wide and curious. Her mouth, such soft full lips, parted slightly beneath his gaze. The freckles that topped her narrow nose and cheeks were playful, making her no less seductive. Even here, beneath his weak and milky sun, she seemed to glow.

"That horrid?" she gasped, taking his silence as his answer.

He nodded. It was.

She slid closer to him, pressing along the length of him. He did not resist her, but drew her closer. She felt warm, the only warmth he'd ever known.

She rested her chin on her folded hands. "Still, it is beautiful here."

Her words surprised him. She thought his realm beautiful?

Elysium was a vibrant jewel upon the brilliant sea. An island of bounty and harmony, it was the most removed from the Underworld, the best of the Land of the Living with none of its frailties. Below them, Asphodel's wheat blew in waves, golden and brown. She could not see Tartarus' entrance, hidden behind an outcrop of rock. Without knowing what lay within that portal, his realm might be considered as she described it.

"In its way, I suppose," he agreed as his attention returned to her.

"Asphodel reminds me of the plains of Larissa or the lands west of Athens," she said.

She was beautiful, too beautiful to resist. He reached forward, smoothing the hair from her forehead. His hand slipped to the side of her face, savoring the feel of her against him.

She smiled at him and the pulling within his chest grew sharp.

A chorus of barks filled the air, drawing her eyes from his.

She watched the hounds. "There are no birds, no cows, no animals save your horses and hounds. I know why you keep the horses, what their purpose is. Do the hounds serve you as well?"

Hades glanced at the dogs. "They are Cerberus when I have need of him. They are hunters, when Thanatos calls. They are hounds, when at play."

The hounds ran, snapping playfully at one another. The smallest fell behind, glancing in their direction with golden eyes.

"He fancies you." Hades' voice was soft. "It was he that brought me to you in Thessaly." He did not tell her that he'd left Theron with her. He did not tell her that Theron would have stayed with her with or without his consent. Theron was most devoted to his master, and the hound chose Persephone as his. Hades could find little to fault in the animal's choice.

She nodded. "I shall remember that when next he's at my side."

"That he feels a sense of loyalty to you is…" Hades grew silent, considering his words.

"He cares for me, something he, like his master, finds a flaw versus a gift?"

Hades sighed loudly. "He would not think it a weakness. He's always been loyal."

"Always? Has he been with you so long, in your realm?"

He nodded. "Long enough. The three of them, mother, father, and son, came to me after their death. But they were not content to simply be. They wanted work and service, to be of use to me."

"And they are happy now?" she asked.

He shrugged. "Happy? They were betrayed by those they loved best. Seeking purpose is enough." He felt her eyes upon him, knew she was finding the meaning behind his words. Indeed, why had he said them?

He continued, hoping to distract her. "They will not tire or slow until their prey is caught. Out of my realm, they move too quickly for the mortal eye to see them. But a soul, one trying to outwit death, stands no chance against them."

He felt her shiver and pulled her closer.

"What were they… before?"

He rolled on to his side. "Tis a sad tale, Persephone."

She looked at him, resting her cheek on her arm. "Oh, I see.

Perhaps later then?"

He nodded, yet another smile finding its way to his lips.

She chewed on her lower lip, lost in thought. When she spoke, she had yet another question for him. He admired her mind, the need for answers.

"Does Death... Thanatos bring them all back? The dead, I mean. Surely not?" She looked doubtful.

"No. He spends most of his time collecting those that run from their fate. Most of the souls he collects are for Tartarus." He watched the hounds, running in circles. "Many times they go with him, hunting at his side. They've not been long at home in recent months."

She turned back to the dogs, thoughtful as she watched their playful antics. "They seem happy to be home now."

"As you can imagine, Thanatos is an even less merry companion than I," he murmured.

Her surprised green gaze met his as startled laughter burst from her. Her head fell back on the grass and her laughter continued. It was the sweetest sound he'd ever heard. And somehow he was the cause of it? The pain, sharp and quick, was like a blow to the chest. But the pain was replaced with a rising warmth, building within him until his lungs felt strained and his throat compressed. Her laugh, her smile, the joy clear upon her features, intensified the sensation.

"Such a peculiar sound to hear here..." His words slipped from him, unaware.

She stilled, her hand coming to rest on his cheek. "In the Underworld?"

"There's little in the way of joy here." He looked away. If he could erase the past, forget what it was to have trust broken so thoroughly, he might have joy. He would take what she was so willing to offer him.

"You've a duty, to be sure. But you've the right for happiness as well, Hades. I know of no one else who's earned such a right, as you." Her voice was soft, almost pleading to his ears. "You deserve happiness, laughter, and love..."

He'd never wanted such things, never known them to be missing from his life... until now. He sat up quickly, ignoring her when she did the same. And yet she continued to watch him, waiting. From the corner of his eye he could see the worry and sadness lining the sweetness of her face.

Again, his chest tightened.

Why was he so acutely aware of her? When she moved, as she did now, he tensed, waiting... for her... to leave... to scorn him?

Instead she moved close beside him, taking his hand in hers. Relief swept through him. He would not cling to her. He would not hold it against his cheek and turn into her touch. He stared at their hands until he'd calmed himself. Then he looked at her.

She looked back at him with color staining her cheeks. "You do, Hades. Do you never long for such things?"

His eyes met hers, stunning him into silence. Could she love him? For there was a sheen to her eyes that went beyond desire. Such affection would fade when she returned to her mother. "I am content with my duties, Persephone. I have no need or longing for more."

She smiled slightly. "No need? You've sacrificed your lack of need and longing to appease my own?" She shook her head, blushing. "No need."

He smiled as well, appreciating the vivid red that stained her cheeks. "I have managed without such...."

She held up her hand to stop him. She laid her head against his chest, speaking quickly. "I thank you for enduring my need and longing, Hades. Let us speak of it no more. Leave me to think that ours is a unique relationship, one that exceeds all others, one you might enjoy. For the peace we both value so."

He laughed, but said nothing. She had little to fear. What they shared was unique. A gift he would treasure.

"What of your duties?" she asked. Her hand slid along his arm, her fingers stroking him gently. "Were you unhappy when the realms were divided?"

"With my lot, you mean?" he whispered, inhaling into her hair and relaxing.

She nodded, slipping one arm about him and burrowing closer.

"No. It was fairly done. Things were different then." He paused, burying his nose in her hair and breathing deep. "We were of one mind, the Olympians. We knew those under our rule would see us with fearful eyes, the Titans had made certain of that. After all, if we could defeat the Titans, what monsters were we? Drawing lots eased the mortals. If we could decide such matters with calm deliberation, we must be civilized... not violent tyrants."

She nodded against his chest. "Wisely done."

"My lot was no different than the rest, to me. It is necessary, helping a soul find its place in the afterlife."

"You rule justly."

"Perhaps. I know what mortals say. Some will not speak my name for fear I will send Thanatos to bring them to me before their time. Others fear death and the eternal horrors and suffering my realm holds."

Persephone tilted her head back to meet his gaze. "I've never seen Tartarus, I confess, I hope I never do, but that is how I imagine it to be."

He searched her eyes, "It does not begin to describe the depths of the abyss... A nightmare."

"Nightmare?"

"One you cannot wake from. Such a place must exist to hold the blackened souls of the damned. And mark my words, Tartarus is full." He felt her shiver and pressed her against him. He pressed a kiss to her forehead, knowing such actions damned him for the fool he was.

"Was your realm as it is today? When you came to be Lord here?"

He shook his head. "It took a great many years... years of work, far from the world above and the life there, and Olympus."

"You said as much before..." She turned, regarding him with curious green eyes. "Tell me, do you accept blame for Poseidon and... her... your wife's actions?"

Anger was there, as always. Not at Persephone, but at himself. "I had a hand in it..."

"How?" Her hand pressed along the side of his face. "Tell me how you had a hand in what they did?" She sighed deeply. "You did what was honorable. You did what was right." Her brow furrowed. "She was a fool."

He shook his head even as he smiled at her. He pulled her onto his lap, unable to deny the feel of her against him... the very need and longing he denied flooded him. His words were rough as he whispered, "Mayhap you are a fool for thinking her wrong?"

His stomach tightened as her hands cupped his face and pulled him to hers. Her lips parted beneath him, inviting him eagerly.

"Then I am a fool," she spoke against his lips. "And I will remain so, happily, to stay in your arms."

Her words touched him, more than he wanted. Each one of them tore at the restraints on his heart. Each unleashed something he could not afford to feel – hope.

Chapter Sixteen

Her heart was so full of love for him.

She ached for Hades and all he had been through – for his poor wife too. And yet a part of her was happy Priska was gone. Not for the woman's suffering or the grief that she'd endured through no fault of her own. Prisca's was a tragic tale, one that haunted her to think on too long. But if she'd lived, Persephone would not have her Hades. And he was hers.

He grabbed her, gripping her shoulders to draw her closer. She did not resist, but leaned into his chest. He had large hands, long fingers that stroked and caressed the length of her arms into the tangle of curls that fell about them. She arched, pressing herself against him as her lips clung to his. His lips traveled along her neck to nuzzle her earlobe, his teeth sent shivers down her spine. Thoughts of Priska, or anything beyond his touch upon her, vanished.

She pressed her own lips to his chest, her nose brushing the line of his neck.

He shuddered against her as he drew her peplos from her shoulder. He was warm against her, warm as he bore her back against the grass. His hands were cool against her hips, gripping her. His mouth and breath brushed her face, his hands cupped and kneaded and she was undone.

She rose, burying him deep within her, a strangled groan escaping her.

He was no more controlled than she, and she delighted in his frenzy. His hand tangled in her hair, while the other cupped her hips. He turned his face into her neck, releasing a ragged moan against her skin.

She let her head fall back, setting a rhythm both hard and deep. Each time she took him in, she longed for more. At length her body tightened, tensing as ripple after ripple of pure ecstasy coursed through her. She clung to him, catching his lips with hers to stifle her cry of release.

Her body throbbed, echoing her climax with near painful spasms. He was still hard inside her, wanting. Such a realization surprised her. She was only vaguely aware of his hands, holding her face as he kissed her tenderly.

She stilled for but a second and found her rhythm quick enough, determined to push him to pleasure. Instead, she was gripped by another climax. It swept over her suddenly, ripping a startled cry from her before she knew otherwise.

Every inch of her still pulsed. And still he'd been left wanting.

She stared at him, passion and frustration blurring her vision. He was so beautiful, his wide eyes fixed on her in fascination.

She moved, shuddering violently at the sweet friction she stirred. And pleased by the flare of his nostril and the tightening of his jaw.

She stopped, slipping her peplos over her head. She loosed his chiton, pushing it about his waist so that his chest was as bare as hers.

He swallowed, making her smile.

But the feel of his skin upon her reduced her again, making her moan hoarsely as her body surged and tightened in release once more.

"I wonder," he ground out against her chest, his lips latching on to her nipple. "How long we might make this last, Goddess?"

She shuddered, horrified that her body would respond so quickly. She'd known it would be powerful, but she'd never thought her body could rule her so. She could not calm the fire in her blood or the delight of them joined so well. She did not want to.

"I know not," her words were husky to her own ears. "But I will see it through 'til you're well spent."

He closed his eyes as his face twisted, almost pained. He

grabbed her to him, wrapping his arms about her as if his life depended upon it. He rolled, sliding her beneath him and lifting her hips. He gripped her hard, cleaving to her once more. She was shuddering, raw and exposed from their lovemaking. She clung to him, whispering, "Hades... how I love you."

His eyes were dark as he stooped, kissing her softly, sweetly as he found his release. She caught his cry, his breath mingling with her own.

He collapsed on top of her. Her hands rested against his back, her arms tangled about him.

She'd never been happier. She bit her lip, stifling the laughter that bubbled up inside of her. It escaped anyway, her soft giggles making him roll to one side. "No, stay–"

But he'd moved and they were no longer wrapped up in one another. She sighed, scowling at him. She'd not expected to hear his laughter ring out. When it did, all traces of her irritation vanished. He had such a glorious laugh.

She laughed too, poking him in the side and leaning over him. "Does my anger really amuse you?"

His hand stroked her cheek. "Are you truly angry?"

She sighed, resting her chin on his chest. "No. How could I be?" She rolled on to her back, sighing again.

"It was you who laughed first," he reminded her.

She shook her head. "I laugh because I am happy. Happier than I've ever been. Because I am here, with you. The things you do to me..." She sighed. "My body is overwhelmed. And I am happy."

He watched her closely, but said nothing.

She looked at him, staring up at his face above her. "And...you are gloriously handsome. I find looking at you very... pleasing."

His eyes went round, the muscles in his throat working.

"Do I... Do I please you at all?" She covered her face, shaking her head. "No..." She sat up, wishing she's not asked such a question.

She stood, refusing to look at him as she dropped her tunic and attempted an air of nonchalance. "Shall we swim?" She did not wait for an answer, but ran to the edge of the water. What had she done? Why had she asked such a thing?

She stepped into the warm water, the steam enveloping her as she descended into its soothing depths. The pond, a shallow hot springs, was deep enough to bathe in. But the waters were clear and shallow enough to see its sandy bottom. She curled her toes into the sand, sighing.

She turned, smiling at him. "It's lovely."

He hadn't moved. He lay, resting on his elbow as his fingers plucked at the grass. His face was still, not rigid or hard, but thoughtful as he watched her. She was relieved. She would not lose this fragile truce they'd found. She must take better care with her words.

She called out to him, missing his closeness. "Will you join me?"

He sat up, shaking his head. But he said, while smiling that smile she loved so dearly, "I will."

Her eyes feasted upon him as he stood. He was lean and tall, his muscles clearly visible with his every motion. She'd been right when she'd first spied him. He was carved, hard and jagged, as the mountains of Greece. Her eyes found his, deep and blue.

He walked into the water, lowering himself with a loud sigh.

"I agree," she murmured, laying back in the water and closing her eyes.

The only thing that would make this day perfect was the heat of Apollo's orb, hot upon her bare skin. She opened her eyes, staring up at the sky overhead. The sun was there, faded behind the layers of cloud and gray that separated this realm from that of the living. But to feel such warmth, she'd be there, in the land above and not here.

No, she thought with a glance at Hades, *nothing could make this day more perfect.*

Water hit Hades squarely in the face, followed by a peal of laughter.

He sputtered, wiping the water from his eyes as he turned to Persephone. Her hands covered her mouth as she continued to giggle. She peered at him over her hand, waiting.

He laughed, unable to stop himself.

And her face, the pure joy that shone from deep inside of her, tore his heart free. Damn her, she left him no choice.

She splashed him again, her laughter giddy as she dove beneath the water.

He loved her.

He stared at the pond's surface, saw her lithe form dart away from him under its depths, and swam after her. He had no idea what he'd do when he caught her, he just knew he needed to touch her. This realization did little to provide him comfort, or happiness. His feelings meant he was vulnerable, and that was a weakness he'd taken pains to avoid these long years.

Fear. True fear, threatened to consume him. He would lose her, in time. He knew it.

She rose up amongst a shower of drops raining down on him. He pulled her into his arms. "Persephone," he murmured, noting the dimple in her cheek, the way her curls were almost black from the water, and her smile... She'd a smile like no other.

And he loved her.

Her face grew serious as he regarded her. Too serious.

He planted his hand upon her head and submerged her beneath the water. She came up sputtering, her eyes wide with astonished outrage.

"You... you..." she blinked, pushing her sodden curls from her face.

"Yes?" he asked, pulling her against him again. He could not deny himself. She slid, silky and soft, along his chest. His hands pressed along the line of her back, gently molding himself to her.

"You..."

"Answered your challenge?"

She stopped, her open mouth curving into a bright smile. "You did."

He sighed. He loved her.

She leaned forward, hesitant, and offered her mouth to him.

He bent his head, kissing her softly. There was passion, yes; he suspected he'd always want her. But the tenderness he felt, the feeling of wholeness and peace... She'd given this to him. Not through the joining of their bodies, but through the joining of their hearts.

Her words tickled his lips, "Your arms... They feel nice. I like it when you hold me so."

His heart thundered as her fingers twined into the curls at the nape of his neck. "Do you?"

"I do. They are strong and capable arms." She leaned back, meeting his gaze. "And gentle."

"Only with you."

The words seemed to startle her. They startled him all the more.

She blinked, her green eyes intense. Her breath was unsteady, fanning across his shoulders and chest. "Only with me?"

Did it matter? It changed nothing. If he told her of his newly discovered affection... No, it was no new discovery. He'd known it, felt it in his bones, but refused to give it credence. Did he dare? No. Admitting his love to himself was one thing. Telling her of his love was another.

He smiled, shaking his head as he lifted her quickly and tossed her into the water. She landed with a squeal and a splash, breaking the spell that held them.

But her squeals brought her defender. Theron arrived, the fur on his back rigid and his ears pricked and alert.

When she broke the surface, she was laughing. "You disarm me with your charm..." she gasped. "And near drowned me..."

"You would not drown." He watched Theron circle the edge of the pond and then settle down and rest his head on his legs, his golden eyes watching them.

She followed his gaze, smiling when she saw the dog. "Hello, Theron," she cooed.

The hound lifted his head, his tail thumping in response to her adoring tone.

"You've made him a lap dog." Hades splashed the animal.

Theron blinked, but did not move.

She shook her head. "A lap dog? You wound him. Can you not see the offense upon his regal face?"

Theron yawned, resting his head once more.

Her laughter filled him, warming him.

"So I see," he murmured.

She shook her head and swam to him. "Hades?"

His name from her lips... He was becoming more besotted by the minute. He scowled.

She stopped. "Are you angry with me? I admit I am fond of Theron, but I would not take him from your side..."

He shook his head. "No, no."

"Then what?" She didn't move, waiting just beyond his reach.

He stopped himself from reaching for her. He shook his head.

She closed the distance between them, wrapping her arms about his neck with ease. "I am hungry."

He shivered lightly as her nipples brushed across his chest. "For food?"

She laughed again, throwing her head back as her arms tightened about him. "Yes... for food. For now."

"Do you think I'd have left you? My men? Men loyal to me?" Erysichthon's voice met silence.

No sound but the wind reached him. The forest grew darker with each passing second, yet they remained hidden from him. He would need them. He would need their help for his plan to work.

"I come to you now, seeking your allegiance." He paused. Perhaps it would be better not to ask too much of them. Not yet. Better to tempt them with words, soothe their wounded pride.

He spoke clearly, his words ringing out. "I would see you avenged. See us all avenged."

One shadow moved, then another, separating from the trees and moving towards him. They were cautious, wary... He could not blame them. It was a strange existence, this in between. And they were as trapped as he was. He'd chosen his fate, forbidding Kadmos and Barak from performing the funeral rites that would send him into the Underworld. But these men had not. Their bodies had been left to rot... A circumstance they might choose to hold him accountable for, if he were not careful.

All of them were trapped here, for one hundred years. One hundred years of living without life. Only then could Charon would give them passage into the Land of the Dead. It was decreed by the Fates.

"My lord Erysichthon," one spoke, his voice gravelly and rough. "The war is over. No battles have been fought. How then, did you meet your end?"

"Taras? Taras, my friend." He paused, happy to see one of his personal guards amongst them. He continued, speaking earnestly.

"Demeter cursed me. She saw me die a low death. One unfitting the king of such a great people. It is through Olympus' part that we stand here, souls adrift."

"Yet you speak of avenging our deaths?" another asked.

"Against the Gods?"

Erysichthon held up his hand, comforted by its solidifying appearance. The dark was thickening, and so were they. "One God. The very God who closed his realm to you. The very God that took Persephone from me, that turned Demeter from us all. Hades..."

"You would fight Hades?"

"I know you all." His vision sharpened as the night fell heavily. "I see you. Taras, Sotirios, Panoptes. I know you, know the strength of your arms..."

Panoptes spoke, "I'd not thought to use my strength against the Gods."

"What have you to fear?" Erysichthon asked. "What can they do to you? That has not already been done?"

There was a hushed murmur then, and more shadows joined him. The forest was thick with them, so many souls – embittered and betrayed. An army. *His* army.

"Your wives and children are left without protection. Demeter has seen the crops fade and wither. So their bellies are empty as well. When I begged for her aid, prayed and sacrificed all, she would not hear me. We must make her listen."

Taras spoke then, "And this will change?"

Erysichthon nodded. "If Persephone returns to me, Demeter returns to us. There is nothing impossible, nothing beyond our reach."

"And Hades?" another asked.

His voice was hard, bitterness tingeing his every word. "If we rule the Underworld, what need do we have for Hades?"

The murmurs grew stronger, questions filling the night.

"How would you overthrow him?"

"What will become of him?"

"What will become of us?"

"What will Demeter do? Olympus do?"

He held up both hands then, waiting for them to fall silent before he spoke again. "He brings death; we are already dead. In truth, he has no power over us, not anymore. If we send him to Tartarus, would not those souls he's imprisoned rise up? Would they not delight in his eternal suffering? And when they join us, he *will* fall. I cannot return you to the land of the living, but we can rule the Underworld. Elysium, Asphodel... all would be within my power. If you choose to serve me."

Panoptes shook his head, "And Olympus?"

Erysichthon smiled. "Will have no choice but to seek an allegiance. We will control one of the three realms. With Hades imprisoned and Persephone my wife, they will yield."

"And if we fail?"

He laughed. "If we fail, we fail. We've nothing to lose. We are dead already."

Chapter Seventeen

Persephone held her sides as she laughed, shaking her head. "Truly?"

Aeacus smiled. "Truly."

Hades smiled as well. It pleased him to see her so. Aeacus' tale delighted her; perhaps he'd have others to share. "No other news?"

"No, my lord. Our court has seen little in the way of arrivals."

"A welcome change, I'm sure." Her voice was soft.

Aeacus nodded. "Indeed, Goddess."

"Thank you," Hades murmured, taking the scrolls from Aeacus.

"My pleasure..." Aeacus' words ended as Hermes entered the hall.

Hades felt a crushing tightness within his chest. It was not unusual to see Hermes, but each visit posed a threat to his newfound happiness. The time would come when Persephone was called home. The look upon Hermes' face was so grave that his fear threatened to overwhelm him.

Persephone rose from the kline, hugging Hermes with a welcoming smile. "Dear Hermes, come, join us. Aeacus was just..."

Hermes glanced at Persephone, his jaw rigid. "You are well?"

She was still smiling. "I am quite well."

Hades waited, knowing Hermes had news of import. His hand tightened about the base of his goblet, bracing himself.

Hermes nodded. "Then you will be able to return to your

mother, now. I have news you must hear." Hermes turned, speaking to them all. "News you must all hear."

Hades did not like the panic that found him. But he held himself stiff, until her green eyes flew to his. Her smile, her laughter was gone. And he saw the worry on her face. If Hermes were not here, he would pull her onto his lap. He would hold her close and...

"Much has changed in the time you've been here," Hermes continued. "Erysichthon... Erysichthon is dead."

Hades turned to Hermes, surprised by this announcement.

"What happened?" Persephone, too, was startled. She stepped away from Hermes, making her way to Hades' side.

Hades breathed deep, aching to pull her against him. Something was amiss, something more. He'd never seen Hermes so unsettled. He busied himself with pouring water in a goblet.

"Too much has happened to share now..."

"Then tell us what you can." Hades' voice was calm, betraying none of the worry that gripped him.

"He'd been cursed for cutting down Demeter's grove. He was obsessed, with food... and finding you." Hermes looked at Persephone, then continued, "He sold everything, including his daughter, to appease his hunger. But he could find no satisfaction." He shrugged. "His madness was so great that he began to eat his own flesh."

Disgust roiled within Hades, robbing him of words. Persephone began to tremble, pressing herself against him. His arms caught her and held her close.

"He did not cross over, Hermes." Hades' voice was sharp. He glanced at Aeacus. "Erysichthon of Thessaly? He has not..."

Aeacus shook his head. "No, my lord."

"No, he hasn't." Hermes said in resignation. "He demanded no funeral rites be performed. His hunger died with his death, but his obsession with Persephone has not."

Hades stroked the length of her back, over and over. Her trembling angered him, but Hermes' words infuriated him.

Persephone whispered, pressing herself into his side, "Why does he do this?"

His arms tightened about her, her presence the only thing that eased him. The look on Hermes' face told him there was more.

"What else is there, Hermes?"

Hermes took a deep breath. "Poseidon..."

Hades sucked in a sharp breath.

"He'd given Erysichthon a draft, one of Aphrodite's potions. He gave the poor mortal a vial when he should have had no more than a drop. He sought to make the match take..."

"So he says," Hades sneered. "Go on."

"It was through Poseidon's hand that Erysichthon fell to madness?" Persephone gasped.

"He confessed all when he learned of Erysichthon's plan. Indeed, he felt such conscience over his part that he sought to offer aid to Erysichthon's daughter. It was through the daughter and the last of Erysichthon's men that Poseidon learned of the plan."

"What plan?" Hades' patience was gone. His grip on Persephone had tightened, but she seemed to need his arms about her as much as he needed to hold her.

Hermes' words spilled out. "He's rallied those left to wander, those souls that cannot cross. He will take Persephone and try to overthrow you."

Persephone gasped, turning into his chest.

"Aeacus." Hades did not hesitate. "Go to Tartarus. Inform Didymos and the Erinyes. Put guards along the Rivers Acheron, Cocytus and Styx. Have Minos rally Asphodel and send Rhadamanthys to Elysium. We will be ready. Send me Cerberus."

Aeacus nodded, bowing low before he left the chamber.

Persephone was clinging to him, her hands twisting in his tunic. "I cannot go. I will not leave you."

Hades' heart throbbed, so sweet were her words.

Hermes watched them, his tawny eyes full of sympathy. "We must take her to Olympus, Hades. Before the sun is set."

Hades nodded.

"I will not go," she cried.

"You will." He gripped her shoulders, pulling her back to look up at him. "You will go."

Her eyes were true green, sparkling with tears. "Please let me stay."

Her words tore at him. He felt an unaccountable ache at the back of his throat, a heaviness in his lungs and stinging in his eyes. "I told you, Persephone. You knew you could not stay here, not forever."

She shook her head, the tears flowing freely down her cheeks. "But... but..."

His hands tightened on her shoulders. He cursed himself as he pulled her against his chest, holding her tightly against him. He buried his nose in her hair, drawing in a deep breath. Her scent flooded him, making him ache with sadness.

He set her aside. "Hermes..."

He did not look at Hermes, but gently pushed her into his waiting arms. He could not bear it, could not bear the pain that gripped him. It was right. She did not belong here, in his realm or in his heart. He would see her to Olympus, see her to safety... as was his duty. And then he would never see her again. He could only wish that his heart, this foolish hope, would stay with her.

He could not think as he called up his horses, lacing them into their harnesses without a word. But when he was done, he leaned against Orphnaeus' flank. His lungs rebelled against the air he sought to pull in. And pain, sharp and hot, almost forced him to his knees. He swallowed, the strange tremor of his mouth and the hitch of his breath angering him.

He pushed off of the horse, climbing into the chariot's basket and snapping the horses forward.

Cerberus ran beside them, claws tearing up the turf. Hades cast the briefest glances upon the beast, but saw his sorrow echoed in their six golden eyes. They, Theron the most, would feel her absence.

"Protect her," Hades spoke harshly. "So that we will only miss her while she is safe upon Olympus, instead of her being lost to us."

Three sets of eyes narrowed, three sets of ears stood alert. The snapping jaws bared their teeth, growling and howling. Rows of serpents, green and brown, crowned Cerberus like a lion's mane. They writhed and hissed, heeding his warning. Cerberus' mighty tail, a spiked rudder, swung forcefully.

The beast heard him, then.

By the time he'd reached the bridge, he'd managed to steady himself. After years of control, he would not reveal himself now. Now, when he needed to send her away... He must. To keep her safe.

Hermes waited, Persephone at his side.

He did not look at her, but drew the horses up.

"We'll not be alone," Hermes assured him, helping Persephone into the chariot. "Every wood nymph of Thessaly has come to your aid. If we go now, they can keep the shades in the trees."

"Why?" Persephone's words were hollow... broken.

He'd not meant to look at her. "Souls are strongest in the shadows... in the night." His eyes found hers and his voice softened under her gaze. "They offer little threat now, when the sun is high."

She nodded, her face drawn. She looked too fragile, too frightened. He scowled, but she'd turned from him. She stared at Cerberus, a small smile on her lips. "Hello," she murmured.

Cerberus whimpered then growled.

"Hermes will lead us out," Hades said.

She nodded again.

"I'll go on ahead," Hermes said, his brow creasing as he glanced between them.

"Thank you, Hermes," she said.

Hades' hands tightened on the reins as he nodded at Hermes. Hermes sighed and turned, disappearing on the wind.

With a crack of the reins, they started off. He was aware of how stiffly she stood, how her hands gripped the chariot's rail. With every bounce and jolt, she grew more rigid.

He could not hold himself silent. "Persephone." She looked at him with tear-filled eyes.

Words failed him then. What reassurance could he offer her? None. "Hold tight. The road worsens ahead."

Her chin quivered, but she nodded.

The chariot bounced, the chargers flying across the ground without pause. His cave, his sanctuary, seemed alive with menace. Every shadow and crevice full of threat. It was with relief that true sunlight poured from the cave's opening. He blinked, the white light strong after so long in his realm. He glanced at Persephone, his heart in his throat.

Her eyes were closed, but her face was tilted to the sun's rays. She glowed, golden, ever brighter as they left the cave.

Cerberus howled in farewell. They could not cross over.

Persephone looked back, her green eyes searching the cave. "Good-bye," she murmured, her breath hitching.

He tore his gaze from her, swallowing the words that welled

up within him.

Her hand reached out, covering one of his, pulling at him unsteadily. He took a deep breath, her touch burning into him, connecting them once more. His hand twisted, gripping hers tightly.

She moved to his side, but did not lean into him. Her face changed, her brow furrowing as they left the cover of the rocky cliffs that bordered his realm. It was the sight of the long grassed plains, their golden stalks grey and brittle, that held her attention now. They did not wave in the wind, but splintered beneath the chargers' hooves.

He watched her dangle her other hand over the edge of the chariot basket.

"What happened here?" she asked.

He followed her gaze. No war had ravaged this place. But something had happened. He'd never seen this realm so untended, so bleak. "I know not."

Her fingers brushed across the grass tips. With a single touch the shoots began to plump, turning a rich green. She leaned forward, stretching her arm, hand, and fingers as far as she could. The path widened, a vibrant stripe of emerald spreading across the meadow. He held his arm out, anchoring her to the chariot basket and further extending her reach.

The wind lifted her copper curls, while the sun gilded her. He feasted on the sight of her.

She laughed softly, glancing at him with sparkling eyes. "They're happy to see me."

He nodded, though it pained him to do so. Of course they were happy, she was returned to them. Her very touch saw them healed and whole once more. He knew all too well the magic of her touch.

Silence fell. She turned her attention to the plants, growing more lovely with every flower she blessed. He knew her magic, her gift, was where it should be. Here, in the land of the living. She did not, had never, belonged with him. And she never would.

Her grip tightened upon his hand. The chariot tilted, leaving the meadow and climbing the base of the mountain.

She could scarce speak the word. "Olympus?"

He glanced at her, nodding. He looked away, but did not release her hand.

"Hades," she started, then took a deep breath, knowing he heard the tremor in her voice.

"Perhaps it's better left unsaid."

She pressed herself against his side, resting her head on his arm. "Perhaps... I love you..."

"Be wary, Persephone." His words were harsh. "Do not reveal yourself to them. They are your brethren, yes, but they will favor you only as long as it serves them to do so. Guard your heart... And your tongue."

She nodded. "Honesty is not so revered here."

His eyes traveled her face, and he shook his head, his smile sad and his brow furrowed. "No."

"Then I will be careful." She paused, stroking his face. "And I will love you..."

His hand covered hers. He turned into her touch, kissing her palm once. "No more. I beg you. Put such thoughts from your mind."

His hand gripped hers, lifting it from his cheek and pressing it to her side.

She watched as he took the reins in both hands. She stared at those hands...

"Will you be safe?" she asked. She would know that much.

He nodded. "Erysichthon thinks there is nothing to fear after death."

She shivered, remembering his description of Tartarus, of the abyss beyond.

"And you will be safe, with your mother," he finished.

"Yes." She had missed her mother.

And the sun, she'd missed it as well. She tilted her face to its rays once more. It was hot, but it did not seem to warm her. She opened her eyes, astonished by the beauty of the mountain. Whereas Greece was brown, Olympus was green and fertile. The higher they rode, the greener it became. She stared behind her, taking in the land that stretched as far as she could see. On the horizon was blue, the sea, perhaps?

The clouds were vapor thin about them. And still the horses ran on.

The world below was lost, swallowed by the white clouds of the heavens.

And then she saw it.

Olympus. Such halls, white columns of gleaming marble shot through with gold and silver. Several halls resting at various levels on the mountains peak. On the tip stood the largest.

"There?" she asked.

He nodded. "The Council Chamber."

She stared at him, feeling close to tears once more. It would be easier if she could hold his hand. She swallowed, looking at his white knuckled grip upon the reins. She knew, no matter how much she might want his strength, that she must stand alone now. He cared for her, she knew that. But not as she wanted. His love, if any existed, had no roots. While hers were deep, connecting him to her always.

"Tell me," she whispered as they drew to the towering golden doors of the Council Chamber. "If I were not Persephone..."

He scowled. "No more. Hear these words, Persephone, and know that I mean them. You do not belong with me, in my realm, at my side, in my bed or my heart. My life is without you. And yours is without me. When I leave here, know that I wish you well. But I will not think on you anymore." His eyes bore into hers, revealing nothing more to her.

If he'd struck her she wondered if the pain would be less. When her flesh had been torn, had it hurt as much? She closed her eyes, ending the torture his gaze inflicted upon her.

She managed to turn, managed to step down from the chariot... but her knees threatened to buckle then. She felt his arms come about her, but held her hands out, warding him away. She would not look at him.

"No," she gasped, fearing the power of his touch. "I am fine."

She steadied herself, resting one hand on Aethon's flank. Each breath was excruciating, but she forced the air into her lungs, forced herself to climb the steps. He was there, pushing the doors wide. She had time to see the detailed carvings, a picture story wrought into the golden surface.

And then she saw her mother.

Demeter ran, lifting her tunic to fly across the chamber and pulling her into her arms. Persephone turned in to her mother's

neck, burying her face against the familiar scent, the warm softness...
And fought the urge to sob.

Demeter shook, her sobs overtaking her.

"Shh, Mother," Persephone soothed. "I am well. And returned to you."

She peered over her mother's shoulder. Hades stood, his strong profile illuminated by the torch flames. So beautiful... so cold.

Demeter's hands cupped her face, pulling back as she spoke. "You are. You are here, in my arms. Something I feared might never again happen." She pulled Persephone close once more, squeezing her.

"We welcome you," a voice boomed, demanding her attention.

Demeter's hold loosened, though she gripped her hand. "Persephone," her mother gasped, wiping the tears from her face. "Welcome to Olympus."

Persephone blinked, blinded by the auras of so many. She knew them, recognized them from the stories her mother and Hermes... and Hades had told her. She'd seen Aphrodite... She steadied herself, remembering Hades' warning.

"You are most welcome," Zeus – Persephone knew it was Zeus – took her hands in his.

She smiled, a small smile, and glanced at her mother. She felt lost. And her pain... pain pressed upon her. "Thank you."

He smiled, flashing white teeth and a charming dimple. His brown hair was cropped short, as was his beard and mustache. His eyes were brown, like her mother's. Rich and warm.

"And you," Demeter spoke again, the passion in her voice surprising Persephone. But her mother was staring at Hades, her face trembling with emotion. "You..."

"You are once more a hero, brother." Zeus clapped Hades on the back.

Persephone clasped her hands behind her back to steady herself. She looked at him then, saw the widening of his eyes, the slight furrow of his brow before it was gone. His face revealed nothing.

"While I am once more the villain." This was Poseidon, then.

Side by side, she could see the resemblance amongst brothers. All were dark, though Hades was darkest. Where his eyes were blue-black, Poseidon's were the palest blue. All were tall, broad, and handsome. But he, Hades, was the only one she would happily look upon...

"You will forgive me?" Poseidon stood before her, one eyebrow arched. His face was the picture of regret and sincerity.

She stared at him, blinking fiercely. She'd never wanted to hit someone before, ever. It was not in her nature to inflict injury, to malign or degrade a being. But, staring into his eyes, knowing what he'd done to Hades... to her, she thought she might be able to make an exception. She turned to her mother, then Zeus. "Must I forgive him?"

Demeter's eyes were round, but the smile upon her face was greatly amused. "Persephone..."

"No," Hades spoke. His voice remained cool and aloof, his eyes fixed upon Poseidon.

"Come now, brother. You cannot believe I would wish such events to take place?" Poseidon's smile was tight and his eyes narrowed. "Persephone, you know little of me. But I can assure you I'd not meant you any ill will..."

Hades stepped forward, between her and Poseidon. "And yet Thessaly, Erysichthon and his people, Persephone and Demeter have suffered, because of you."

It should not please her so, to see him defend her, to see him stand up to his horrible brother. But it did. She felt a smile rise up within her. Only the memory of Hades' warning kept it from her lips.

"I see no reason why she should forgive him." A woman, a warrior, approached. The look she sent Poseidon removed any doubt; this was Athena. She was bigger than Persephone imagined, taller and well muscled. That she was a fighter was no surprise. That she was lovely, was. Her light brown eyes flashed as she continued, "He's done little to earn it. I applaud your choice, Persephone. Do not forgive him."

"Will there ever be peace on Olympus?" Zeus asked, his tone low.

"Peace?" She heard Hades whisper, saw him glance at her. His jaw hardened as he tore his gaze from her. "At what cost?"

"Forgive him or not, daughter. It is your choice and one you've the right to make on your own." Demeter moved forward, taking

Hades' hands in hers. "But you, Hades, I would give you some reward for caring for my daughter. I can never repay you for that, never. But I would try. Please, Hades, there must be something you desire?"

Hermes cleared his throat, causing all eyes to turn upon him. He smiled, wiping a hand across his face. "Sorry."

Aphrodite came forward, the picture of grace and beauty. Her blond curls swayed about her hips as she joined Demeter. "Surely, there's something that might ease your loneliness?"

Persephone remembered the Goddess' visit. And heard the Goddess' words. She felt the urge to cry once more. This would not end well.

"What say you, Persephone?" Aphrodite turned to her. "You were with him, in his realm. He cannot be happy there. What might make his realm more comfortable?"

She stared at the ground.

Every detail, every memory flooded her. The feel of the furs on his bed, the strength of his arms, the smell of his skin, the rich tone of his laughter, the scent of his soap, and the caress of his hand upon her... She blinked, suddenly warm. She shook her head, feeling the world tilt... go fuzzy... then black.

Chapter Eighteen

"What say you, Persephone?" Aphrodite spoke. "You were with him, in his realm. What might make his realm more comfortable?"

He looked at her, saw the rose fade from her cheeks and the tremor of her chin. She swayed on her feet and then crumpled to the floor. He stepped forward, anxious, his arms instantly reaching for her.

Zeus' hand gripped his shoulder, holding him in place. Hades did not pull free from his brother's grasp, but glared at him. And Zeus stared back. With a slight shake of his head, he spoke volumes. Hades went rigid, assessing those around him. None but Zeus was aware of his misstep, none but Zeus saw his anxiety... and pain.

It was Hermes who caught her. Hermes who cradled her against his chest. Hermes who stared at him, looking disappointed.

She looked so pale and small in his arms.

Hermes carried her, following Demeter from the room and taking her away from him.

"Come now, Hades." Hera regarded him with her luminous brown eyes. Her full lips parted in a sincere smile. "We are all eager to show our appreciation to you. You've done so much of late."

He glanced at Hera. "Out of duty." Which was true, somewhat. He stared after Persephone, holding himself rigid. She was gone from him, no longer his concern... But Poseidon's pale blue eyes were also fixed upon the door, the door Persephone had gone through, and a roar of fury filled his ears.

He clenched his fists, his hatred too near the surface for his liking. His tone was hard. "I need no payment."

Poseidon laughed. "You astound me, brother. Twice now you've turned from immeasurable pleasures. I begin to think you've befriended Hephaestus in his fiery workshop."

And still his fury raged.

Zeus shook his head. "You are my brothers. I remember a time when we stood together, as one, against our enemies. Have we truly fallen so far? That we would look upon one another with such malice?" He looked at Hades, then Poseidon. "With ill intent? Are we no better than those we overthrew? Are we doomed to follow their example?"

"I make an observation and am slandered with ill intent?" Poseidon scoffed.

"I will not deny malice on my part." Hades' words were biting. One day, Poseidon would be caught by a net of his own making. If there was any justice left, he would see it.

Zeus regarded Poseidon, his frustration plain. "Brother..."

"It is his nature, Father," Athena said. "He is only content when wounding others."

"Athena." Poseidon smiled. "Pity your tongue is only skilled with making words..."

Athena's face reddened at the dig. "Pig."

"Harpy," Poseidon returned.

"Can you not banish him?" Athena asked Zeus.

"Banish him?" Hera asked. "Such a punishment would serve you both, I think."

Zeus regarded his outraged daughter, then his brother. "Perhaps, wife."

Hades sighed. "I leave you to your justice, then. And go to serve my own. My *enemy* waits to challenge my dominion over the Underworld. Though I seek no help from you." He glared at Poseidon, meeting his brother's pale gaze with his most ferocious scowl. "Such a request would earn me a sword in the back."

Poseidon hesitated, his face awash with confusion, sadness, and anger. But Hades no longer cared.

Apollo stepped forward, his grin quick. "I would help. And

promise not to stab you."

"As would I." Ares smiled, pushing up from his chair for the first time. He rubbed his hands together. "As long as I get to stab someone."

"I fear there's little stabbing to be done," Athena offered. "Since those you would challenge are dead."

Ares' eyes narrowed. "Fire."

Apollo nodded, clapping Ares on the shoulder. "Light, yes. It weakens them."

"Clever, Ares." Athena nodded. "Clever indeed."

"How does one harness light?" Aphrodite asked.

Ares' gaze lingered on her briefly. "There's no need to harness it."

"Demeter will not thank you for destroying her..." Hera interjected.

"There's little to destroy," Apollo said with a shrug. "Demeter's grief ravaged most of Greece."

Hades took this news to heart. If he'd sent Persephone home, would less damage have occurred? Would Erysichthon be dead? Or would his curse have been discovered, and cured? Would the crops...

"So we burn it," Ares' voice was hard.

"Greece?" Poseidon regarded them with wide eyes.

"The risk is too great." Hades looked at them, one at a time, surprised by their readiness to help. "I would have them driven to my realm. Once inside, they cannot escape and they cannot win."

Ares nodded. "Fire will flush them out."

"Fire will flush who out?" Hermes joined them.

Hades glanced at the door, again. She was well. She was with her mother. She was not his concern.

"Erysichthon and his men," Apollo answered. "We're to drive them into the Underworld."

Hermes nodded. "Ah."

"Hades is right. The mortals have suffered enough." Zeus shook his head, his brow creased in concentration. "You must control the fire."

"How?" Hera asked.

Hera echoed his very thoughts. Fire would serve his purpose, but...

"Rain. Rain would be the best choice." Athena glared at Poseidon. "So we must come up with another plan."

"A storm, perhaps," Aphrodite turned to Poseidon, entreating. "A storm would ensure success. And leave the mortals unharmed."

Zeus glanced at Poseidon, his expression holding little hope. "What say you? Will you help?"

Poseidon nodded quickly. "Of course."

But unlike the rest of the Olympians, Hades was distracted by Poseidon. There was a look about him, a tenderness that surprised Hades. More surprising was that Poseidon looked upon Aphrodite so. He forced himself to join the others, but not before he saw Poseidon stroke Aphrodite's rounding stomach... Not before he saw her blush and shy away from Poseidon's touch.

What attachment had formed between them? And what would happen upon its end? He knew, without a doubt, that such an affair would end. His brother had no capacity for devotion, no comprehension of loyalty. And poor Aphrodite, so desperate to find love herself, would find herself soon alone. He glanced back, watching the Goddess arrange the gathers of her voluminous robes over her stomach.

Her condition was well hidden, covered as she was.

But in time, he suspected a babe would join Olympus. And then, with or without Poseidon, the Goddess of Love would no longer be alone.

"Hades," Apollo beckoned to him. "Ares' plan is promising."

It eased the pain, knowing they would help him confront this new foe. In truth, he almost pitied Erysichthon and his army of souls. They'd no notion of what would be waiting for them when they chose to attack.

"Persephone?" Her mother's voice?

She blinked. Where was she? Why were there so many faces staring at her?

Her eyes settled, focused. She was floating... No, someone held her. She turned, looking at a chest.

Her eyes traveled up.

Her voice wavered. "Hermes?"

"She needs rest, Demeter. I can only imagine the conditions she's become accustomed to..." a woman spoke, her regal face lined with concern.

Persephone laid her head back and closed her eyes, the strong beating of Hermes' heart filling her ears.

"Yes, rest," she heard her mother's voice. "Follow me, Hermes. We've chambers here... Until this matter with Erysichthon is done."

Persephone did not open her eyes when she heard him; indeed, she turned into Hermes to stifle her cry of pain.

"I need no payment," Hades voice was cold.

"Shh," Hermes' voice was in her ear. He carried her, the voices from the Council Chamber fading behind her. A door shut, she heard it, and could hear him no more.

She sobbed, clinging to Hermes' chiton with trembling hands.

"Shh," he whispered, his breath tickling her ear. "I am sorry, Persephone. Let your mother comfort you."

She shook her head, searching for her control.

"In here," Demeter was speaking. "Oh, child, cry if you will. I will cry with you."

Hermes set her on the bed, covered in thick white furs and woven blankets of the softest fabric. She stared at the bed, then the room, through bleary eyes. It was so bright, so white... Her eyes felt heavy and swollen. She sniffed.

"I shall leave you," Hermes murmured.

She met his eyes. "Thank you."

"Yes, Hermes, thank you." Demeter hugged him, escorting him to the door and whispering. "I beseech you. Find out what might tempt Hades. He's too quick to dismiss his needs. I will hound him relentlessly on this, you may tell him as much."

Persephone flopped back onto the bed, covering her face with her hands.

"He will not take..." Hermes tried.

"He is a man," she snorted. "He will not refuse such an offer forever."

"Mother," she pleaded. "Leave him be. I've troubled him long enough. He will savor the quiet now that I'm gone from him. Perhaps that will please him above all else."

She did not look at them, but turned on to her side and waited.

She heard the door close, felt the bed move.

"Was it horrible?" her mother's voice was soft. "I know he's a brute..."

Persephone glanced at her, too weary to sit up or move. "Do we speak of Erysichthon? Or Hades?"

Demeter's chin quivered, tears flowing freely. "Both... Oh, Persephone. Forgive me for putting you at the mercy of such men. All your life I sought to... to protect you... Instead..."

Persephone sat up, fighting the leaden weight of her arms to pull her mother close. "All is well, Mother," she murmured , holding her mother until her sobs subsided.

Demeter leaned back, her face wet with tears. "You are right. All is well now that you are home." Demeter wiped the tears from her face and patted her cheek. "We have time to share and catch up. You must tell me about Hades' realm, later. First... a bath?"

She watched her mother, quickly recovered and demanding a bath be delivered.

"And Zeus has given us these chambers. If Poseidon had not learned the thrust of Erysichthon's plan, you might well have been taken. And Hermes had the good fortune to come across that water nymph..."

"What water nymph?" Persephone's head was beginning to throb.

"The one that saw you... When you were injured." Demeter began to cry again. "She saw Hades, saw him take a woman into the Underworld the day Erysichthon battled the Persians. She thought no more of it until Hermes explained you were missing. But that you were carried into the Underworld, by Hades himself, prompted Hermes' search. As he and Hades share little in the way of camaraderie, Hermes had never thought to ask Hades... It is no secret that Hades has little love for mortals, or company of any kind, really. But he must have known who you were..."

Persephone listened, stunned into silence.

Did Olympus truly see him so? Did no one see him as the hero he truly was?

She regarded her mother, flitting about the chambers for fresh linens, soap and a comb.

What would happen if she told her mother the truth? That

Hermes had joined them at their supper table more than once while she was there?

The bath arrived, steaming and fragrant. Demeter held her hands out, smiling. "Come, Persephone. It will do you good to sit a while."

She stood, letting her mother unwind her tunic.

Demeter winced, drawing Persephone's attention. Her mother's hand trembled, pressing along the pale line that edged her ribcage. It was faint, so faint Persephone had all but forgotten the wound. Hades had said nothing about it when... Her heart twisted sharply.

"This shall be burned," her mother's nose wrinkled. "What a strange smell. I suppose the Underworld would have no use for flowers? Was it a strange place?"

Persephone sat in the warm water. White petals floated on the water's surface, scenting the air heavily. She curled her toes, but the basin had a metal bottom. She missed the grit of sand and the perfume-free warmth of his pond. His arms, his smile, his touch...

She shook her head. She must forget. She must.

"Persephone? Forgive me," Demeter bent over her, kissing her forehead. "I've missed you terribly. It's been so long, so very long..."

"How long have I been gone?"

"The moon has come ten times since last I saw your sweet smile." Demeter stroked her cheek. She sighed, took the soap in her hands and began to wash Persephone's hair.

"I... I had no idea..." Persephone stammered.

"Were you ill for much of it?"

Persephone nodded, unable to speak.

Demeter's hands were gentle, massaging her scalp as she chattered on, "I searched. Know that I searched, but there was no news of you. And when I went to Erysichthon... Well, he was no help."

Persephone listened in silence, letting her gaze wander about the room to avoid her thoughts.

"... Zeus was less than helpful. Hera seemed to think you'd run off with a lover. I could convince no one of the truth. So I searched. When I came to Eleusis, I'd lost all hope." She paused, pouring water over Persephone's head. The water clouded about her knees, disturbing the surface. Her reflection vanished, lost beneath the foam and oil.

She swallowed, feeling lost too.

Her mother chattered on, wrapping her in a clean tunic and brushing the tangles from her hair. She was never quiet, Persephone noticed.

"Sleep now," Demeter said, hugging her close. "Rest and forget all the ill you've seen. You've the sweetest soul, one too long missing from this realm."

Persephone lay back, pulling up the furs and blankets as her mother crept from the room. Once the door was shut, Persephone rolled into the furs and sobbed until she could sob no more.

"The entrance is guarded by the three-headed beast," Sartirios whispered.

"I see no one, nothing else..." Erysichthon's eyes scoured the darkness of Hades' caves.

The men, souls fading in the rising sun, crouched behind a boulder.

Taras hissed, "Can we kill it?"

Cerberus was staring at them. Cerberus would not leave the darkness of the cave, but stood ready. Their eyes, all six, flashed yellow in the gloom. When the wind fell still, the hiss of the serpents was audible.

"No. It is dead, like us," Sartirios responded.

Erysichthon smiled, meeting the eyes of the monster. "It will have a weakness."

The creature growled, rising up on thick legs. The jaws snapped, drops of drool flying out onto the grass beyond the cave's mouth. The grass curled, turning brown then crumbling to black.

"What a vile beast." Taras shuddered, turning away from the cave's entrance to lean against the boulder.

"Be mindful of what you say," Erysichthon laughed. "It will serve us soon enough..."

"Or drag us to Tartarus," Sartirios warned.

Erysichthon ignored them, too transfixed by the vicious brutality that shone from Cerberus' gaze. Did the animal know him? Or did it gaze upon all souls with such hunger? It mattered not.

He pushed off of the rocks, walking in front of the cave. He heard Cerberus howl in fury, but ignored it. He'd nothing to fear, for now. He motioned for the men to follow, speaking to them as they made for the cover of the trees.

Sunlight broke over the mountains, erasing all traces of them in the light.

He hated the sun, almost as much as he hated Hades... And Demeter. The sun took his strength, his form, his being... While Demeter and Hades had taken his purpose. His anger warmed him, buoying his confidence.

"Time is our ally," he assured the men. "Night will come soon enough. But now, make use of the light. Go and learn all you can about the beast. There must be some who know how to tame it."

Sartirios nodded, leaving them as they entered the trees. Men waited, too many for Erysichthon to count. More came every day. Broken souls, lost and bitter. Erysichthon was learning quickly, nothing was more dangerous than one forgotten. He offered them a way to be remembered.

"Panoptes," Erysichthon continued. "What of the rivers?"

"We cannot cross them. Some force, some magic, prevents it." Panoptes sounded defeated.

"What of Charon?" Erysichthon asked. "What of making him an ally?"

Panoptes took no pains to hide his disbelief. "Charon?"

Erysichthon stood, towering over the man. "Charon. You whine and complain and belittle too much of late, Panoptes."

Panoptes did not look at him.

"I never promised this would be an easy fight," his words were low. "What else would you do?"

"Watch my boy," Panoptes said, glancing at him now. "See him grow."

Erysichthon felt a moment's pain at the words. He did not think of Ione often, he saw no point in it. But when he did, he felt the pull of loss. He knew there was no hope for a reunion, not while she still lived. And knowing that, he had no desire for a reunion any time soon.

But Persephone... she'd lived long in the Underworld. She would do so again.

He reached for Panoptes, to clap him heartily upon the back and rally his spirit. But his hands were too insubstantial to do so. His form passed through Panoptes, and unsettled all who saw it. For none of them had made peace with their state. It was why they kept fighting. They hoped, somehow, to change it.

"Go then," Erysichthon urged. "Watch them. They cannot see you in the sunlight. But know that while you are stuck, they move on. What will you do when you visit them and find a man in your bed? When your wife finds your children a new father, will seeing them still bring you comfort? I warn you now, prepare yourself for such things. It is the way of the living, to move on and forget."

"I would see them happy," Panoptes murmured, his voice anguished.

"Would you?" Erysichthon asked. "Then go now. Your visits will end when we cross over. So go now, and savor what time you have left."

Panoptes hesitated, then set off at a fair pace toward what had once been his home. Erysichthon watched him, and seven others like him, vanish under the sun – chasing a life that was no longer theirs.

He felt that familiar ache, the faint twinge of longing for Ione, but shrugged it aside. They'd a new path before them. Panoptes and the others would come back. And they would fight. There was no other choice. Erysichthon would make certain of that.

Chapter Nineteen

"What do you think?" Demeter stood back, tilting her head this way and that as she regarded the bountiful arrangement of flowers.

Persephone stood beside her. She tried to smile. She did try. "They're lovely, Mother."

Demeter sighed. "They are. Yet you are not pleased."

"I am," she hastened to assure her mother.

"They're flowers," Athena said with a shake of her head. "Nice, certainly. But flowers nonetheless. Would such sights normally send her into raptures?"

"Stop being churlish," Hera snapped. "We all know you'd rather be off chasing ghosts..."

Demeter clicked her tongue.

"Sorry." Hera looked truly remorseful as she smiled at Persephone. "I meant no offense."

Persephone smiled back. "No, no, of course not." She walked slowly, moving around the massive vase of flowers. It was a small distance, but she savored it.

"I'm more capable than Hermes," Athena complained.

"At fighting perhaps," Hera said.

The women laughed, making her loneliness complete. She did not share in their banter. She felt no camaraderie amongst these women, no comfort in their discourse. And yet, they seemed determined to keep her close.

She could not leave Olympus, not while Erysichthon was still free. But she'd been denied the right to walk the mountain top, to explore the nearby valley or Olympus' vineyards. Demeter was near crippled with the fear of losing her again.

"You're heartsick." Aphrodite came round the other side of the arrangement, trailing her fingers along the rim of the vase. She smiled slightly, her blue eyes full of sympathy.

She should deny it.

"Being away from home for so long, perhaps?" Aphrodite stroked the petal of one blossom between her fingers. "You miss your plants and the earth beneath your touch?"

Persephone opened her mouth, but could find no answer.

Aphrodite stared at her then, inspecting her face intently. "Or is it something more?"

Persephone blinked, the prick of tears startling her. "No, nothing more. It is as you said. I... I have been too long without tending to those that need me."

Aphrodite lowered her voice. "Your plants?"

She nodded.

"Nothing else?" She moved closer, placing a hand on Persephone's forearm. "There's a sadness in you... it is familiar. You long for something... something that has nothing to do with your plants..."

Persephone pulled her arm away, shaking her head.

"Persephone?" Demeter joined them, "Did you hear?"

"No," she spoke quickly, if a bit breathlessly. "I was admiring your gifts. We both were." She glanced at Aphrodite. The Goddess of Love smiled easily enough.

"Curious." Demeter touched her forehead. "I wonder..."

Her mother looked at her. Aphrodite regarded her as well.

"You wonder what?"

Demeter wrapped an arm about her shoulder, pulling her back to the padded cushions and klines where the others sat.

"Water," Demeter ordered, waving Hebe forward. "For Persephone."

Persephone took the cup and drank deeply, aware that all eyes were on her. When the cup was empty she gave it back to Hebe with a small smile. "Thank you."

Hebe smiled back.

"What did you eat while you were away?" Demeter asked.

"Away?"

"While you were in..." Hera's voice faded.

Aphrodite's voice was softer, gentler as she finished what Hera could not. "In the Underworld."

"Eat?" Why did such a question seem to trouble them so?

Demeter sat beside her, taking her hands. "You've been so... melancholy since your return, Persephone. I'd hoped you would recover, in time."

Recover? She clasped her hands in her lap, staring at them as pain welled up in her chest. Could one recover from a broken heart?

"But you seem to fade every day."

Persephone sighed, a forced attempt to dismiss her mother's concern.

"You're not as Demeter described you," Athena offered.

Demeter clicked again. Had she always done so? Persephone couldn't recall, but it was a most grating habit.

Her gaze traveled from one Goddess to the next. "I'm not sure I understand."

"Your mother may not have brought you to Olympus, Persephone," Hera spoke. "But she often spoke of you. Your laughter, your easy smile."

"Your fondness for singing," Aphrodite added.

Athena joined in, "Your stories... What a gifted story teller you are."

"Oh." She would gladly feign a headache, but she'd claimed such a malady too often of late.

"Are you well?" her mother asked.

Persephone drew in a slow breath, "I am. I am well."

Hera and Demeter exchanged a look, clearly unconvinced.

"Are you sure, daughter?"

Hera asked, "Can you recall what you ate while in Hades' home?"

Images, too painful to recall, too painful to ignore, filled her head and her heart. She stared at her hands again. Her knuckles were white, her fingers bloodless. She wiped her hands over her knees, under the guise of smoothing her skirts. When she looked up,

Aphrodite's blue eyes were full of tears.

Persephone felt her nerves rise up, and tore her gaze from Aphrodite.

"Nectar," the word spilled from her lips. "And ambrosia... Nothing else."

Demeter sighed, her face overcome with relief. She clasped her hands to her bosom, smiling at Hera. "I knew he would not..."

Athena shook her head, "Then why did you worry so? He's done nothing to cause such suspicion... ever."

"He avoids anything that might cause him upset," Aphrodite added. Why were her blue eyes so intent?

"Look at her," Hera argued. "Demeter has reason to worry..." Hera leaned forward, patting Persephone's knee. "Sorry, dear. I only mean that it is a relief to know you're not suffering from something more permanent."

"Permanent?"

"From the food..." Athena shook her head.

"The food grown in Hades realm can only be eaten by those that reside there," Hera explained.

"Oh, well." She nodded. The apple she'd picked, for Orphnaeus. The apple he'd knocked from her hands...

"If you'd eaten it..." Demeter shivered, taking her hands. "I'd not think on such a thing."

"You've no need to." Athena rolled her eyes. "Shall we walk? In the gardens?"

Persephone stood, eager to find some occupation. "Oh, yes, please."

Demeter patted her arm. "Then we shall walk."

"There, you see." Hera smiled and took Demeter's arm as she spoke. "You've no reason to worry on that front."

They walked on ahead, and Persephone found herself trailing behind.

"Can you blame? If it had been your Hebe, and not my Persephone... One bite would have ensured she was never free of the Underworld–"

"It matters not," Athena's impatience rang out. "She did *not*, not one bite. The Fates will *not* send her back... She is free. Enough. Let us enjoy the day with no more pointless worrying and carrying on."

Persephone could not breathe. The world was spinning. Her mind was spinning.

She felt an arm, soft yet solid, slide around her waist.

"Careful," Aphrodite murmured.

Persephone stared blindly, clinging to the Goddess. "But..." Her heart throbbed, as if some new wound had formed. "Why?"

If she'd had one bite, her fate, his fate, would have been sealed. The Fates would demand she return... As her heart demanded with its every beat.

"Men are foolish creatures, Persephone," Aphrodite murmured, a slight smile on her lips. "I will not force my confidence upon you. But I will hear your tale without judgment... If you choose to confide in me."

Persephone took short steps, unable to ease her grip on the Goddess.

"For now," Aphrodite said squeezing Persephone's hand, "Savor the warmth of the sun on this glorious day. Speak to your plants, see them grow and bloom. Love them as they love you."

She nodded, descending the steps into the most bountiful garden she'd ever seen. Her hands reached out, trailing along their plump leaves and making them rise and stretch. She watched, unable to ignore the throbbing ache in her heart. She had so much love to give. If he did not want her, she would find something, or someone, that did.

❖❖

The mouth of the cave roared with fire brought from Tartarus. The Erinyes had been pleased to help Hades. New souls were all the enticement they needed. These souls were bound for Tartarus, for torture.

"No one leaves," he yelled to Cerberus, Thanatos, the Erinyes, Aeacus... All fought with him, to protect his realm.

The souls poured into the cave. From translucent shells to full bodied men, the souls of Erysichthon's army were ready for a fight. The fools did not know they were now trapped.

Behind them, the flames of Tartarus roared high, sealing the entrance and rolling over those souls bringing up the rear. Hades did not relish the look of surprise, of terror, that gripped those caught within the flames. They could feel it, the burning and pain. They'd not known the truth. Death would not end their suffering, there would be no reprieve. Such agony was their fate now, one they would never escape.

He doubted they'd known what Erysichthon had brought upon them. If they had, this pathetic attempt at revolution would never have happened.

And yet, it was happening. And he had no more time to think.

A soldier, now the echo of his mortal form, came at him. Hades waited, the rise and fall of light within the cave his ally. As the light surged, he grabbed the weightless soul. In his hold, the soul moved, swinging his sword and kicking out at Hades. He felt a moment's sadness, for the man's eyes were filled with understanding.

It was all for naught. They would not bring the Underworld down. And Hades would not be merciful.

An Erinyes swooped, her talon-like fingers plucking the shade from Hades' grasp and carrying it below.

Another was on him. A fist, solid and heavy, slammed into his side. He turned, but the shade weakened and faded. With every leap of flame, its light filled the cave. Its heat devoured everything in its path.

The soul stood, knowing it was trapped. It gaped at Hades then turned, running for dark. But Cerberus was faster, and leapt, shredding the soul with poisoned teeth and dragging it to the flames.

Before Hades turned, he felt the sear of the blade slicing through his forearm. He winced, but welcomed the pain. His hand gripped the soul's wrist, forcing it to release the weapon.

"Hades." Hermes was at his side, pulling the sword from his arm.

"Behind you," Hades warned, pushing Hermes aside.

An Erinye reached the soul, lifting it into the air. The soul's screams echoed eerily in the cave. But it was the gleeful laughter of the Erinye that sent a ripple of disquiet along Hades spine.

Hades nodded towards the door. "It is sealed?"

"I've seen no one... no soul escape," Hermes assured him.

The flames crept higher, licking the top of the cave. None would escape.

"We have won. But Poseidon must bring the rain soon," Hermes spoke softly.

Hades forgot the soul he gripped, his rage was so great. He knew the risks of trusting his brother. But he'd thought, with such stakes at risk, even Poseidon might honor duty.

I am a bloody fool. His mouth twisted sharply as he hissed, "Poseidon..."

"No harm has been done beyond your realm..."

He shook his head. "Not yet." His eyes narrowed, searching the cave for what he knew he wouldn't find. "Erysichthon?"

Hermes shook his head. "I've not seen him. Apollo swears he was not with his men."

"What?" the soul gasped.

Hades looked at the man. "He left you once, to a less noble foe. It surprises you he would do so now?"

The soul stared at him, defeat lining his features. Hades would not grieve for it.

"Minos," he called, thrusting the soul into his judge's hands.

He left Hermes' side, tracing the light to capture what few souls remained. As the roar of the flames died down, the Erinyes joined him. They spared no time plucking those that clung to the cave walls. The flap of their wings, the cackle of their delight accompanied the screams of men, men no more.

None would leave; he'd declared it. It would be so.

He drew in a steadying breath, his nostrils filled with a strange scent.

"Rain." Hermes returned to him, smiling broadly. He clapped Hades on the shoulder.

The cave rumbled, thunder echoing inside the chamber as sheets of rain fell heavily upon the smoldering grass. He'd done it; Poseidon had kept his word. None of Greece would fall prey to today's conflict. No mortal would ever know...

Hades drew in a deep breath, his relief overpowering him. He would see no more suffer this day.

"Erysichthon was not amongst them," Aeacus said as he joined them.

Hades knew as much. The great king had sacrificed his men for some purpose. He had no doubt Erysichthon was far from finished with him… And Persephone. Anger faded, but his fear remained.

"I shall tell Ares." Hermes was in a good humor. "He'll enjoy such sport."

Hades nodded.

Aeacus waited, his face troubled.

"Speak, Aeacus."

He cleared his throat. "If Erysichthon is not amongst them… Is she not still in danger?"

"He will join them soon enough," Hades answered. "And she remains on Olympus. Safe."

He met Aeacus' gaze, willing himself rigid. Forcing himself to believe the words that he said.

The cave rumbled again, the floor pooling with muddy water. He sighed, staring out into downpour.

"It will serve Greece well," Aeacus murmured as he watched the rain. "'Tis a sadness, to see our country turned so brown and brittle."

Hades held his tongue. He knew that Poseidon sought to prove a point, not to help restore Greece's crops and fields. If, however, his actions aided their people in some small way, he would not rise to the bait Poseidon thought to taunt him with.

"Yes," he agreed, then headed to the cave's entrance.

Ares, Apollo and Hermes stood, their heads bent as they gathered beneath the shelter of overhanging rocks.

"A fine day," Apollo said, flashing his golden smile.

Hades nodded. "My thanks."

Ares shrugged. "I prefer fighting to herding, Hades."

Hades laughed.

A silence fell. Even the storm stopped.

He'd laughed.

They stared at him, each more astounded than the last. Where Hermes smiled, Apollo gaped. Ares' cold gray eyes narrowed, his brows furrowing deeply. The silence held until Apollo asked, "What of Erysichthon?"

"He will come for me." Once he'd spoken the words, he knew them to be true.

They looked at him again.

Apollo shook his head. "He cannot defeat you."

Ares shifted restlessly, as was his way, but his eyes remained fixed upon Hades.

Hermes rubbed a hand over his face. "Not tonight, surely."

Hades peered out of the cave. The rain had chilled the air, leaving the sky thick with clouds. The sliver of the moon that hung low in the sky cast almost no light.

Yes, tonight.

"No, not tonight," he agreed.

It took little encouragement to send them on their way. Apollo and Hermes were eager to return to Olympus to share the day's events. But Ares lingered, turning his stony gaze upon Hades.

"You're ready then?" he asked.

Hades did not pretend to misunderstand him. He nodded.

Ares' eyes narrowed. "He cannot kill you, he knows that. But he would see you suffer, dearly, I think."

Hades nodded.

He bid Ares farewell. In the darkness their auras shone brightly. Apollo, golden. Hermes, yellow, and Ares, red.

He removed his tunic, leaving the cave and scaling the mountain face to wait.

Erysichthon had watched closely.

It took one touch. Once in Hades' hold, they fell. Not once, but twice, these men had tasted defeat. For him. And he would not let their sacrifice be in vain. He would see this thing through, and be successful.

The night was black. No wind stirred the trees or lifted the shadows.

He was strong. He was ready.

Three spears, tipped with poisoned barbs, were strapped to his back.

He watched them leave, heard the boasts and jokes of Apollo and Hermes. Heard the bark of Ares as they left.

And when they were gone, he saw Hades remove his tunic and climb, with no shield or clothing, to the top of the mountain.

It galled him. Did the God think he needed no protection? Did he doubt Erysichthon's prowess, his power?

He smiled, slipping through the trees.

Each footfall sounded, the squish of mud, the snap of trees. But Hades did not turn. He stood, alert and ready.

Erysichthon ran, darting about his foe to flank him. He waited, pressing himself flat against the tree. Why did he not move?

"Why do you hesitate?" Hades called out.

Erysichthon tensed, then circled closer. He could see Hades' face now, but there was no fear. Not yet.

Hades' voice was cold, hard. "Did you send them all to me knowing they would fall?"

He would not be baited. Not now, when he was so close.

Hades' eyes narrowed, searching the dark. But Erysichthon knew he had the advantage.

He slipped the spears free, careful of his every movement. He gripped the spear, steadied the shaft, and aimed in silence.

"What do you hope to gain? You are no immortal, Erysichthon. No God..."

The spear flew true, piercing through Hades' right shoulder and driving deep into the tree behind him.

Hades attempted to step forward, his teeth bared as the shaft of the spear jarred.

Erysichthon gripped another spear, took aim and released it. The spear sailed, ripping through Hades' left side and slamming him into the tree.

"What do I hope to gain?" He left the cover of the trees, using the last spear as a walking stick. "Pain. Your pain."

Hades' face was covered in sweat, the heavy muscles of his chest rising and falling rapidly. "You have it. Are you satisfied now?"

Erysichthon stopped, a low chuckle escaping him. "It's a pity that bravery is your only strength. How would this satisfy me? How would this–" he gripped the spear that split Hades' side– "satisfy me?" He pushed the spear, forcing the wood ever deeper into Hades' pale flesh.

Blood flowed, pouring from his chest and hip to stream down his leg.

"But I know what will." He stepped back, realizing he lingered too closely to Hades. He could not indulge his ego so, or he would be lost to Tartarus as his men were. And this time he knew what their reception of him would be.

Hades' eyes were black when he opened them. "Tell me. So that we might end this conflict."

Erysichthon smiled, shaking his head. "Why would I wish such a thing? You are immortal. These wounds will heal, though I fear the poison may linger for some time yet."

Hades glared at him, gripping the spear at his shoulder.

"They're Persian." He smiled. "A nasty adversary, barbing their arrows and spears. It will not be easy, pulling free. You'll see the spear shaft widens, either way will be most uncomfortable. I looked for a sword, with their serrated blades. But seeing you today, I knew the only weapons I might use against you required distance."

"Your cowardice is surprising." Hades' voice betrayed little.

Damn you, I will make you suffer.

Hades continued, "You were once a great warrior. A generous king..."

"Once, but no more. Now I have but one purpose. Making you suffer." He paused. "Not with spears or arrows or swords, but through your heart. I will find her. And I will take her..."

He'd expected Hades to fight, expected him to hurl curses and threats upon him. But he had not anticipated the fury his words would unleash within Hades. Hades was not possessed of inordinate strength, yet he managed to pull the spear in his side free. And as he did so, the night rang with the barbarous growl that tore from deep inside.

Erysichthon stepped back, smiling. "And you cannot stop me."

Hades pulled, his hands slipping along the bloodied shaft that refused to release him from the tree. "I will..."

Footfalls reached Erysichthon. They were no longer alone. And while he'd planned to savor his last spear, his time was up. He smiled, disappearing into the trees as he promised, "When she visits her flowers, sings to her trees, tells her stories, or sleeps in her bed... I will be with her. And, when the time is right, I will claim her. She is mine. Persephone is mine."

He stood within the cover of the trees, a satisfied smile upon his face.

Hades jerked and pulled, but he'd driven the point through the tree, pinioning the Lord of Death in place. But his pathetic attempts to free himself were weakening, and the venom that coated the spear tips began to take effect. If not for the arrival of Ares, who stood staring at Hades in apparent disbelief, he would have laughed out loud at the tremors that overtook Hades. Instead, he enjoyed the view from the safety of the dark forest, savoring every trickle of blood that ran from Hades' failing body.

Chapter Twenty

"*This* is ready?" Ares' voice reached him though his ears throbbed. No, it was not just his ears... His head, his body... Something was not right. He lifted his head, narrowing his eyes to focus. Ares stood, assessing him without sympathy. "You are no warrior, Hades."

He drew in an unsteady breath. "I never claimed to be."

"I will take her..." Erysichthon's words echoed in his ears.

Ares took four long steps, wiped the blood from the shaft of the spear and gripped it in both hands. "This will hurt."

He could endure this pain, but Erysichthon's threats... He must protect her.

"Hades?" Ares' stare was hard.

Hades nodded. Ares pulled, making the spear shift in Hades' shoulder. The shaft bounced off his collarbone, unleashing nauseating pain. He glared at Ares as the sensations choked him.

"Yell, Hades. Even the bravest fighters do," Ares encouraged, gritting his teeth as he jerked and twisted the spear. It would not give. Ares sighed, circling Hades. "It's sunk too deep to remove. I'll need to break the staff."

He could scarce breathe, but forced the words out. "Do it."

Hades heard Ares' sword slide from its scabbard. The blow was fast, freeing him with one swipe. He swayed, no longer held up but no less skewered. He stared at his chest, placing his unsteady hands upon the shaft and pulling it from his shoulder. He did not stop the groan that ripped from him, for the splintered end of the spear sliced its way through the open wound. His chest was blanketed in his own hot blood, the iron smell sharp in his nostrils.

He leaned back heavily against the tree. The spear fell from his trembling hand, spraying a fine mist of blood upon his feet as it landed on the dirt at his side. He stared at his hand. Was it his hand that shook, or the throbbing within his eyes that made them appear to shake?

"Well?" Ares asked.

Hades spat out the blood filling his mouth. "Well..."

"Explain yourself."

Each breath seemed thinner, while his body grew hot and heavy. "He watched the day's battle. He stayed outside my reach..."

Ares laughed. "He is clever, learning your weakness and using it against you."

His weakness... How had Erysichthon learned of his real weakness? *"When she visits her flowers, sings to her trees, tells her stories, or sleeps in her bed... I will be with her. And, when the time is right, I will claim her. She is mine. Persephone is mine."*

Hades tried to move, tried to push himself up, but he fell back. He rested his head against the tree trunk, feeling trapped within his traitorous body. His blood boiled within him, scalding his insides with each pump of his heart. "He is..."

"He tipped the spears in poison. I know the smell well enough." He heard Ares sigh. "Fever will find you..."

He glanced at Ares. Erysichthon had said as much. He'd said a great many things... "Poison?"

"Your wounds will turn putrid. You'll need attention." Ares stooped at his side, placing a thickly muscled arm about his waist. The God of War spoke gruffly, hauling him to his feet, "Lean on me or fall flat. It makes no difference to me."

Hades laughed softly, his throat convulsing. He coughed, hungrily pulled in air, and then spit more blood from his mouth, weakly offering, "My thanks." He gripped Ares' waist, willing himself to stand erect even though it pulled at his injuries. "But you must go on to Olympus. I will manage..."

"You will manage?" Ares shook his head. "My hearing is as sharp as my sword, Hades."

"Then you know we must get word to Olympus," he hissed in

pain.

Ares retorted, "Send your hounds if you must. None face danger on *Olympus.*"

Hades would argue, but knew there was no help for it. He could not force Ares to action. He lifted his foot, to step forward, but his leg began to spasm and shake.

Ares snorted as his iron-like arm wrapped about him, dragging him along.

It took time, for each step jarred the gaping wounds. The pounding intensified, the pain rising in steady waves of heat. When Hades could bear it no more, he stopped, retching blood and bile.

"You will manage?" Ares asked gruffly, mocking him.

Hades lifted his head to glare at Ares, but the sudden movement sent the world spinning.

"Ah," Ares voice rumbled in his ear. "Damn fool..."

Hades agreed. He was a fool.

Blackness swirled when he tried to stand, but Ares' arm supported him once more. He had no time for weakness, no time for distractions.

Ares moved quickly, all but dragging him along the narrow path to the cave below. He was thankful Ares had come back, even if the God of War rejected the threat to Olympus.

Each step took effort. His blood flowed freely, running down his chest and legs and sapping his energy. He was weakening quickly... almost too weak to breathe.

He was helpless when she needed him.

And then they were standing before the cave. He released Ares, leaning against the rocks to stand. Could he make it to Olympus?

"Good," Ares said, sounded winded.

Hades turned, his vision blurring. He blinked as Apollo's handsome features came slowly into focus.

"Hades?" Apollo stared at Hades' wounds.

"A trap," Ares explained. "Punctured, twice. Both poisoned."

"How did a noble king become such a cowardly villain?" Hades heard the disgust in Apollo's words, but all he heard became distant and muffled. Erysichthon had used a most effective serum indeed. No, he would not make the journey to Olympus. He must rely on them, then.

"Hermes?" Hades managed, the faintest whisper.

"What?" Apollo asked, his voice moving closer.

Ares sighed loudly, complaining, "His blood stains *my* chest and yet he calls out for Hermes..."

"Hermes?" Apollo's voice was soft, reassuring. "He's gone on to Olympus."

Ares spat out the words, his disdain evident. "Erysichthon threatened Olympus. He would see Hermes deliver a warning."

Apollo laughed. "Would that he reaches Olympus soon, Hades. Athena was most affronted to be kept from the fight. Let her vent her frustration on the arrogant soul and see how quickly he comes running to your realm."

Hades heard Apollo, heard the ring of their laughter, but the sound grew distant. His eyelids drooped, shutting away the hazy images. He could not open his eyes, he could not speak. But Apollo's words were a comfort. Athena would offer some resistance. She was most fearsome when angered.

"Hades?" He heard Apollo but could not answer him. Apollo's next words were a whisper. "The fever?"

Ares grunted, but said no more.

"I shall fetch Aeacus," Apollo offered, the sound of his footsteps fading.

He would rest for a moment, no longer. He was no use to her now, burning from the poison. An image of her, smiling at him atop the black furs of his bed, found him. He sighed, clinging to that image until the fever forced his mind into blackness.

Time had stopped, or so it seemed. Every day was like the one before it, with little of note or consequence.

Each night Persephone slept on her white furs and finely sewn blankets, dreaming of him. Each morning she'd risen with the sun, grief-stricken when sleep refused to linger just a moment longer... And once again she was without him. And his absence weighed upon her most heavily.

But for her mother's sake she dressed and smiled. They would visit the Council Chamber together and she would attempt to listen to matters discussed there, she must. She was a Goddess. She must act as one.

And this time, when she sat at her mother's side, she would not stare at his throne.

She'd known it was his even though she'd never seen him in it. And she knew better than to ask. But she didn't have to ask. It sat, imposing and black, out of place amongst the muted tones of the Council Chamber. Just as he did.

As they drew close to the Chamber, Demeter's hand tightened on her forearm. Persephone forced a smile, hoping it would ease her mother, for it did not ease her. Demeter's brow dipped ever so slightly, but she said nothing. Instead she patted Persephone's arm.

Voices spilled into the hallway, echoing off the walls of the Council Chamber within.

"They're back," her mother said, smiling more brightly.

This time Persephone would not have to work so hard to find her smile. With Hermes returned, she might not feel so alone, so out of place.

Apollo, Ares, Hermes... they'd been gone since she arrived. And while she had no opinion of Apollo, she feared Ares more than a little. She had missed Hermes, but was wary of him now. She did not want to speak of Hades. While all on Olympus assumed Hermes indifferent to Hades, Persephone knew the truth. And she knew she was not strong enough to hear news of Hades, missing her not at all.

Her mother's pace quickened as they entered the Chamber, but Persephone held back. Her mother released her then, moving to greet the returned Gods with warmth and sincerity.

Persephone's heart hardened. Of course he would not be here. She was foolish to hope... She'd not known she'd hoped. She wrapped her arms about her waist.

She circled the room, absentmindedly making her way to the place she sat on the opposite side of the chamber. Her fingers moved over the marble, the fervor of conversation eventually reaching her.

"He is free, then?" Her mother's frightened voice drew her attention.

"Peace, Demeter," Zeus soothed. "A shade can do no harm to her."

"We live in the light," Hera agreed.

Persephone saw Hermes look at her, but she turned from him.

If she looked at him, if their eyes met, would he see the truth? He'd taken pains to hold his peace, but for how long? Hades' warning still rang in her ears. Trust was not a wise choice amongst the Olympians. She could not trust herself yet, she should not expect it from others. She continued slowly, eager to find her seat.

"And Hades?" Athena asked. "He is recovered?"

She froze. Recovered? She turned, searching out Hermes. He was waiting, his brow furrowed and his expression troubled.

"Tis a foul poison," Ares grumbled. "And Hades was a fool..."

Ares' gaze settled on her, narrowing. She met his gaze, narrowing her eyes alike. Hades was no fool.

"He's not meant for battle. He's too easily inflamed and distracted," the God of War continued, his gaze sweeping Persephone from head to toe.

She lifted her chin, refusing to be cowed by his brazen inspection. She reached her mother's throne then and leaned against it for support.

Poseidon laughed. "Inflamed?"

Apollo shrugged, casting a brief glance upon Poseidon. "So it would seem."

"But his wounds?" Aphrodite asked. "He was injured?"

Persephone gripped the throne back in front of her. Injured?

Ares nodded, his attention returning to the others. "Two spears." His fingers pressed against his hip. "Here..." His hand moved, pressing against his shoulder blade– "...and here. He was speared through, pinned to a tree when I came upon him."

She would not falter. She would not collapse.

"He pulled one free himself," Ares went on, "But I had to cut through the other."

She swayed, pressing her face to the cool marble throne.

"It would be no great matter," Apollo said with a shrug, "But Erysichthon tipped the spears with poison. From a viper. A nasty toxin, eating flesh and causing fever."

She clung to the chair, speaking without thought. "He will recover?"

All eyes turned to her.

Apollo smiled, his forehead crinkling as he did so. "He will recover."

She nodded, moving around the chair to sit. She stared at her hands, clasped tightly in her lap. She knew the others still watched, knew that she'd revealed too much. But she no longer cared. It was enough to know he would recover. She must find solace in that.

"And Erysichthon?" Demeter asked. "Surely there is a plan to rid ourselves of him?"

Persephone looked up.

Athena took a cup from the tray Hebe offered. "What need is there for any action, Demeter?"

"We would return to our home." Demeter glanced at Persephone with a smile.

Home. Persephone stared at her hands, willing her tears back. Did such a place exist for her now?

"In time–" Zeus began.

"Time?" Demeter interrupted. "I've lost enough time with my daughter. We are Goddesses of the earth, Zeus. We must return to it–"

"Demeter." Zeus' tone startled Persephone, the command sharp.

"Walk with me?" Hermes appeared at her side, smiling. He offered his hand. "The gardens?"

She swallowed, taking the hand with a slight nod.

"Have you not looked upon the grasses? The crops?" Demeter continued.

Apollo nodded. "Greece is brittle. Perhaps we should–"

The voices were lost to Persephone then, closed behind the doors of the Council Chamber.

"And how do you find Olympus?" Hermes asked.

"Odd," she answered. "White. Cold."

"Cold?" He laughed.

"Yes. Cold."

"But you can be no closer to the sun," he said, leading her into the gardens. "Unless you rode with Apollo in his chariot."

She shook her head. "I am cold."

Hermes stopped, tilting her chin up. "You have lost your smile."

She felt the prick of tears in her eyes. "I will find it again."

He sighed.

She shrugged, pulling gently from him to stroke the burgeoning bushes and vines.

"You've spent much time here?" Hermes laughed. "I've never seen it so abloom."

She nodded.

"It is an improvement," he continued.

"Tell me." She turned, ignoring the tears that rolled down her cheeks. "Tell me, honestly, that he is well, Hermes. My heart aches to know the truth."

Hermes took her hands in his. "He will be well."

How she wanted to believe him.

"Have you found no happiness here?" he asked.

She sighed. "I have tried…"

"But?"

"I miss him."

"Who?" Demeter's voice was soft. "Who do you miss, daughter? Tell me, so that I might help ease your sorrow."

Persephone spun. "Mother? I… I–"

"You thought you were alone with Hermes." She took Persephone's hands from him. "What does he know that I, your mother, do not?"

"I shall leave you," Hermes murmured, though neither Persephone nor her mother acknowledged him.

Persephone stared at her mother, considering her words. Would her mother understand? Had she ever felt such love? Or been rejected so completely? She trembled, whispering, "Hades. I miss Hades."

Demeter's brown eyes went round, her hands tightening. "Hades?"

Persephone nodded. "I love him."

Demeter continued to stare at her.

"But he does not love me," Persephone's words choked her. "He does not."

Demeter pulled her to one of the stone benches. No sooner had they sat than Demeter drew Persephone into an embrace.

"He knows little of love," Demeter's breath brushed her forehead. "If he did, I'm sure he would love you. None is more deserving than you, sweet child."

Persephone clung to her mother, crying in earnest. "It hurts, to be parted from him. I ache... ache for him. To see his smile, and hear his laughter. I can scarce breathe from the hole in my heart."

Demeter held Persephone pulled back, regarding her daughter with surprised eyes. "You have seen him smile? And laugh?"

Persephone nodded. "Many times."

"I thought he'd forgotten such things." Demeter's thoughtful gaze swept over her. "Did you give yourself to him?"

Persephone felt heat scalding her cheeks. Not from shame, she felt no shame in their joining, but from the memory. "Most happily."

Demeter drew in a deep breath, releasing it slowly. Persephone watched, regretting her words.

"I am sorry," Persephone began. "Not that I gave myself to him. I cannot and do not regret a moment of our time together. I am sorry that I kept it from you. But I feared your reaction... That he might be punished for such things."

"I can hardly punish him when you were willing." Demeter's smile was tight. "I can punish him for hurting you–"

Persephone shook her head. "No. You cannot. He told me," her voice wavered. "He told me he could not give me what I wanted. He held me at arm's length as long as he could. It was I that forced his hand, I that took what he would give. If you would punish anyone, punish me."

Demeter's hand cupped Persephone's face. "Oh, Persephone. There is nothing to punish, child. You found love. That is a gift."

Persephone allowed him to enter her thoughts, then. And with his memory, she found her smile.

Chapter Twenty One

Hades' gaze swept the meadows. How quickly the green had returned. The grasses waved, supple with life. Flowers bloomed and fruit hung heavily from the trees. All about him were signs of life.

Signs that she had returned to those that loved her – and needed her. As he needed her.

He offered silent apologies to the plants but did not slow his team as they reached the base of Olympus, tearing up the trail in his haste to reach the Council Chamber and Persephone.

He knew what he had to do. That he would humble himself before all. And he was ready to do so.

He leapt from the chariot and took the steps two at a time, entering the gleaming white hall and heading swiftly to the Council Chamber. He paused only long enough to draw in a fortifying breath, then pushed the doors wide.

She was not there.

Neither was Hermes. Or Apollo. But the rest of the Olympians regarded him.

"Hades?" Zeus stood, coming to greet him. "Tis a surprise to have you with us, brother. But I am pleased to see you recovered."

Hades clasped Zeus' forearm in his. "I am."

Zeus wore an odd expression. Amused or expectant, Hades could not be certain.

"You are most welcome." Hera smiled stiffly.

Hades nodded, but said nothing.

Zeus stepped back, encouraging Hades to take his seat.

None spoke as Hades moved towards it.

Hades hesitated. He stood tall and moved to Demeter.

She stared at him. "Hades."

"Demeter. I..." He paused. "You offered me a gift."

Her eyes narrowed. "I did. For you cared for my daughter, did you not?"

His throat tightened as he nodded. Would he be forced to do this in front of all?

Her eyebrows rose. "What do you want, Hades?"

"Yes," Poseidon laughed. "This should be interesting."

Hades turned and smiled at his brother.

Poseidon grew still, his face wary.

"I will tell you," Hades' voice rose. "So that there is no worry that what I want might be misunderstood. You will all hear, and know, so that none can claim ignorance."

Hades ignored the rest, turning back to Demeter. "I would have Persephone as my wife."

Her reaction startled him. There was no surprise, no anger, only the slightest tightening of her mouth.

"My Persephone?" she asked. "Tell me, Hades, are you the cause of all her tears?"

Demeter's words struck him. "I'd never meant to be."

"Wife?" Hera gasped. "But, but she's a Goddess of the earth. How can she go... there?"

"There is balance in life and death," Zeus spoke carefully. "One fuels the next. Does it not?"

Hades did not turn from Demeter.

"Will she have you?" Demeter asked.

He did not know. He'd hurt her, he knew that. He'd intended to, to force her from him. His plan might have worked too well. "I know not."

Her eyes narrowed. "I will not part with my daughter."

He sucked in a sharp breath. "I would not keep her from you."

"She is safest in his realm, Demeter." Ares' voice startled Hades.

"The Fates–" he began.

"You visited them?" Demeter's face was startled now.

He nodded. "I did. I would not enter into such an arrangement without knowing their mind. I've never betrayed their call for balance. I would not start now."

"And what did they say to such a union?" Hera asked softly.

"She is life, I am death. One balances the other. She cannot stay gone from her realm, nor I from mine. Her time would be divided, between her realm and mine—"

"Children?" Demeter asked. "In the Underworld?"

"There will be none." Hades swallowed. Of all the conditions the Fates had demanded, this was the harshest. "Any child of our union would be too powerful. A threat to many. So none will be born."

"You ask too much of her." Demeter's voice trembled.

He nodded. "But I ask it anyway." He turned then, coming to stand before Poseidon's throne. "I will watch over her. I will keep her from harm. And if Persephone agrees, you will remember who she belongs to."

Poseidon smiled. "If she is truly yours, I cannot take her from you."

Hades felt fury. "And you will not try. Whatever scheme or plot, ruse or mischief you devise. You will leave Persephone alone. Or I will see you suffer." Hades stared into his brother's pale blue eyes, his every word a promise. "I will make you crave death. I vow it."

Poseidon sat forward in his chair, his body stiffening with tension. "You forget yourself—"

"No, Poseidon." Hades didn't step back. "I've given you a choice. All here have heard it. What you choose to do with my vow, I can only wait and see."

"She will not choose you," Poseidon hissed.

Hades smiled.

Athena cleared her throat. "Well. I look forward to the future with great anticipation, Hades. You surprise me."

"He surprises us all," Hera said, then went on, "I think?"

Hades saw her glance at her husband. Zeus looked pleased. A little too pleased. Had his brother known? Hades sighed, making his way back to Demeter.

Her face was no longer remote. For the briefest moment, Hades saw Persephone in Demeter – vulnerable, yet strong. She looked away, shaking her head. "I cannot undo the damage you have done to her. She grieves–"

"She hardly eats," Athena agreed.

"We feared she was ill," Aphrodite added. "And she is, I think. Her heart suffers."

Hades clenched a fist, hating himself.

"I have much to think on," Demeter muttered. She frowned at Hades, then turned to Zeus. "What say you, Zeus? Are you in favor of this match? Would you give my only daughter to... Hades?"

Hades saw the smile on Zeus face, saw the immediate nod. "Most happily, Demeter. But she is yours to give. I leave the choice to you."

Demeter stood, looking up into Hades' face. Her voice was low. "I want nothing more than her happiness. Her smile is lost since you've returned her to me. I will be forever thankful to you for saving her from Erysichthon. But I will never forgive you for breaking her heart." Her eyes bore into his. "I will leave this choice to her. If you love her–"

"I love her." The words were a strangled whisper.

Demeter's face softened. "You do." Her hand touched his cheek. "But does she still love you?"

"There is still the matter of Erysichthon," Ares interrupted. "If your Persephone is willing to return to your realm, she will still have to travel from here to there. He will be waiting."

Athena nodded. "If he knows she belongs to Hades, he'll want her all the more. Isn't that right, Poseidon?"

Poseidon smirked, "How would you know what it is to be wanted by a man, Athena?"

"Have you a plan, Ares?" Hades asked. As much as he wanted Persephone to return, he would not risk her safety.

"I do," Demeter sighed. "If this, if *you*, are what she wants."

Persephone leaned against the tree, savoring the calm within her. She had missed much, and the spruce was eager to tell her all it had seen and heard. She was in no hurry, either, and savored each and every word.

Her fingers pressed against the slight gash on the tree's trunk.

"I'm pleased that you were spared." She pressed her cheek against the rough bark, sighing.

Too many great trees had been cut down for ships, spears, and makeshift camps for Grecian and Persian troops.

"How much longer?" Hermes asked her.

"It's not finished."

Hermes sighed. "The sun is setting, Persephone."

Her eyes flew to the horizon. When the sun slept, the light went with it. She had no desire to be found by Erysichthon. She pressed her hands upon the tree. "I must leave you. But I will come soon. Keep the rest of your stories 'til then?"

The tree wasn't happy with this, so she wrapped her arms about the trunk. "I missed you so. But never fear, I shall never be so long away from you again."

The tree was somewhat mollified. But its next question startled her.

"No," she whispered. "I didn't come here to get away from him."

The tree continued. Hades had ridden by, headed for Olympus...

"Today?" she asked. The tree answered quickly.

She swallowed, unable to deny the heaviness that flooded her chest. "Hermes?" She turned, placing a hand upon his arm. "Why would Hades go to Olympus?"

Hermes had been watching Persephone's nymphs with wide-eyed interest. "What?" he asked.

"Why would Hades travel to Olympus?"

"Today?" He shook his head. "I know of no cause."

"None have summoned him?" She knew her mother would not do such a thing. Surely not.

Hermes shook his head again. "Why?"

"The tree says he passed by, headed for Olympus." She glanced toward the distant mountain.

"Did it?"

She nodded. "I'm glad I'm here, then."

Hermes sighed, loudly. "Why? You don't ask after him, or speak of him. You don't want to see–"

"No," she spoke quickly, scowling at him. "Why would I want to see him? Why would I want to be reminded of such joy, only to know it was gone forever?" She blinked back tears before they could betray her. "I would not look on him. Not ever again." Her heart twisted at her own words, refuting every word she'd uttered.

He stared at her, then scanned the dimming sky. "I'm afraid we've no choice now. Come, let us return to Olympus."

She nodded, pure anticipation stealing her breath. She waved farewell to the nymphs and placing her arms about Hermes' neck. He carried them both, swift as the wind, to Olympus. When they arrived, the Council Chamber doors were closed. And still, she could hear yelling from inside.

Hermes set her down and moved to the door, but she stood back.

Hermes glanced at her. "Persephone?"

She shook her head. "I shall retire... I cannot face...." She did not finish, she could not. Instead she ran to her rooms, far from the Council Chamber and any hope of seeing him.

Was he here?

She picked up the comb Demeter had given her, brushing through the tangles in her long hair. It calmed her, busying herself. But once her braid was tied, her thoughts returned to him.

Time had passed, yet her heart held onto him. She did not draw breath without thinking of him. She did not dream without feeling his presence at her side. His voice, in memory, was sweeter than any she'd heard. And she did not want to be without him. She knew what she must do... but was she brave enough?

"*Be brave, Persephone.*" His words brushed over her.

She stared at her reflection. "I will," she murmured. In no time, she'd tied her heavy white cloak, filled its pockets with apples, and crept from her room, down the hall, past the doors of the Council Chamber and down the steps of the mighty Temple.

Night was quickly falling, but she could not wait.

There was no sign of Hades' chariot in the fields. The horses that came to meet her were tawny and sleek. Apollo's steeds perhaps? She raised a hand up, offering an apple. As the horse chewed its second apple, she pulled herself onto its broad back. She gripped its wheaten mane and nudged its side, remembering all that Hades had taught her. The horse responded, setting a brisk pace as they descended the mountain path.

The plains greeted her, stretching without end. The sun's rays retreated, stretching long fingers of black and gray in their wake.

She squeezed the horse with her knees and tangled her hands in his mane. The horse quickened its pace, flying so swiftly that Persephone bent low over his shoulder. Her hood blew back and pulled her hair free from its braid. She looked to the light, following its path as they raced across the plains.

The tall grasses whispered to her, welcoming her as they brushed against her calves. The sun was gone, blocked by the towering trees that edged the plain. Patches of light dappled the plains, but not enough. She would not reach the rocks, or his cave, before darkness reached her.

Still she tried, tugging the horse towards each break in the dark. Until there were none.

The grasses faded, kissed by neither sun nor moon. She looked up into the blackening sky. While the stars had begun to sparkle and dance, the moon would clearly be of no help. The slightest sliver, the thinnest crescent moon, offered no protection on her journey.

The rocks rose up ahead. Their jagged peaks offered her no menace, only comfort. His cave, her home, was close now.

And then all fell silent. The grass hushed. No bird or owl called out. Nothing but the whistle of the wind against her face.

She felt a rush of cold upon her back, and closed her eyes against it. She had no reason to feel fear. She was so close.

The horse shied, pulling against her and rising on his hind legs. She clung to the animal, whispering frantically, "Shhh, there's nothing to fear here. I promise. Help me. Help me, and I will free you soon enough."

The animal danced sideways, flicking his ears back again and again. She stiffened, and glanced back – knowing she shouldn't.

In the creeping gloom that followed, she felt him – Erysichthon. But she could not see him.

She nudged the animal, pleading with it to hurry.

The horse bolted, tearing forward and knocking her back. Her hands flailed, snatching at the horse's mane before she was knocked off.

Closer, so close she could see the cave.

The horse reared once more, managing to toss her from its back. She fell, landing heavily and knocking the breath from her lungs.

"You should be careful," Erysichthon's voice caused her to shudder.

She sucked in breath and rolled, ignoring the ache in her side and the tear of her tunic. She did not look at him, but pushed herself up and forward, to the cave.

His hand grabbed her cape, twisting the hood and jerking her sharply back. The strings, tied securely, dug into her neck and pinched her throat. She pulled back, yanking the tie and releasing her from the cape. She ran, frantically, to the mouth of the cave. With one step she was inside, her tunic grabbed by three sets of pointed teeth and drug to safety.

She fell to her back, her head smacking the stone floor before she could catch herself. Pain and fear found her, dredging up memories of the last time she lay – unprotected – at Erysichthon's feet. She swallowed back her panic. She was not alone.

She heard a whimper, then the tell-tale rumble of Cerberus' roar. Even with the beast before her, white teeth bared and spiked tail thrashing, she felt no fear. Cerberus would protect her. She knew it and took comfort in it.

Two sets of blazing red eyes tracked Erysichthon's every move, their growl reverberating through the cave. There was no mistaking their warning. She suspected Cerberus longed to drag Erysichthon straight to Tartarus. But her presence stopped them. They would protect her first.

She stood, the throb of her head making her wince. She lifted her hand, finding the knot her fall had formed. She drew her hand away, aware that her fingertips were wet.

"If only you would accept your place with me, Persephone. Such injuries would not occur." His voice was soft, soothing.

Cerberus stepped forward. Their serpent mane roiled and hissed, their tail whipped suddenly, snapping in the air.

"I prefer a bloodied head to falling captive to you again," she answered. She stepped back, further into the cave – further from Erysichthon.

"In time, you will come to accept me. You will see." Erysichthon laughed. "I bid you good evening, Persephone."

She waited until he'd faded into the darkness. When he was

gone, Cerberus circled her, pressing her deeper into the cave with alternating growls and whimpers. She nodded, stroking each head in turn. "I know," she whispered. "Lead me to the orchard in Asphodel. I would eat before I go to your master."

Chapter Twenty Two

Hades wiped his face on his cloak. His skin was heated from the tunnels, covered with sweat and sulfur, rock and dirt. He ran the cloth over his arms, then tossed it onto the ground. It had done him good, chipping away at the catacombs of Tartarus. It had helped the day pass without his every thought wandering to her. And now, the bracing winds of Asphodel brushed over him, easing the weary ache of his muscles. If not the longing in his heart.

He thought it was a trick of the wind, at first.

But a voice reached him, a whisper upon the wind. A slight growl, then a muffled bark followed. Why were the hounds here? Why was Cerberus not guarding the cave?

He crept forward, his irritation rising. He was not the only one battling restlessness, then.

He walked on, welcoming the exhaustion. Perhaps he would sleep tonight. His eyes followed the path of the sun, long since gone in the mortal world, as it began to lower in the skies of the Underworld.

"I have it," a voice, one more dear than any other, reached him.

He froze, his eyes searching. Was she here? Or had he finally succumbed to madness?

"Thank you," she spoke softly. "I'm sure it is most delicious." She sighed then, sounding forlorn.

She was a flash of white, glimpsed between the closely grown trees. She took one step from the trees, turned in a circle, then slipped amongst them once more.

He hurried then. Was she here? In the orchard? "Persephone?" he called out to her.

She did not answer.

He ducked beneath a low lying branch, all the while searching for her white tunic.

He saw her then, moving away from him.

"Persephone?" Why did she run?

She stopped suddenly. He did not; she was too far from him. When he could reach her, she turned to him. Her eyes were green in the milky sunlight, fixing on him with an intensity that made him pause. She swallowed forcefully, her hands gripping the sides of her tunic.

Her tunic.

He stepped forward, inspecting her. Her tunic was torn and dirty. His eyes lingered on the red line upon her neck, the drops of blood upon her shoulder. "What happened?" he asked, his voice rough.

She blinked, her forehead furrowing.

He reached for her, clasping her upper arms in a loose hold. He stifled the sigh that rose from within. How he'd missed touching her. "Persephone?"

"I am well, Hades." She shook her head, brushing his hands from her. "No... No I'm not. You have made me... angry."

He could not help the smile that touched his lips. Angry or no, she was here, speaking his name.

"Angry?" he asked, moving closer to her.

She scowled and stepped back. "Yes... very angry."

"You came here? To tell me that?" He brushed her hair from her shoulders, caressing the curls slowly.

She nodded, her eyes upon his mouth. "You gave me up."

His hand stilled, the hurt in her words more than he could bear. He had betrayed her time and again. And yet she was here. She was here.

"You left me," she whispered.

He shook his head. "To protect you."

Her face softened for an instant before she scowled again. "No, to protect you."

Again, there was truth to her words.

"But I realized I was not as helpless as I thought. I have a say in this." She stepped closer, her eyes flashing. "And I say you are wrong. You've no reason to harden your heart against me. No reason to turn away from the happiness that comes when we're together. No matter how you would deny it, I know you care for me. I know I make you happy. And that, Hades, is why I am here."

He shook his head, confused. But she spoke before he could.

"You cannot send me away now." She held up her hand, the sweet smell of ripe fruit filling his nostrils.

He tore his eyes from hers and stared at her hand. A half eaten pomegranate lay upon her palm.

"What have you done?" he whispered. His hands gripped her shoulders, dragging her against his chest. He was torn between shaking her and kissing her. Did she realize the consequences?

"You cannot make me go back." She lifted her chin and met his gaze.

"You are trapped," he whispered, his joy overshadowed. His arrangement with the Fates had been determined by Persephone's choice. He'd never meant for it to be permanent. When she'd tired of him, as he knew she would, he would ensure she was not beholden to him or bound to his realm. But now, now... "Why, Persephone? Why would you do this?"

"Because I love you." Her voice broke. "And though I tried every day not to think of you or look for you... or miss you, I accept my fate. I cannot *be* without you." Her sweet words hung in the air, demanding his response. "So I will not."

He crushed her against him, her last words muffled against his chest. Burying his nose in her hair, he drew her scent deep within him. He could not deny his happiness, as misplaced as it was. "You act rashly..."

"No. Not rashly." Her breath brushed across his chest, her silken arms wound about his bare back. "Desperately, perhaps."

She did not know of his visit, that much was obvious. Would she regret her actions once she learned there was another way? One that would have afforded her freedom when she wanted it? He spoke softly, "I visited Olympus today–"

"And did not stay to see me." Her hurt was obvious.

"I was told to leave," he continued, "After I'd spoken with your mother."

She looked up at him. "My mother?"

He spoke quickly, willing himself to voice all that he'd fought so long to keep from her. "I missed you," he murmured. "Desperately. After I'd gained the Fates' approval, I sought Demeter's blessing–"

She silenced him, most effectively. With a startled gasp, she tangled her fingers in his hair and pulled his face, his lips, to hers. He would not fight her. And her lips... He shivered. Her mouth parted, catching his moan. His hands slid from her arms, caressing the line of her back, the flare of her waist, beneath the softness of her tunic. It was then that he felt the ripped hem. What had happened to her?

Her lips lifted from his, allowing him to draw in a ragged breath. But the question was lost. Her smile overwhelmed him once more. She expressed, openly, the joy that so completely filled him.

"I knew it," she spoke clearly, still smiling.

"Yes," he nodded, letting his eyes look their fill. His voice was rough, heavy with emotion. "You did."

Her hands cupped his face and she sighed. "All will be well."

"You have such faith," he whispered.

"As do you," she paused. "You bargained with the Fates..."

His hands covered hers. "A bargain I will have to revisit."

"Why?" her smile did not fade.

"That was not part of the bargain," he pointed at the fruit, fallen on the ground at their feet. "I'd meant for you to keep your freedom..."

She sighed, shaking her head.

He continued. "You were to have a choice, to come and go as you pleased. But now..." he scowled at the fruit. He could not bring himself to scowl at her.

"This is my choice," her voice hitched. "There is nothing I want more... than to be with you."

"Truly?"

She nodded. "Nothing, Hades. It is no passing fancy. My heart is yours."

He turned, pressing a kiss against her palm. His heart was all too willing to accept her words as truth. It would take time for the rest of him to believe as well. He glanced at the fruit. Time they had.

"There is balance between us," she added, drawing his attention back her.

"Oh?" His fingers traced the line of her jaw, then her neck. He smoothed a heavy curl from her shoulder, savoring every touch. "Balance?"

"You've my heart and you... I..." she swallowed then, uncertain.

He nodded. "And you have mine."

She smiled, her eyes closing for a moment before she sighed happily. "Yes."

He shook his head, astounded. He was blessed above all Gods. And he would do whatever the Fates asked of him to keep her with him. "I must make them understand what's happened."

"And what has happened?" she waited.

His eyebrow rose. "You've come home."

She nodded, pressing herself against him once more. "Yes, I am home."

Epilogue

"You must learn patience." Demeter smoothed the long white veils over Persephone's braid. "He has waited these six months, I see no reason for your agitation now that you're about..." She sniffed, once, then twice.

"Mother," Persephone soothed, pulling Demeter into her embrace. "And I shall return to you in six months more." Her heart felt heavier at the thought. No, not now. Not yet. She would not worry over the goodbyes when she'd yet to say hello to him.

Demeter nodded. "It is foolish of me, I know. For I have what I've wanted. I know you are safe with Hades. But you are so... so..."

Persephone sighed and hugged her mother to her once more. "You must not forget the plants while I'm away, Mother. They may sleep through my absence, but keep them living – I entreat you."

Demeter nodded. "Yes, yes."

"It's time." Aphrodite peered around the door.

Persephone smiled at her. "I'll be there in a moment."

Aphrodite smiled, but there was a sadness in her eyes that Persephone was all too familiar with. Something troubled her new friend, the Goddess of Love–

"You look lovely," Demeter interrupted her thoughts. "Today I give away my daughter and gain a son."

Happiness settled upon Persephone, warm and strong. She did not let her mother dally any longer, but took Demeter's hand and led them to the Council Chamber.

He stood, swathed in gray silk. He cut a regal figure, handsome and tall. So handsome that she released her mother's hand and ran to him. His smile greeted her before she tangled her arms about him and demanded a kiss.

"Well," Hermes laughed. "It would seem she has no resistance to the union."

Apollo laughed heartily. "Would that all women greet their men in such a fashion."

"Truly, Persephone," Hera chided her. "Remember who you are."

His lips lifted from hers then, making her fingers tighten upon the front folds of his tunic.

"She remembers well enough," Hades words were soft, amused.

Persephone smiled at him, taking his hand in both of hers.

"Come." Zeus waved them forward, holding a single golden coronet in his hand. He lifted it, placing it upon Hades' head, then her own. It was the lightest touch, yet it marked them as partners before Olympus.

"Go now, before the sun sets." Demeter hugged her daughter. "And remember the ritual that will bring you home. These ceremonies, the Eleusian Mysteries, will keep you safe and with us."

Persephone nodded. "I will not forget. I promise you."

Hera's words were praising, and faintly envious, "The city Eleusis honors you greatly, Demeter. That they place their daughters in harm's way, to ensure Persephone's safe crossing, knowing Erysichthon waits–"

Hades' hand was warm about her. "I will not rest until Erysichthon is a threat no longer. Thanatos has seen him. The hounds hunt him still."

Demeter shook her head. "They are a good people, and cared for me well while I grieved for you, Persephone. They do no more than I. If their Goddess must risk her daughter for a fruitful harvest, they will do the same. It is the will of the Fates, is it not? If they require such dramatics for their cursed balance, I can scarce deny them." She paused. "Nor could I deny the desires of my daughter."

Aphrodite was quick to ease the worry Demeter's words raised. "You have no need to fear for them. They know what they do, and why. It is more than a harvest that brings these Mysteries into being.

It is your love. A love that leaves us all in awe." She met Persephone's eyes. "Besides, Ares is most desperate for battle. Perhaps these Eleusinian Mysteries will offer him a conquest?"

"It has been too quiet of late," Ares muttered. He glanced at Aphrodite, then Persephone, with an ever increasing scowl.

"Then I shall worry no more," Persephone smiled at Ares. "And thank you for keeping watch."

Hades' hand tightened about hers, the slightest pull revealing his impatience. She met his eyes, so blindingly blue she paused to gaze at him.

"Have you any more good-byes, Persephone?" Hades' words were soft, meant for her ears alone.

She shook her head, smiling up at him. "No, my lord. I'm done with good-byes for now."

"Come then," he lifted her hand, pressing a kiss atop her fingers.

She nodded. "Take me home, Hades."

Sasha Summers

Sasha is part gypsy. Her passions have always been storytelling, romance, history, and travel. Her first play was written for her Girl Scout troupe. She's been writing ever since. She loves getting lost in the worlds and characters she creates; even if she frequently forgets to run the dishwasher or wash socks when she's doing so. Luckily, her four brilliant children and hero-inspiring hubby are super understanding and supportive.

Sasha can be found online at sashasummers.com.

Acknowledgements

Thanks to Suzanne Clark and the 'Shakers' for your unwavering support.

To Stephanie Dray for loving Medusa, A Love Story enough to put her name on it.

To my parents – thank you for nurturing my dreams & teaching me to love stories of all kinds.

Sincere thanks to Candice Lindstrom for getting 'me' and my books, and wanting them to shine as much as I do!

Very special thanks to my little family: Shane, Summer, Emma, Jakob and Kaleb. You keep my roots firmly grounded while letting my imagination soar.

Glossary Terms & Reference Index

Chiton – men's tunic of lightweight fabric

Chlamys – a short cloak, worn by men and women, made from one seamless piece of material

Doru – a spear, 7-9 feet long, used by the Greek infantrymen

Ekdromos/Ekdromoi – skilled infantrymen used for special missions or close combat

Epiblema – a woman's shawl

Himation – thick cloak. Large enough to be used as a blanket or folded into a pillow

Hoplite – Greek infantrymen

Kline – a fainting couch or day bed used for social gatherings

Linothorax – armor worn by more military leaders or affluent soldiers. Made of thick padded leather, fabric covered in metal scales of metal – depending upon the soldier's ability to pay. Not all soldiers could afford armor.

Oikos – the household – not the house itself but the property, livestock, family and slaves

Peplos – a full length tunic worn by women, usually made from one large piece of fabric to be pinned, sewn or draped.

Peltasts & Psiloi – foot soldiers without extensive training

Shades – souls or ghosts

Strategoi – ten generals chosen from ten Greek tribes

Trireme – a ship, propelled by three rows of oars, possibly 25 or more oars, on each side.

Xiphos – soldier's short sword used as a secondary weapon to the spear/doru.

Levels of the Underworld

Elysium or Elysian Fields – reserved for heroes or special mortals, this was 'Heaven' to the Greeks.

Asphodel Fields – Most occupied level of the Underworld, it was neutral – shades that came here had neither good nor bad

Tartarus – Feared by all, this was 'Hell' to the Greeks.

Rivers into the Underworld

River Acheron – River of Woe

Lethe River – River of Forgetfulness

The River Styx – River of Hate

Pyriphlegethon – River of Fire

Cocytus River – River of Wailing

Myths Revisited in For the Love of Hades

The Abduction of Persephone – According to most myths, Hades was taking a chariot ride, spied Persephone, and could not resist himself. He kidnapped her, took her to the Underworld, and kept her there until she'd eaten food grown in the Underworld, preventing her from ever being able to return permanently to Earth & Olympus.

Erysichthon & Demeter's Sacred Grove – Erysichthon had nothing to do with Persephone, he was simply a king with an ego. He started chopping down Demeter's sacred grove (and killed a wood nymph in the process). Demeter appeared to warn him from his course of action, but he ignored her. His goal: to build the most amazing feasting hall in existence. So Demeter cursed him with insatiable hunger and he did end up selling his daughter and eating himself.

Cerberus – The three headed dog of Hades was never three separate hounds. His job was to guard the entrance to the Underworld. He had a fondness for human flesh and a nasty temper. He was on the list of Hercules' Twelve Labors and was carried from the Underworld by Hercules.

Sneak Peek: Eclipsing Apollo

The Loves of Olympus, 3

Apollo, do not desert me now. Guide me. Show me the way.

Apollo heard Coronis' prayer, though she uttered no words aloud. His curse was muffled for he knew his fate was sealed. Denying her was impossible. He glanced at the only woman who threatened everything he stood for. It would be easier to still the very blood in his veins than to turn from her when she called upon him.

"Apollo," Hermes cautioned. His friend would know his mind, know it was pointless to add, "King Phlegyas thinks us gone, he'd expect no aid from us. This is not our fight, brother."

Help me bring honor to my father. Save me from shaming myself. I ask you...I beg of you.

Beg? Coronis? His proud, fierce woman. His chest ached with unfathomable longing. His gaze feasted upon her beauty, her vibrant spirit. For it was her spirit that drew him in and bound him to her.

Hear me, Apollo. Her eyes pressed closed, her hands fisting, pressed rigid against her hips... *Please, I give myself to your care... I give myself to you.*

Her words consumed him. Damn this weakness she stirred in him, he had no choice.

"Apollo," Hermes all but growled.

"You were always the wiser." He clapped Hermes on the shoulder before striding through the crowd.

His presence was noted amongst the spectators. From jubilant approval to hostility at his interference, their reaction varied. But the silent prayers offered, seeking Apollo's aid against the new threat Damocles posed against their good king and these people were those he heeded. He was their God, not just Coronis', his duty was here-to all of them.

When he stood straight and proud before Coronis' father he spoke clearly, his words ringing out in the now hushed clearing. "King Phlegyas."

Coronis' amber eyes flew open, her sudden intake of breath sharp and unsteady. Was that delight upon her face? Or did his wishes cloud his vision as well as his judgment?

Apollo knelt. "I offer my strength, in your champions' stead, oh King."

Silence fell.

King Phlegyas could refuse him. He'd made no secret that he and his queen wanted Apollo gone, away from their daughter. And yet, Phlegyas loved his daughter dearly... too dearly to give her to the fool Damocles without a fight.

He glanced at the mortal King-a good man-and saw relief upon Phlegyas face. Phlegyas' queen gripped his hand, drawing her husbands' attention. Her nod was quick but enough for Phlegyas' to answer, "Your offer is accepted, most heartily, Apollo."

Apollo nodded and rose. The crowd jumped as he clapped his hands together, rubbing them together with childlike enthusiasm. "The games were through before I'd had my fill. 'Tis a fitting way to end such celebrations, is it not, Damocles?" Arching one golden eyebrow, he smiled at his opponent.

He heard her again, the sweet satisfaction in her silent prayer. *My thanks, Apollo.*

Apollo could not stop himself. He turned, his gaze fastening upon her. She blinked, but met his gaze with a defiant tilt of her head-as was her way. If she knew he was the same Olympian she prayed to, not a mere man named to honor her city's deity, she would never again seek his aid.

Her amber gaze held his, blazing with disdain... defiance.

He smiled. No. She would not. And he would miss the sound of her voice.

He winked at her, knowing his irreverence would gall her and chase away his grief for the moment.

And, oh, how she balked. Her face revealed all. Her control, her relief, vanished – replaced with wide-eyed incredulity, then consternation. Had she not chided him before for his lack of humility... of decorum? How he had laughed, as he longed to do now.

She was too easy to bate... to react. Her anger was quick, hot, and glorious. He reveled in the heat of it.

He smiled broadly, letting his eyes sweep over her. He did not care if all saw his admiration for this woman. She was worthy of it, deserving of it.

And tomorrow he would be gone. His hands fisted, briefly.

Tomorrow.

Her nostrils flared, the muscles of her jaw fighting to hold back what he suspected would be an admirable diatribe. But she succeeded – much to his disappointment.

Damocles low breath, almost a growl, caught his attention. The mortal was livid, his face blood-red and his body coiled for battle. It would be a good match-one all here would remember.

Do not let him fall. Her prayer startled him. Urgent. *Give your namesake the strength to be victor this day. Apollo must win. He will honor you.*

His gaze met hers. For the first time in his existence, he wished he were mortal. Regret, something he'd little experience with, all but choked him.

"Go with Apollo, Coronis." Phlegyas bent closer to his daughter, whispering something in her ear.

She nodded, her gaze still locked with his. "Yes, father." Her final plea was heavy with desperation. *Do not let him fall.*

Apollo smiled broadly, his brow rising high. Could this prickly, haughty woman actually care for him?

"Coronis," Queen Tasoula grasped her daughters' hand. "He saves us all, daughter. Take care."

Coronis nodded at her mother's words, tearing her gaze from his as she descended the dais. Her long stride carrying her to her father's tent. He followed, watching her every move. The flex and shift of muscle beneath her gilded skin. Yet, the lush swell of both hip and breast left no doubt of her femininity. 'Twould be easier if he could deny it, for then leaving her would offer no challenge at all.

He followed her into the tent, waiting for her reprimand, her fight. Yet she held her tongue, setting to work. That her father had sent her to help him bathe, to anoint him with oil, before his match with Damocles was a gesture he'd not expected. Phlegyas was indeed thankful.

As was Apollo.

She shivered, her long fingers trembling as she lit a lamp and cast the tent in long shadows. He heard her draw in a deep breath, her slight pause as she set the taper aside. Was she truly troubled? For him? Or did she doubt his prowess and fear the claim Damocles would make upon her if he lost?

She was not a fretful sort. He'd no desire to see her so.

He moved closer, searching out some words to soothe her. He would win, he knew it. But such claims would make him a greater ass in her eyes – if such a thing was possible. So he waited, unable to pull his gaze from her lithe form. His gaze traveled down the back of her neck and over her shoulder. Her arm was trim, muscled – shifting slightly in the dim light as she poured water into a beaten copper basin. When the ewer was full, her long fingers grasped a bottle of oil. With another deep breath, she turned to face him.

He frowned.

She did not meet his gaze, staring all about the tent - save him. He smiled, the ache in his chest surprising him. With one step, he removed all but a hairsbreadth of space between them, allowing him the luxury of staring down at her.

But she simply regarded at his chest, her lips pressed flat, her breath shaky.

"Do not fret. You've not broken your vow. You said you would never ask for my help. And you did not."

When she looked at him, he fell silent. Her gaze bore into his very soul. He would promise all to this woman, give all to her... for her.

But she was not his. And would never be.

He did not reach for her, no matter how his hands ached to touch her. Instead he whispered, "You will never have to ask. I give it to you freely. I always will."

Made in the USA
Middletown, DE
22 July 2022